AT FIRST HATE

AT FIRST HATE

K.A. LINDE

ALSO BY K. A. LINDE

COASTAL CHRONICLES

Hold the Forevers

At First Hate

Second to None

WRIGHT

The Wright Brother | The Wright Boss

The Wright Mistake | The Wright Secret

The Wright Love | The Wright One

A Wright Christmas

One Wright Stand | Wright with Benefits

Serves Me Wright | Wright Rival

Wright that Got Away | All the Wright Moves

CRUEL

Cruel Money | Cruel Fortune

Cruel Legacy | Cruel Promise

Cruel Truth | Cruel Desire

Cruel Marriage

AVOIDING

Avoiding Commitment | Avoiding Responsibility

Avoiding Temptation

Avoiding Extras

RECORD

Off the Record | On the Record | For the Record

Struck from the Record | Broken Record

DIAMOND GIRLS

Rock Hard | A Girl's Best Friend | In the Rough

Shine Bright | Under Pressure

TAKE ME DUET

Take Me for Granted

Take Me with You

BLOOD TYPE

Blood Type | Blood Match

Blood Cure

ASCENSION

The Affiliate | The Bound

The Consort | The Society

The Domina

ROYAL HOUSES

House of Dragons

House of Shadows

STAND ALONE

Following Me

At First Hate

Visit my website at
www.kalinde.com

Cover Designer: Staci Hart, www.stacihartnovels.com
Photography: Wander Aguiar, www.wanderbookclub.com
Editor: Unforeseen Editing, www.unforeseenediting.com

ISBN-13: 978-1948427524

PART I

1

SAVANNAH

PRESENT

The long life of Meredith Christianson was over.

I just called her Gran.

And she was still gone.

No more phone calls. No more visits. No more Gran. She wouldn't make fun of my driving or roll her eyes when I back-talked or be my forever cheerleader on my way to success. She wouldn't be anything because she'd died.

I was still in black from the funeral. A knee-length lace dress that my best friend, Lila, had pulled out of her closet for me. She'd known before I did that I'd need the help today. She'd practically been raised by Gran too.

"Mars," my twin, Maddox, said with a wash of sadness as we stood before Gran's empty house.

I closed my eyes to fight back the tears. "I'm not ready."

"I can wait."

Maddox knew as well as anyone how hard this was. We'd been dropped off on this stoop at the age of two and never left. I didn't remember anything before the old Victorian home with light-blue siding and a wraparound porch with peeling white paint. The Spanish moss–covered oak in the front that we'd climbed on as children. The smell of Gran's cooking in the kitchen—her famous biscuits and gravy, fried chicken, and cornbread. I'd do anything for her biscuits right about now. To see her wrinkled face pinch with consternation at my insufferable mouth.

"You don't have to," I told him.

Maddox had been inside the house since Gran had passed. He still lived in Savannah. He'd been the first one to get the call from the caretaker we'd hired so that Gran didn't have to leave the house she loved. The house she'd lived and died in. The house that now belonged to us, clean and clear. It was worth a fortune at this point since Gran and Gramps had owned it for generations. Not that we ever had any intention of getting rid of it. Other than my memories, the house was all I had left of Gran.

I squeezed my eyes against the pain. Gran was gone. She was *gone*. Okay. That was how it was. She'd been going for years anyway. But now that it was here, it felt more surreal than I'd ever imagined. Final.

Maddox wrapped an arm around my shoulders. He didn't say anything. He didn't have to. We had that twin thing where we knew what the other was thinking. It had always been like that.

He pressed a kiss to my temple. "Take your time. You can come inside whenever you're ready. We don't have to make any decisions today."

I nodded and watched him head up the front stone path to the house. He was gone inside a minute later. I swallowed back tears. I'd cried enough of them to last a lifetime. My eyes were still red and puffy from the funeral.

It hadn't helped that my mom and aunt had shown up. I'd expected Aunt Ruth, who lived in Savannah even if I hadn't seen her in at least a decade. But my mom...

My teeth ground together. She shouldn't have been there at all. She didn't deserve to mourn the woman she'd all but sent to her grave. The last argument they'd had, the one I'd been there for, I'd wanted to strangle her. It wasn't enough that she'd been a shit mom, abandoning me and Maddox at the age of two to be taken care of by Gran, but she had to continually make everyone's life *worse* by her sheer existence.

I didn't want to think about her. I never did. How Gran had afforded her sympathy and compassion year after year, day after day, was beyond my comprehension. At least I'd gotten the last laugh when I found out Gran had given us the house and not her own children.

My hand hovered on the gate. It was just a house. It wasn't haunted or anything. Despite everything else in Savannah seemingly being haunted. Gran had lived a long, long life. She'd passed with peace in her heart, knowing she'd done the best she could with her circumstances. But it didn't make it any easier to step over the threshold. I'd been avoiding it all weekend after driving in from Atlanta with Lila, where I worked as a professor at Emory. She'd graciously let me stay with her mom down the street. Deb always had warm hugs and an open heart. I was grateful for her this weekend, but now, I finally had to face that the empty house.

With a deep breath, I stepped into the yard. I kept my focus forward as I mounted the small stoop, reaching the iconic bright yellow door. I twisted the worn silver knob in my hand. The hinges gave with a slight creak as I crossed over onto the original hardwood floor. Everything was precisely where it had always been. The floral couch against the far wall. A color-coordinated pink and brown set of chairs on either side of it. Gramps' brown leather recliner tucked in the corner. The rug was a threadbare multicolored thing that Gran had always taken special care of since it had belonged to her mom. The TV was way past outdated and veering toward an antique. She'd never cared for new, fandangle things. Though she secretly watched soaps on the nicer TV in her bedroom. I'd crawl into bed with her to find out what Stefano was doing to Marlena.

Pictures littered the walls, as they always had, collecting dust as much as memories. Gran was the third oldest of eight with pictures of her immense family all over the room. A scant few pictures of her own two daughters. They'd almost all been replaced by photographs of me and Maddox throughout the years.

"The kids I never had," was what she always said.

I'd laughed then. I just found it sad now.

I pressed my fingers to a graduation photo nearest the door. Maddox and I stood in baby-blue cap and gowns at the local high school. Gran and Gramps had their arms around each of us. Lila and our other best friend, Josie, beamed. I'd never seen Gran as happy as when I got that full scholarship to Duke.

"*Off to bigger and better, chickadee.*

It was too much. How was I supposed to survive a wake here? How could I fill Gran's house with strangers? How had we gotten wrangled into this in the first place? I wanted to be left alone. I didn't want any well-meaning cakes and dinners. I didn't want people to tell me they were sorry for my loss. I didn't want pity at all. I wanted Gran back. I wanted the impossible.

My heart constricted. That was the last thing I needed.

I could hear Maddox stomping around upstairs. Who even know what he was doing? I wanted to tell him to keep it down, but if stomping around helped him grieve, then who was I to tell him to keep it quiet?

Then the doorbell rang, saving me from making a decision.

I checked my reflection in a giant brass mirror that Gran had always called the Lipstick Mirror. My eyes were still puffy, but they weren't lined with tears. My curly brown hair was actually manageable since Lila had gotten to it before the funeral. My cheeks rosy from the Savannah summer humidity. My lips a perfect neutral pink, just as Gran had always preferred. I'd even picked her favorite Estée Lauder color, Pinkberry.

"I got it," I called out to Maddox and then swung the door open.

My heart stopped as I found Derek Ballentine standing before me in a three-piece navy-blue pinstripe suit. As impossibly tall as ever with his sideswept brown hair and those too-damn-keen hazel eyes. His lips were pouty with an exaggerated Cupid's bow and always appeared as if he'd been kissing all afternoon. He looked like he'd walked off the set of Savannah's quintessential film, *Midnight in the Garden of Good and Evil.* He'd always been gorgeous. And he was the very last person I wanted to see.

"Derek," I growled.

"Minivan," he said, rolling over the nickname I'd always hated.

"No."

"Aww, Mars, you didn't miss me?"

I glared at him, and then without a second thought, I slammed the door in his too-smug face.

2

SAVANNAH

OCTOBER 29, 2004

The first time I saw Derek Ballantine, I thought he was the most gorgeous person I'd ever met. Then he opened his mouth.

"Hey, y'all," he drawled, low and smooth. "Any of y'all have Halloween plans other than losing to Holy Cross?"

He pulled his Holy Cross letterman jacket more firmly around his shoulders and then leaned forward against the chain-link fence. His other basketball buddies chuckled at his *incredible* wit.

While Danielle and Leigh stumbled over their words to see the hot private school boys talking to us, I narrowed my eyes. Yes, we were losing the football game to the all-boys private Catholic school 42 to 10. Yes, we undeniably *sucked*. But this guy wasn't even playing. His letterman jacket was for basketball, which *they* sucked at. I'd cheered through enough basketball games to know that we destroyed them every year. They had, like, one good guy on that team, and it probably wasn't even *this* guy.

"Is that supposed to be a pickup line?" I demanded,

planting a hand on my hip and stretching the baby-blue miniskirt.

His eyes dropped to my long, pale legs and back up. "I don't know. Is it working?"

"No," I said flatly.

He shrugged, undeterred. "Well, I'm having a Halloween party tomorrow night. My parents are out of town, and y'all should swing by."

"Oh wow, yeah!" Leigh said with wide blue eyes. "That'd be fun, right?"

Danielle bit her lip. "I'm supposed to go to Jack's gig. So... I don't know."

"What about you?" he asked, nodding at me.

"I mean, the invitation just sounded so tempting, what with the insults and all, but no."

Of course, I didn't say it was because Gran and Gramps would never in a million years let me go to an unchaperoned Halloween party. Let alone a Holy Cross party. They'd never liked the local Catholic schools. They had vocally opposed Lila going to St. Catherine's, the sister school to Holy Cross. But it was hard to argue when her mom got her free tuition because she working there.

"She's got you there, Derek," the tall Black guy next to him said with a laugh. "Why don't you show them some manners? I'm Trask." He held his hand across the fence, and Leigh shook it. He smacked the obnoxious one in the chest afterward. "This is Derek. And Hooper."

Hooper waved shyly, a blush forming on his cheeks. He was easily the tallest of the lot—well, they were all tall, but he was a giant. "Sup."

"I'm Leigh," Leigh said, jumping in for us. "Danielle and Marley." She pointed out a few other cheerleaders who had wandered over to find out what was going on.

They all waved, and I heard Christina Arlington whisper in awe, "That's Derek Ballentine."

Derek grinned broadly when he realized he had the attention of the entire cheer squad, and again, he invited everyone to his Halloween party tomorrow night. Only I seemed uninterested. Not because he was unattractive, but because I knew his type.

I'd spent long years analyzing people like Derek Ballentine. The ones who wanted sex after the first date, who expected the world but refused to give anything back in turn, who thought they were entitled to respect when they hadn't earned it. I'd seen them flounder in and out of my mother's life since I was a baby. One after the other after the other. She'd never been around enough for me to really know their names, but in my mind, they were all the same guy anyway. A placeholder for the real thing. And Mom *never* saw it, but I certainly did.

"Ladies!" Coach called furiously. "The game is still happening."

The rest of the girls giggled and headed back into positions. We ran through a few cheers to try to get the crowd into the crippling defeat, but nothing could make them rally. And Derek stood by and watched me.

I'd never felt self-conscious in the tiny blue skirt and crop top before. I'd actually started cheering so that I could wear something other than pants or knee-length skirts. Gran was traditional, and she believed deeply in modesty. I thought she was trying to make up for how Mom had turned out, but I'd only said that once before in her presence and had the shit smacked out of me. So I wasn't prone to saying that one again.

Either way, cheer wasn't my passion by a long shot. I preferred dancing and did so at a local studio, but the high school didn't have a dance team, and Gran wanted me to be "involved"—i.e., she thought it looked good on my transcript. And now, I was strutting around in a skirt that my ass nearly hung out of, and the hottest guy I'd ever met was looking at me like I was a puzzle he wanted to figure out.

A cheer rose from the other side of the stadium. Holy Cross had scored another touchdown. Their quarterback, Ash Talmadge, had run the damn ball in himself. I sighed heavily as they made the extra point, bringing the final score to 49 to 10. Depressing.

"Better luck next week," Coach called.

I grabbed my cheer bag and slung it over my shoulder, heading for the stands to find Lila and Josie. I hadn't seen them at all in the stands the second half. That likely meant that Josie had gotten them into trouble. What else was new?

I crossed the fence and squinted for my girls when Derek stepped into my path. He was enormous in person, towering over me with bulk I hadn't expected from a basketball player. And I hated to admit, he was hotter up close.

"So, you really don't want to go to the party?" he asked with a quick grin.

It was hard not to look at his lips. They were the kind of lips girls spent money on fillers to achieve. Perfectly pouty and oh-so endearing. I snapped my attention away from those lips.

"Why are you following me? It's creepy."

He shrugged. "Public school girls don't normally say no."

I rolled my eyes. "To you or your party?"

He shrugged again.

"Well, let me tell you, *Derek*," I said, "I'm not like any other girl you'll ever meet."

Then I shouldered past him to find Josie flirting with a football player, Kyle Curtis. Lila looked generally miserable.

"Hey," I said, dropping my bag at Lila's feet.

"Mars," she said. "You killed it out there. That high kick put everyone to shame."

"Obviously," I joked. I glanced at Josie. "How long will she be like this?"

Lila raised her eyebrows. "How long do we have?"

"Josephine Reynolds," I called. "Can we keep the flirting to a minimum? I want to go home?"

Josie put her hand on Kyle's arm and then turned all dramatic to face me. "Marley Nelson, you will wait your turn. I am occupied."

I rolled my eyes at her. Most days I wished that my last name was Christianson like Gran's. Nelson was from my father, whoever he was. He'd ditched mom when she found out she was having twins at the ripe old age of eighteen.

"Maddox is going to be picking us up any minute. If we're late, he'll drive off without us. I've watched him do it."

Josie huffed. "Fine." She twirled her fingers at Kyle, mouthing, *Call me*, and then followed us out of the stadium. "You got your ass kicked."

"Yep," I said, "Lila's team is better."

Lila groaned. "Let's not. I've only been at St. Catherine's for three months, and I want to die. I will never fit in there."

"Well, it's better than being in Atlanta," Josie complained.

For as long as I could remember, Josie had spent every summer in Savannah with us. Her dad would drop her off the day after school got out to stay with her mom, who had a reputation in these parts the size of Mount Rushmore, and pick her up the day before school started. But we'd all gotten so attached, and she loved Savannah like it was home that her dad had agreed to let her drive down to see us now that she had a license. Another thing Gran would *never*, ever let me do.

Maddox was waiting in an old Ford pickup that used to belong to Gramps. Even though we were twins, I didn't have my license. We'd both turned sixteen three days ago, and Maddox had passed his driver's test with flying colors. It was the only test I'd ever failed in my entire life. And so Maddox got the truck and the fun job of chauffeuring us around.

"Get in," Maddox said, reaching across the seat and opening the passenger door.

It only had one long seat across the front, and we had to squash inside to fit. Josie practically crawled onto Maddox's lap, then Lila, and then me after I threw my bag into the bed. He zoomed away with all the freedom that I was lacking.

Maddox parked on the street, like everyone else in Savannah, and we trudged inside. Gran was waiting up for us, as usual, with Gramps snoring softly in the old brown recliner. She got to her feet as her eyes went to the clock. As if she didn't already know the time.

"Late game," she said, pulling us each in for a hug. "Y'all win?"

I shook my head. "Nah. We're no good."

"Ah, next time, chickadee," she said with a kiss to my forehead. "Now, change out of that ridiculous skirt. Y'all hungry?" A chorus of yeses followed. She nodded. "I'll whip something up. I got some biscuits in the freezer, and I can make some gravy."

"Thanks, Gran," Josie said, knocking her hip against Gran's. "You're the best."

"Nothing like Gran's biscuits," Maddox agreed.

"And fried chicken," Lila said. "Makes my mouth water thinking about it."

"I'm going to change," I said and headed up the creaking stairs to my room.

It was still decorated in a splash of pink from the days when I'd liked the color. I was more partial to dark colors now, but it wasn't like we could afford much to renovate. So, pink it was. Lila and Josie followed in my wake, crashing into my room and dropping onto the bed.

"So, who was that hot guy you were talking to?" Josie asked.

I slipped out of my cheer uniform and into oversize sweats and a T-shirt. "Some Holy Cross guy."

"I missed it," Lila said.

"He invited me to a Halloween party."

Josie perked up. "Party?"

"We're not going," I told her.

"But..." She pouted.

Lila laughed. "As if Gran would let her go."

"Tell her that you're staying with Lila. Works like a charm."

"I don't want to go."

"Well, I do!" Josie said. "Hot guys are my specialty."

"You're boy crazy."

"You say that like it's a bad thing!"

Maddox cracked his head in. "Gran said food'll be ready any minute."

"Excellent," Josie said. She leaned against the door and fluttered her eyelashes at Maddox. "Do you think you could cover for us tomorrow if we go to a party?"

"I, uh... have a gig," he stumbled over his words, as he always did around Josie.

"For what?"

"Maddox is in a band," I said, "remember?"

"Local Carnage," he said with a grin. "We're, uh, we're playing a local Halloween party for some rich dude."

I groaned. "It's probably the same party. Gran is letting you go?"

He scratched the back of his head. His dark hair falling into his eyes. "Well, I told her it was for a charity thing."

Lila cackled. "Brilliant."

Josie squealed. "Let's do it!"

Everyone turned to stare at me. The only one who had no interest in a Holy Cross party on Halloween. But how could I say no with everyone else on board?

I sighed heavily. "*Fine.*"

3

SAVANNAH

OCTOBER 30, 2004

I didn't have a costume.

Josie was going as Marilyn Monroe, iconic white dress and all. Lila had gone for Greek goddess, complete with a skimpy toga that Josie had sewn into place. I'd declined a dozen suggestions. If Gran saw me in any of Josie's outfits, I'd be in trouble for the rest of my life.

Which was how I'd donned Lila's St. Catherine's uniform. A plaid miniskirt that Josie had hiked up against my protests, white button-up, and tie. Lila had fished out some knee-highs and braided two pigtails to give off the perfect Catholic schoolgirl effect. I felt like a fraud.

"You look hot. Shut up," Josie said.

I rolled my eyes. "Easy for you to say."

I gestured to her. Josie was... Josie. Tall and tan with flowing black hair and hazel eyes. She was extroverted and flirtatious. She dominated a room. She always had. And then there was sarcastic, cynical, brainy, introverted me.

"You do look hot," Lila said with a shrug.

Her blonde hair was loose and lips painted bright red. Long dancer legs were exposed against the white toga and black high heels. The benefit of having really hot friends meant no one spent too much time looking at me at least.

"All right," I said with a sigh. "Let's do this."

Maddox was waiting out front in his truck. He wasn't dressed up, except to look like a rocker, which wasn't that different than his normal attire—ripped black jeans, a white Nirvana T-shirt, and his hair brushed forward to look emo. I was pretty sure he was even sporting guyliner.

"Hot, Maddox," Josie said, shimmying in tight next to him.

He went nonverbal. Typical.

"Just drive. Let's get this over with."

Lila and Josie laughed at my lack of enthusiasm, but it was short-lived. It was hard to be with my two best friends and not be happy. We were so rarely all together that it would be a travesty to not revel in it.

Halloween weekend in Savannah meant three things: one, my birthday, two, parking was shit, and three, the ghost tours were packed. If we had to lay on the horn at one more oblivious tour, I was going to go mad. I remembered why we never did anything other than birthday shenanigans for Halloween. Savannah was one of the most haunted cities in America. Any local could probably rattle off a half-dozen ghost stories without blinking, but the tourists made it all so over the top.

"We are never going to find parking," Lila said, craning her neck down Gaston as we passed Forsyth Park. "Literally just park anywhere, and we'll walk."

"In these heels?" Josie complained.

"Deal with it," I said. "We're never going to find a spot near the square."

Josie huffed but nodded at Maddox. Then she pointed. "Oh there! Parallel park."

Maddox huffed. "Great."

Maddox sucked at parallel parking. Meanwhile, I was a pro from years of parking Gran's minivan in the spot across the street. I'd baffled the person who administered my driver's test by blowing the parallel park test out of the water and failing the actual driving part.

"I'll do it," I offered.

"You don't even have a license," Maddox said.

"So? If you hit that Beamer, Gran will never forgive you."

Maddox sighed heavily and shot me a pained look. As if how dare I make him look bad in front of Josie. But he relented, and I swung it around with practiced ease.

Maddox pulled out his guitar from the back, and then we headed down Whitaker. A gentle mist hung over everything as the humidity doubled the size of my hair. I tried to flatten it, so it looked long and glossy like Josie's, but there was no hope.

"This is the place," Maddox said.

All four of us gawked at the enormous Victorian. It didn't matter that I'd lived in Savannah all my life; there was always a new mansion with giant oaks covered in Spanish moss, which left me slack-jawed. And this one came complete with a gold plaque, listing the residence as The Ballentine House, built in 1833. Well, at least that confirmed that it was Derek's party.

"Man, I want one of these," Josie said, swinging open the giant wrought iron gate that led to the courtyard.

"Don't you have a house like this?" Maddox asked with a grin.

She arched an eyebrow. "No, that's Mom's."

His smile faded. We all knew she had issues with her mom, which was why she was staying with us this weekend.

My head craned ever upward, past the massive double

doors to the sprawling white brick with tiered balconies. On some level, I had known that Holy Cross guys were rich, but there was knowing, and then there was *knowing*.

"Holy shit," I muttered.

"Seconded," Lila said, looping arms with me. "How the hell do I deal with this every day?"

That was a fantastic question. St. Catherine's and Holy Cross felt like a completely different world. A world we were about to enter.

Maddox didn't bother knocking; he just stepped into the mansion, which was already full. Everyone held a red Solo cup and laughed and chatted as if they'd all known each other their entire lives. I kept my mouth glued shut as we passed through the immense entranceway with its marble floor and two giant staircases leading up to the second floor.

Josie dragged us through the house as if she owned it. We stopped in the kitchen, where booze covered every available surface. Josie grabbed us each a drink and passed them out.

"I can't," I said, trying to pass it back to her.

"Just hold it," Josie said. She took a good long sip of hers. "Then no one will ask why you aren't drinking."

"Fine," I said with a sigh. I wasn't opposed to drinking, but I preferred to do it in safer scenarios. Not at some random Holy Cross guy's house miles from home.

Lila winked at me as she took a sip of her drink and then pulled a face. "You're not missing anything anyway. This tastes like shit."

I laughed as we followed Josie through the kitchen and into a living room the size of my entire house. Maddox was tuning his guitar as the rest of the guys got set up. I saw Danielle dressed like a black cat and waved. She pulled me into a hug once we walked over.

"I didn't realize until I talked to Maddox that this party was the same as his gig."

"Me either! But I'm glad you came," she said with a smile.

"I kind of got roped into it." I gestured to Lila and Josie.

Danielle grinned and hugged Lila. "We miss you at school. This year is just not the same without you."

"Tell me about it," she said, taking another fortifying drink. Her eyes roamed the room. "I certainly don't fit in with these people."

Danielle laughed. "No shit. This place is ridiculous." She glanced back at the band. "I'm really just here for Jack. I don't know if Leigh is coming."

Josie leaned in. "Is that your boyfriend?"

She bit her lip, and the lead singer looked up from his guitar. His smile ignited when he realized we were all looking at him, and he sideswept his dark brown hair. His eyes were so crystal-clear blue that they seemed to see straight into our hearts. All of us melted at the same time.

He hopped off the makeshift stage and slung an arm around Danielle. "Hey, y'all. You here for the Local Carnage show?" Then he nodded at me. "Mars."

"Hey," I said.

"Don't think we've met." Josie held out her hand. "I'm Josephine Reynolds. My friends call me Josie."

He grinned at her. "I'm Jack Howard. Friends just call me Jack."

"It's so nice to meet you."

Lila shot me a look that said everything I needed to know. We needed to get Josie far away from Danielle's boyfriend, or she'd have her claws in him by the end of the night. Which I'd hardly blame her. Jack was two years older than us in school and easily one of the hottest seniors. Not to mention, he had this charisma about him. If I were Danielle, I'd watch out where that smirk landed.

"We're here for Maddox," Lila interjected.

Josie shot her a look. "Yes. Maddox."

"Cool. Cool. Enjoy the show."

He winked at us and hopped back on the stage. Maddox waved, and Josie was already distracted again. Welp. My poor twin.

"He's great, isn't he?" Danielle said in awe.

I laughed at Josie's expression and then let her drag us around the room as she made friends. Local Carnage began their set, and Josie went in search of more drinks while I watched my brother perform. They weren't bad, but they weren't going to blow anyone out of the water.

"Look at what we have here," a voice sounded behind me.

I turned to find Derek Ballentine standing over me. For a second, my breath caught at the sight of him. He wasn't in a costume that I could discern, just a pair of white shorts that revealed a few inches of tanned thighs with a thick brown belt, a blue button-up with the sleeves rolled up to his elbows, and boat shoes. His dark hair looked wind-whipped, and he had these mercurial hazel eyes that were more gold than anything in the lighting of his mansion home. His perfect lips tilted upward at the sight of me.

I managed an ounce of bravado. I lifted my chin up and met his gaze. "Can I help you?"

"Marley, right?"

"Yeah," I said with an annoyed look.

"Thought you were too good for my party?" He grinned this little half-smile, his lips curling up on one side, as insufferable as I could imagine. His eyes crawled my outfit. "And dressed like a St. Catherine's girl. The girl not like anyone else is dressed just like everyone else."

I gritted my teeth. "I'm here for the band."

"Right. The band," he said disbelievingly.

"My brother plays guitar." I pointed Maddox out.

Derek barely glanced that way. "We both know you wanted to see me."

I actually snorted. "Keep dreaming, Holy Cross boy."

"You know, Holy Cross boys and St. Catherine's girls go together."

"Is that what you're supposed to be dressed up as?"

He laughed. "No. I'm a sailor."

I looked him up and down. He just looked like a regular dude. "Right. Obviously."

He opened his mouth to say something else that I'd likely detest, but then his gaze shifted past mine, and his face dropped. I turned to search the crowd, but it was just a bunch of drunk people.

"Excuse me," he said and then brushed past me as if I weren't there.

He stormed right up to some girl. I didn't recognize her, but she was beautiful. Waist-length, pin-straight brown hair in an all-white tennis outfit, complete with a racket. He grabbed her arm and furiously spoke to her.

I shrugged and turned away. Probably his girlfriend. Maybe she wasn't supposed to be here, so he could flirt with everyone else. Sounded like something Holy Cross boys would do.

"Hey, who were you talking to?" Lila asked, coming back with drinks.

"No one," I said, putting Derek out of my mind. I took one of the drinks out of her hand and sipped. Then I sputtered around the harsh taste. "You're right. This tastes horrid."

She laughed. "Right?!"

* * *

Despite Derek being a dick, the party was actually—as much as I hated to admit it—fun. Local Carnage played a full set, and then a DJ showed to play dance music. Maddox tried to talk to Josie and failed. Josie was too busy flirting with half of the room to notice or care. Lila and I danced our asses off. Both of my friends had probably had too much to drink.

"I'm going to find the bathroom," I yelled to Lila.

She nodded. "Want me to come with?"

"I'm good. Just stay with Maddox."

Lila grabbed my twin's arm and put her head on his shoulder. "Got him."

I laughed and went in search of a bathroom. But the house was enormous, and after a few minutes, I gave up and asked someone. The girl pointed me in the other direction, and I headed that way, only to stop and curse. There were at least ten intoxicated girls in the line for the bathroom.

"Motherfucker," I said under my breath.

There was no way that I was waiting in that line. There had to be more than one bathroom in this huge house. I backtracked to the main foyer and ducked under a rope that blocked off the stairwell. I assumed it was to keep drunk people from having sex in the upstairs bedrooms. Not that it likely did a good job of that either, but I was here for the bathroom.

I just made it to the second-floor landing when I heard a thunk. I turned around and found Derek holding a guy up against the wall. The pretty girl from earlier was standing behind him, crying.

"Derek, stop it!"

Derek ignored her protests. "Don't ever let me catch you touching my sister again."

Sister.

Oh! Well, that explained everything. No wonder he'd looked so pissed when he saw her.

Whoever the guy was, he looked a lot older than her, which was a red flag.

"Derek!"

"Mia, shut it," Derek snapped.

"What the fuck, man?" the guy said.

"Did you fucking hear me, Chuck?" Derek snarled. "Nod your head if you can't open your big fucking mouth to do anything but shove your tongue down her throat."

He smartly nodded his head once. "I hear you."

I obviously wasn't supposed to be witnessing this. But as I stepped backward to find my escape, the hardwood under my foot squeaked. I winced at the noise.

But all three of them whipped their heads in my direction.

I cleared my throat and waved awkwardly. "Uh... sorry to interrupt. I was looking for the bathroom."

Derek released Chuck with a shove. "We were just finished. Weren't we?"

Chuck glared at Derek and then brushed out of the upstairs, passing me and darting down the stairs. He all but ran down them. Personally, I thought he was getting off easy. Derek looked half-ready to kill him.

His sister swiped at her tears. "You're such an asshole, Derek."

"Fine, Amelia. I'll be the asshole, but Chuck Henderson is not good enough for you."

She shoved his arm, and as she rushed away, she said, "God, I hate you."

Derek watched her leave with his jaw clenched. A door slammed hard from somewhere down the hallway. He winced at the sound and then closed his eyes. He stayed that way for a few seconds before releasing the tension from his shoulders and finally turning to face me. All of it had happened so quickly that I'd been too frozen to move.

"Uh..." I managed.

Because the Derek Ballentine that I'd seen at the football game and downstairs in front of his row of adoring fans was not the person standing in front of me right now. This Derek only cared that he'd saved his sister from a creep. And then tried to act as if he didn't care that she was mad at him, but he did. He definitely cared. For some reason, that made him twice as hot.

So now, my words were fractured and forgotten. So much for all the SAT vocabulary prep.

Our eyes met across the distance, and my face flushed at the attention. I'd found guys hot before. I'd even found Derek hot before. But in that one interaction, something shifted. I witnessed something private. A side of himself that he clearly didn't show everyone else. That he *cared*... even if throwing a guy against a wall maybe wasn't the best way to show it.

"Sorry you had to see that," he said.

"Yeah. Well, that was my bad. There are a dozen people in line for the one downstairs."

"Sounds right."

He pointed down the hall, the way that Amelia had gone. "The bathroom is the second door on the left."

"Um... thanks."

"No problem," he said and then sank into the sofa in the second-story landing. It was large enough to be a whole other living area, complete with a giant television and all the video game consoles.

I scurried past Derek and found the bathroom with ease. I took my time in the bathroom, hoping that I could avoid any more of the awkwardness. After I finished, I peeked back out to find him still sitting there, staring off into nothing. I could scurry away like Chuck Henderson and not ever have to talk to Derek again. It would be easy.

And somehow, it wasn't.

I bit my lip as I walked out onto the landing and then took the seat next to him. He looked up in surprise. Those hazel eyes searching mine for an answer for my continued appearance.

"That was a nice thing you did for your sister," I said.

He chuckled, a low rumble in the back of his throat. "She sure doesn't think so."

"I'm well acquainted with the Chucks of this world. Seen a bunch of them up close and personal."

He arched an eyebrow, and my cheeks heated again.

"My mom," I said quickly. "She's dated her fair share of jerks. I'm usually pretty good at spotting the Chucks. Which is kind of why I was like that with you."

"You thought I was a Chuck?" he asked. "What a pickup line."

I laughed. "I'm not trying to pick you up. I'm trying to say that I think maybe you're not as terrible as you make yourself seem."

He straightened on the sofa next to me and swept a curly lock out of my face, tucking it behind my ear. "I wouldn't go that far."

"Oh? You think you're terrible?"

"I know what I want."

I laughed and pulled back. "You were doing so well."

He arched an eyebrow. "So why are you still here?"

"Really asking myself the same question," I admitted. "You'd think I was smarter than this. I'm in Duke TIP and everything."

"Ah, good old Duke TIP," he said with a sneer.

"What?" I asked, automatically offended. "You have something against smart kids getting opportunities for one of the best schools in the South?"

"Nah. Now, hold on. I didn't say that. I was offered for TIP, but we don't do Duke in this house." He grinned broadly. "Go Heels. Go America."

I snorted. "Oh, I see. You're a UNC fan."

"Tar Heels all day, every day, baby." He leaned back on the sofa and stretched his arms out wide.

"That's nice and all, but Duke is a better school."

He snorted. "No."

"No, what? Objectively, that's true."

"Meh."

I shook my head at him. "You do realize that rivalry is clouding your brain so that you can't think clearly about this."

"You can say that, but I will continue to disagree. UNC is better than Duke on every metric."

"Wow. That is *blatantly* false." I threw my hands wide at his rejection of the one thing that had made me special for so long. The one way to get out of this town. My brain, my supposed brilliance, the scholarship that would put me on the road to bigger and better.

"Look, Marley, you're hot when you're all riled up," he

said, tipping my chin up. "But UNC is just better at basketball, and that's a fact."

"Basketball," I said slowly with a disbelieving head shake.

"Priorities."

"You're absurd."

He grinned. "I've been called worse."

"I don't—"

But I didn't get to finish my sentence.

His hand slid back into my wild brown curls. His perfect lips formed the word, "Shh," and then he fitted his mouth to mine.

My brain malfunctioned at the touch of his lips against mine. Those damn lips that I'd thought were too pretty and perfect for one person. Now they were touching mine, and fuck it, they were even better in person. Soft and tender.

My heart raced as he dragged me closer. He laughed softly when I didn't immediately respond and pulled back to look deep into my eyes. When I didn't run in the other direction, he slid his thumb across my bottom lip. I shuddered at that touch. God, he knew what he was doing, and I was so inexperienced. This was my first kiss, and I was sure that I was botching it.

"Should I stop?" he asked sincerely.

Though he'd stolen my first kiss, he was offering me my second.

And to my surprise, I responded, "No."

He tugged me forward, harder this time. And I forgot all else but the feel of his lips against mine. I moved against him, letting instinct take over. For the first time in a long, long time, I didn't *think* at all. Not even a little. I just gave myself over to the moment.

He dragged his tongue across the seam of my lips, and I

gasped. I felt his smile against my mouth at my response, and then his tongue moved forward and brushed against mine. I moaned at that first sweep of him inside my mouth. Everything felt so amazing and overwhelming. I was hot all over, and his hand moved from my neck down my back. I could feel every point that our bodies touched like it was superheated. A small inferno down my back, all the way to my hip, and then across my thigh to the hem of my skirt.

I gasped as he slipped a hand under the tiny St. Catherine's skirt and pulled back. His breathing was ragged as he stared down at me. He didn't apologize, but his hand moved back on top of my skirt.

"I should probably…" I managed.

"Marley," he breathed my name like a prayer. His hazel eyes swirling all over my face.

I didn't want to go. My lips felt swollen. My body hummed in a way I'd never experienced before. Was this how I was supposed to feel? It was exhilarating. And I was going to make a huge mistake if I stayed.

I tried to stand, and he tugged me down into his lap. My eyes widened as I felt exactly what our kiss had done to *him*.

"Stay," he pleaded.

I shook my head, even as I leaned forward and kissed him hard and in earnest. In that moment, I understood drug addicts. Because Derek Ballentine could very easily be the most addictive substance on the planet.

"Derek, I…" I tried again.

"Keep kissing me like that."

And so I did. I'd always followed logic. I'd always been the smart one. And I didn't want to be.

But I wanted to be my mother even less. With twins at eighteen, right out of high school, and no husband to show for it. A desperate need for love, chasing stupidity around every block and never taking responsibility for a damn thing in her life.

I pushed him backward, ignoring the pitter-patter of my heart and the ragged quality to my breathing. "I should get back to my friends."

"Marley..."

I stumbled to my feet. "I should go."

I didn't wait. I just hurried back down the stairs. A second later, a hand grabbed my elbow at the base of the stairs.

I whipped around to find Derek had followed me.

"What?" I got out.

"I just..."

"Yeah, Derek!" a group of guys yelled nearby.

I jolted at the noise, sharply bringing me back to reality.

Derek laughed and shouted out to them. I looked up at him and saw the same guy that I'd seen at the football game yesterday. It hardly mattered that he'd given me my first kiss and made me lose my ever-loving mind. We existed in two separate worlds. And I couldn't end up like my mother.

So, I snuck away while he talked to his friends and headed back to Lila, who was still attached to Maddox.

"You were gone forever!" Lila said. "Did you find the bathroom?"

I glanced backward to make sure Derek hadn't followed me again. "Uh, yeah. Yeah, I found it."

I'd found a whole hell of a lot more than the bathroom.

4

SAVANNAH

PRESENT

"Come on, Mars!" Derek yelled from the other side of the door.

I leaned back against the front door and squeezed my eyes shut. I didn't need this. I didn't need Derek Ballentine in my life especially right after Gran's funeral. I had hoped to be in Savannah and never, ever have to see him again. Ever. Not after all the shit we had gone through together for years. I couldn't lose Gran and deal with him at the same time.

"Open the door."

I didn't move.

Maddox peeked down at me from the stairs. "What's going on?"

"It's Derek," I told him.

He grimaced. "Oh. Want me to tell him to leave?"

"Do you think that would work?"

Maddox shot me a disbelieving look. "I'd do it anyway."

"No. It's okay. It's my own mess. I'll clean it up."

"Yell if you need me."

I nodded at him, took a deep, fortifying breath, and then

yanked the door back open. Derek stumbled forward a step and then righted himself immediately.

"What do you want, Derek? This isn't a good time."

"Yeah, I heard about Gran," he said. His hazel eyes crinkled at the corners in sympathy. "I'm so sorry. She was a great woman."

"She... was," I said, stumbling over the past tense.

"I always think of her fondly."

"Thank you," I ground out. "That doesn't explain why you're here. I thought I'd made it pretty clear that I didn't want to see you."

"I understand. But can we go somewhere and talk?"

I blinked at him. "On what planet do you think I'd say yes to that?"

He shot me a look that I knew well. It was a mix of exasperation and just a hint of desire. How many times had I heard him say that he liked me riled up? Well, that part had never been our problem anyway.

I swallowed hard and backed up a step. "It's a no. Just go."

"All right," he said, running a hand back through his dark hair.

Then, those hazel eyes met mine again, and something hardened in them. I wouldn't have noticed if I wasn't so attuned to his various looks. But he almost looked like he was psyching himself up for something.

"What?" I asked. "Just spit it out."

He smirked. "I forget that you know me so well."

Which only made me scowl and cross my arms. "Fine. Don't."

I started to shut the door in his face again, but he reached out and stopped me.

"I came for this."

When he was sure I wasn't going to close the door, he extracted an envelope from his briefcase and held it out to me.

I narrowed my eyes at him and took the packet. "What's this?"

I broke the seal on the large envelope and pulled the stack of papers out of the inside. My eyes scanned the top of the document in confusion. They were court papers. Derek's name was on it. But that didn't make sense.

"You're... suing me?" I asked in disbelief.

"Keep reading," he said softly.

And for some reason, the softness in his voice made me realize that this was a lot worse than I'd thought. I ripped the entire thing out of the envelope and let it flutter to the ground at my feet. Then, I read the top document. My eyes widened and then widened further.

I looked up at him with uncertain eyes. "My *mom* and aunt are suing me? What the hell, Derek?"

"Technically, they're contesting the will."

The world dropped out from below me. My vision dipped, and everything felt momentarily disorienting. As if up were down and down were up. Not a thing about this made sense. Not the paperwork. Not the words coming out of Derek's mouth as he explained to me in legalese what was going on.

I held my hand up to get him to stop fucking talking as I tried to hold down the scant breakfast I'd had this morning. I put a hand to my mouth. I wouldn't throw up. I wouldn't cry. I'd had enough tears. I just needed to fix this.

"Mars?"

"Just shut your fucking mouth," I snarled.

I shook my head and righted myself again. My mom—who had never been there for us, who had all but sent Gran into an early grave—thought *she* deserved a cent of Gran's wealth? My aunt—who I hadn't seen in a decade despite living in the *same* small town—thought she deserved Gran's *house*? Were they out of their ever-loving minds?

Derek straightened at my words, swiftly dropping back into his attorney mode. "I'm here on behalf of my clients—"

"I said, *shut up*. I don't need any of your bullshit, Derek. I certainly don't need you to *explain* what this is to me. I understand completely. What I don't get is why the fuck it's *you*."

"I'm an attorney."

"You're the owner's kid. You have a Harvard law degree. Why are you taking this on? Is this about me?"

His eyes narrowed. He always hated the reminder that he'd only gotten what he had because of his dad's money. Tough shit. "No. Contrary to what you think, not everything in my life is about you."

I laughed harshly once. "Nothing in your life is about me. I remember that all too well."

"My dad gave me the assignment. I'm up for partner, and when he says to do it, I do."

I shook my head at him. "Same old, same old, huh? He says jump, and you say how high."

"This isn't personal."

"It sure as fuck is," I snapped at him. "And you knew it, or you wouldn't have been trying to sweet-talk me."

"Trust me, I know sweet-talk doesn't work on you."

I ignored him and walked back inside. I snatched Maddox's keys off of the hook. Then, I pulled Gran's Pinkberry lipstick out and added another coat to my lips. Body armor.

"Marley, are you even listening?"

"No."

I was far past done listening to him. He had a snake's tongue, and I'd fallen for it time and time again. This time, I had no intention of listening to another word out of his mouth. I needed to deal with this issue at the source. And Derek was just the intermediary.

I slammed the door shut and then brushed past him, taking the stairs two at a time to the street. Maddox's shiny, new Jeep Wrangler Rubicon, which he'd named Nancy, was parked in Gran's old spot across the street. He wasn't any better at parallel parking than he'd been in high school.

"Marley," Derek groaned, following me down the stairs. "Where are you going?"

"I'm going to fix this," I told him.

He grabbed my elbow before I reached the sidewalk. "Wait, wait, wait. Are you going to go talk to your mom?"

I shook him off with a pointed glare. "Yes."

"As an attorney, I must advise against that."

"Well, you're not *my* attorney," I said, getting up into his face. He still towered over me, but I had pent-up fury on my side. "So, I don't give a fuck what you advise."

I pushed his chest. It didn't move him an inch, of course. It only moved me backward, but I'd done what I wanted, and that was all that mattered. I left him standing there and jumped into Nancy. I tossed the packet of paperwork into the passenger side.

"You're making a mistake," he called from the other side of the street.

I flipped him off as I maneuvered out of the spot and out onto the Savannah streets. I didn't even look back. My body was vibrating with anger at the entire interaction. That I'd had to see Derek today of all days when I buried my Gran was bad enough. But that he was actually representing my mom and aunt was absurd. He *knew* all the shit I'd gone through with my mom through the years. Not that it made a difference in the long run. I didn't know why I'd expected it to. Derek would always do what was best for Derek. He wanted partner. Why *not* throw me under the bus to get it?

Despite never seeing my aunt, I knew where she lived. She'd been in the same house in town with my alcoholic uncle since I'd been a kid. It was a run-down one-story on the edges of the rough part of town. It looked even more like a dump than I remembered. The fence was destroyed in one section, the yard was overrun with weeds, and the entire house looked like one good hurricane wind off the Atlantic would knock the whole thing over.

Uncle Bobby sat on the porch, shirtless, with a litter of Budweisers surrounding him. He nodded his head at me as I parked in the driveway and stomped up the steps. "Hey there. Now, that's a face I haven't seen in a while."

Bobby hadn't always been like this. He and Aunt Ruth had four kids, and he'd been a doting dad until the youngest left for college. I'd joked once that being alone with Aunt Ruth had sent him to the bottle. Gran had called me unkind, but I didn't think that I was wrong.

"Hey, Bobby. My mom here?" I asked, my Southern accent—which I'd thought I'd gotten rid of—coming out in full force.

He glanced at the door and back. "I wouldn't go in there if I were you. They've been yelling since they got back."

"That why you're outside?"

He held up a beer. "Smarter than being in there."

I nodded and then pulled open the screen to knock on the door. The shouting ceased for a blessed minute before Aunt Ruth jerked the door open. She was a portly woman with thinning blonde hair and a mean sneer on her lips.

"Oh, Miss High and Mighty dares to bless us with her

presence," Aunt Ruth said with an eye roll.

"I want to speak to my mom," I said, ignoring her jab at my education.

"Hannah, one of your brats is here."

I clenched my jaw. How the hell these two women had been raised by my Gran was beyond me. How was it even possible that they'd come from the same house that I'd grown up in? Gran had told me that they made their choices, just like I made mine, but it didn't seem like a sufficient enough reason.

"Marley Sue," my mom said, stepping into the light.

She'd always been such a contrast to her sister with beautiful, long, flowing brown hair with just a hint of curl—where I'd gotten mine. Even in her late forties, it was obvious how she'd always gotten men interested in her with her wide brown eyes, perfectly painted lush lips, and lithe figure. Gran had said that I looked like her when I cared about my appearance. I'd scoffed and vowed to only care about where my brain could get me and not my body. It hadn't always worked.

"What the fuck is this, Mom?"

I thrust the paperwork out at her. She took it in her hand, tapping her fresh French manicure against the papers. Then, she arched an eyebrow. "You're the smart one. Shouldn't you know?"

"How *dare* you challenge Gran's will!"

My mom straightened at my words. "Oh, I dare. I was in that will until a few short months ago. Your precious Gran left me and Ruth everything. Clearly, you had something to do with it to get her to hand over everything to you and your brother and leave us with nothing. She wasn't in her right mind in the end anyway."

I glared at her. "*I* didn't do anything. You had that enormous fight with Gran. It's not my fault that she finally saw you as the leech you always were and cut you out."

"Can I quote you on that?" she asked with a smirk.

She made me want to scream. I took a breath and asked, "What do you even want?"

"I want the house."

I shook my head. No fucking way was that happening. "I'll give you money if you need money, but you're not getting the house."

"I don't need your money. When I sell that house, I'll be doing just fine."

"You can't sell Gran's house." My voice hitched, and I hated it. I hated that my mom could make me fall back into that scared little girl all over again. I'd worked so hard to get rid of her.

"You'll find that I absolutely can."

I shook my head. "You're a monster. You were a terrible daughter and an even worse mother. I will fight you tooth and nail over this. You can't win."

She grinned. "Then you'd better lawyer up, Marley Sue. And oh, I already have the best in town."

She slammed the door in my face, the same way I'd done to Derek. This time, I did actually scream. I closed my eyes and let loose.

Uncle Bobby stood and patted my shoulder. "Sorry about that, kid."

I took a deep breath. "I'm going to win."

He nodded but knew better than to say anything where his wife could hear. I stomped away from the house, getting back into Nancy and driving away.

My mother was right about one thing—I needed a lawyer. And I needed one right now. Because there was no fucking way that they were getting the house. Not ever.

5

SAVANNAH

NOVEMBER 1, 2004

I vowed to stop thinking about that kiss at Derek's Halloween party. It was Monday morning, and I needed it to stop. Derek Ballentine was a Holy Cross boy. We might have had a connection in that moment and a series of incredible kisses, but again... Holy Cross boy. I wasn't stupid enough to think that it'd meant anything to him.

Danielle met me in the school parking lot when I hopped out of Maddox's truck. Jack was speed-typing on his phone, hardly paying attention until he saw Maddox. He pocketed his phone, and they started in on the show and future rehearsals and the running theme about the band name.

"Local Carnage is a cool name," Maddox complained.

"It sounds violent," Danielle piped up.

Jack slipped an arm around Danielle as his phone noisily pinged again. He glanced at it and then put it back. "We need something else. Something that fits our sound better."

"Who's texting you?" Danielle asked.

"Just my mom," he said and then arched an eyebrow at Maddox. "Thoughts?"

I let them get ahead of me. Personally, I thought Local Carnage was the best of the ones they'd gone by before. This had to be the third or fourth name they'd picked. Next concert, it would be something else since Jack never seemed to be able to make up his mind.

I stepped inside, and immediately, a guy that I'd only vaguely seen before whistled at me. I jumped, turning around to see if maybe he was whistling at someone else.

"Looking good, Marley," he said with a wink.

My cheeks flushed. What the hell was he talking about? I looked exactly the same as I always did—nondescript. I had on bootcut jeans with a white tank top, layered under a baby-blue T-shirt with a jean jacket over top and a backpack stuffed to the brim. My hair was in a ponytail, and I had on zero makeup. There was no reason for whistling.

I hurried away from the guy, tucking the book I was holding tight to my chest. I stopped at my locker, opening it with the combination and filling the space from my over-stuffed backpack. I was only a sophomore, but I was already taking three AP classes, and my class load was intense on top of dance and cheer.

"So, Marley," a guy said, leaning against the side of the locker next to mine. This one I *did* recognize. Brandt Johnston was a senior and on the baseball team. He was being recruited by Alabama. "You want to go out this weekend?"

I gawked at him and looked around as if I might know another Marley. As far as I knew, I was the only one in the school. "I... what?"

"I was thinking you could come over to my house." He winked.

I blushed deeper. "Um..."

"Maybe eight o'clock."

The bell rang. "I... I have to get to class."

"I'll find you later," he said and then touched my arm as he passed.

I was so flustered that I was nearly late to my homeroom, where I slid into a seat next to Leigh. She had a compact out and was powdering her face as our teacher wrote out our assignment for the period.

"Leigh something strange is happening. Brandt Johnston just asked me out in the hall."

She snapped her compact closed. "What?"

"Yeah, and some guy whistled at me." I gestured to my nerd outfit. "*Me.*"

Leigh frowned and then bit her overly glossed lips. "Well, I might have heard something about that in the hall."

"About what?"

"So... it's going around school that you slept with a senior Holy Cross guy this weekend."

I gaped at her. "I *what*?"

"Yeah," she said with a wince. "I tried to tell someone there was no way that it was you. It had to be someone else."

"Of course it wasn't me! I've never... I mean, I wouldn't..."

"Mars, I know. But I guess some guys from the football team saw you coming downstairs with some guy who has a reputation for fucking everything that walks."

I blinked at her as my stomach dropped out. "Derek?"

"Yes!" she said, pointing at me. "That's the guy."

"I was just looking for the bathroom!"

Leigh winced. "I'm sorry, Mars."

"Did he tell people we slept together?"

Leigh shrugged. "I have no idea."

"So, these guys whistling and asking me out... they think

it's because I'm easy?" I whispered in horror. "Oh my God, am I the new school slut?"

"I'm sure it will all blow over. Try not to worry about it. They're stupid high school boys."

"Ladies," Ms. Matthews called. "Do you want to continue your conversation, or can the rest of us get started?"

"Sorry, Ms. Matthews," we said in unison.

But my mind was not on the subject. Not that I really had to pay attention as she finished up homeroom and started our Honors English class. I was getting a hundred just by reading the books. Apparently, that was rocket science in my school of CliffsNotes.

I was out of it the rest of the day. I was asked out twice more. Brandt Johnston cornered me at my locker again. And a half-dozen other assholes made catcalls like I was working a fucking corner. All that time I'd been working so hard to be the smart girl had just gone out the window with one interaction with Derek Ballentine.

When we got back to the parking lot that afternoon, it was clear that Maddox had heard some bastardized version of what had happened. He looked pale. "Mars."

"Just don't." I held my hand up. "It didn't happen. If I have to hear about it again, I'm going to be sick."

"I didn't think it happened! I didn't think about it at all." He grimaced.

"Ew, Maddox. Stop!" I threw my backpack in the bed of the truck and got into the passenger side as Maddox started the engine. "I need you to do something for me."

"What?"

"I need you to take me to Derek's house."

Maddox looked at me as if I'd sprouted a second head. "Why would I do that? We have to be home on time, or Gran will freak."

"Then, tell her I had a cheer meeting or something."

"Lie?"

"You lie all the time! Just take me to his house, Maddox!"

"Fine. Fine," he grumbled as he took the truck out of the parking lot. "For the record, this is a bad idea. What are you even going to say to this guy?"

"I don't know," I admitted.

I was running on adrenaline and anger. A potent combination on a good day, and today was not a good day. But I couldn't do nothing. As much as Leigh had said it would blow over, it wasn't going to blow over tomorrow or the next day. And I was going to sock someone in the nuts if they tried to proposition me again.

Maddox pulled over in front of Derek's house. "Don't be too long. I can only run interference with Gran for so long."

"Yeah, okay."

I hopped out of the truck and crossed to the front of his mansion, pulling open the intimidating wrought iron gate. The house was even more impressive in the daylight. Also somehow, it looked twice as big. And I looked like a sixteen-year-old sophomore. I pushed back my stray curls and then yelled internally at myself for trying to make myself look nice for him. It was his fault this had all started to begin with.

I rang the doorbell, and a minute later, a woman pulled the door open.

"Hi, honey!" she exclaimed in a straight Scarlett O'Hara Southern drawl. She was also stunning with platinum-blonde hair to her waist and immaculate makeup. She wore a pastel-pink minidress with a square cut, revealing ample cleavage, and four-inch wedges. Her legs were long and fake tan. She could have been a model.

I had no idea who she was. Maybe an older sister. Though they didn't look anything alike.

"Hello."

"You must be Derek's date."

"I..."

"Come in. Come in," she said, ushering me inside. "I'm his stepmom, Kathy."

Stepmom. Well, that explained why she looked twenty-five.

"Hi, I'm Marley."

"Marley, darling, it's so nice to meet you. Let me get Derek for you."

I opened my mouth to object, but this was probably the easiest way to get his attention. Anyway, who had a date on a Monday night during the school year?

"Derek, your date is here!" Kathy called up the stairwell as her heels clomped on the hardwood.

Derek appeared at the top of the stairs in a variation on what he'd been wearing at the party—khakis and a pink striped button-up with the sleeves rolled up to his elbows. "I don't have a date today."

Kathy laughed. "Well, your little girlfriend is here, honey."

Then Derek caught sight of me standing at the base of the stairs. He cocked his head to the side, and a smirk caught on his pouty lips. "Thanks, Kathy."

"Anytime," she said with a wink. "Go get 'em." She turned to me, coming back down the stairs. "Marley, do you want a drink?."

"Um, no, thank you."

"Well, y'all let me know if you need anything."

"Okay."

Derek trotted down the stairs, adjusting the sleeve of his shirt before stopping in front of me. "Hey, Marley."

"Hey," I said, momentarily stupefied in his presence again. Seriously, how was he this hot?

"Didn't expect to see you again after you ran out on Saturday."

I cleared my head. I wasn't here to look at how pretty he was. That didn't matter. What mattered was the shit that had happened at school.

"Yeah, well, apparently, I didn't run away fast enough."

His brow furrowed. "What do you mean?"

"The entire school thinks we slept together!"

"Oh," he said smoothly. He shrugged one shoulder. "So?"

"News flash: we *didn't* sleep together."

"I know that. You know that. Why else does it matter?"

"Because I'm getting hit on by a ton of guys at school. I'm getting leered at and catcalled, and some guy smacked my ass in the hallway."

"Okay." He nodded his head. "And it's bad that guys at school want to ask you out?"

"Yes! They are only doing it because they think I'm easy!"

"I don't think you're easy."

"You are missing the point!" I nearly shrieked at him. Then I took a deep breath and let it out. "I want this to stop. So, whoever you told that we slept together, I need you to tell them the truth. I need you to make it stop."

He shrugged again, unperturbed. "I didn't tell anyone we slept together."

"Well, can you let people know that's the case?"

He held his hands out in front of him, all casual and cool. "No one would believe me."

"What? Why not?" I demanded.

He laughed softly and shot me a look of pure sexual appeal. "Why do you think?"

"Oh God, Derek, gross. You're such a whore that no one would believe if you said we didn't sleep together?"

"Hey, you should take it as a compliment."

"You're a pig," I snapped. "And the entire thing is fucked up. You get to be this awesome guy for having slept with a lot of girls. Whereas I'm suddenly the town slut for being associated with you?"

"It's not like I asked for that to happen to you," he said, his voice turning sharp after I called him a whore.

"No, of course not. None of this is your fault. And you're not going to do anything about it."

"There is one solution," he said with a grin that said I wasn't going to like the suggestion at all.

But I wanted a solution. So, I sighed and asked, "What?"

"You could just go out with me. I didn't get your number on Saturday."

I blinked at him and then burst into laughter. "Oh dear God, no. You think I'd want to go out with you after this shit? Do your pickup lines actually work on people?"

"All the time," he said, tilting his head at me in a way that I sometimes looked at my Calculus homework.

"It's not going to work on me. You can't sweet-talk your way out of this."

"Look, it's not my fault that some guys are hitting on you at school. What exactly do you want me to do? Show up to a school that I don't go to and hold an assembly to let them know that you didn't get laid?"

"No," I grumbled.

"Right. There is no way that would happen anyway."

I glared at him. He was right. This wasn't going to fix it.

He wouldn't tell anyone because he had his precious reputation to uphold. And there was no way I was going to go out with him and let the rumors be true. He was dangerous in all the ways that made me forget the world. I had no intention of letting him dig in deeper under my skin.

"Whatever. This is still your fault," I snapped at him.

He laughed. "I like you, Marley."

"You don't even know me," I said as I headed for the door.

"Not yet," he called as I yanked the door open.

"Not ever!"

His laughter followed me as I slammed the door shut. What an asshole! This was his fault. His damn reputation was ruining everything for me, and he didn't even care. And worse, just being in his presence got under my skin. I could have very easily said yes when he asked me out. And I didn't want that. Did I?

* * *

"Marley and Maddox Nelson!" Gran called as soon as we walked into the house. "Where were you?"

"Uh... cheer meeting," I tried.

She shook her head. "I called the cheer coach, and she said practice was tomorrow. Try again."

I sighed heavily and let my head hang. "It wasn't Maddox. I asked him to drive me."

"Oh?" She held her hand out. "Maddox, keys."

"Oh man," he grumbled, passing them to her.

"No rehearsal this week. Go do your homework."

"Yes, ma'am."

"Marley, sit."

I sat. "Gran, it's not what you think."

"What do I think?" she drawled as she eased back into her favorite chair.

"I don't know," I admitted.

"I think you lied to me. Tell me the whole story. Start from the beginning."

I didn't know how she knew, but she did. She always did. So, I told her what had happened—the party, the kiss, the kids at school, going to see Derek. She listened without comment through all of it. Even the kiss.

When I was finished, she finally asked, "And do you like this boy?"

"No!"

She arched an eyebrow. "Don't lie to me."

I huffed. "I don't know him."

"Yet you kissed him."

"I… yeah."

"I see."

"I mean, we did talk before it happened. I felt connected to him. Like he wasn't going to be a bad guy. But obviously, he was."

"I'm going to tell you the same thing that I told your mom at your age."

I groaned. "I don't want to hear about Mom."

"Don't speak ill of your mother, chickadee. She gave you life. She deserves your respect."

"Even if she hasn't earned it?" I grumbled under my breath.

"Yes," she said confidently. "Now, I told your mom that every person is going through their own struggles. You can never know what someone else is dealing with or why they act the way they do."

"But, Gran…"

She held a hand up. "But if you let them take advantage of you once, they'll do it forever."

I froze in surprise at the words she'd uttered. I had expected a Christian lecture about treating people the way you wanted to be treated.

"So, if this boy did you wrong and you showed him kindness, you gave him a way out. Then, you need to make sure he understands that he can't hurt you again."

I tilted my head. "I like the way you think, Gran."

She laughed and patted my hand twice. "Your mom never quite learned that one, but I think you will. You have to assert yourself, or you'll be walked over your whole life."

"Thanks, Gran. For everything."

"You're welcome, sweetie." She kissed the top of my head. "Oh, and you're grounded for a week too."

I groaned. "But my driver's test is Saturday."

"I guess you'll need to spend all your extra time studying."

"And the game Friday?"

"It's an obligation. So, yes, but there and back, and I'll be driving you."

I huffed in frustration but nodded before she could tack on more time. "All right."

"Love you."

"Love you too."

She headed for the kitchen. "Get your brother, and I'll grab Gramps out of the garden for dinner."

I watched her go in frustration. The grounding sucked. But her words gave me a few ideas about what to do in regard to Derek.

6

SAVANNAH

NOVEMBER 6, 2004

I twirled in a circle. "I did it! I passed."

"Good job, loser," Maddox said, punching my arm.

"Jerk!"

"Children," Gran said with a shake of her head. She held her old-school Polaroid up to her eye. "Now, smile."

We got close together and smiled wide. She snapped the shot, and the picture popped out of the camera. She shook it twice and then handed it to me.

"Congratulations, chickadee."

Gramps pulled me in for a hug. "I always knew you could do it."

"Aww, thanks, Gramps."

"Celebratory ice cream," Gran suggested.

"Leopold's!" Maddox and I cheered at the same time.

"Of course. The one and only. Marley, you can drive." She tossed me the keys to the minivan. "It's all yours."

"Mine?"

She nodded. "I spoke with Melody at the church, and

she sold me her Camry. I thought you needed your own vehicle."

I clutched the keys to my chest. A minivan was the last thing that I wanted. Literally any other car would be preferable. But tears still came to my eyes as Gran handed it off to me. I had my own car. My *own* car. No more relying on Maddox to not be a jerk. No chauffeuring to and from dance and cheer and school.

"Thank you, Gran"—I hugged her tight—"and Gramps."

He squeezed me too. "You deserve it with all those straight As."

I laughed. "Thanks."

"If only you could convince your brother to care," Gran said, arching an eyebrow at Maddox.

"Hey, I care," he said with a shrug. "Sort of."

I laughed. That said all that we needed to know. Maddox was easily as smart as me. He just wanted the challenge, and if it wasn't there, he got bored. His grades suffered from his boredom.

"All right," Gran said. "Let's go."

I trailed my family out of the DMV and stopped before exiting when I heard my name. I turned around in surprise to find Derek's stepmom, Kathy.

"It's Marley, right?" she asked, all bubbly. Today, she was in black cigarette pants, a frilly white blouse, and nude high heels. Her hair and makeup were as immaculate as ever.

"Yes. So nice to see you."

"Ah! I thought it was you. You're Derek's little girlfriend."

I laughed and shook my head. "We're not really dating."

She buttoned up her lips. "I know how things go these days in school." Which was hilarious because she couldn't be that much older than us. "He's been talking about his date at the marina all weekend."

I arched an eyebrow. "Oh yeah?"

"Yes. I'm glad to see that he's interested in a sensible girl."

I kept my comment to myself as my brain started working. "Mrs. Ballentine..."

"Kathy, please, dear."

"Kathy, do you have the address for the marina? He never sent it over."

"You know, I think I do." She pulled out her phone and scrolled through. Then, she wrote the address down on a piece of paper. "Have a good time! Sunset sailing in Savannah is to die for." She clicked her tongue. "Ah, to be young and in love."

I grinned as I waved good-bye to her and pocketed the address.

"What was that about?" Gran asked.

"Just saw someone I knew."

"Stop taking so long. A banana split is calling my name," Maddox complained.

"Shut it, Maddox," I said with a laugh as we headed to the car and I plotted my revenge.

* * *

Leopold's had an hour-long line, but it was always worth it. Anyway, it was better than waiting that time in the summer heat and humidity. At least November was sort of manageable here. But more importantly, neither me nor Maddox were grounded anymore as a treat for me passing the driver's test. Which meant I had real freedom for the first time. So as soon as we got home, I planned to use it.

"I'm going out, Gran," I said, grabbing the keys to the minivan with a little too much enthusiasm. They dropped off of the hook and fell to the ground. I picked them back up in a hurry. Maybe I was more nervous than I'd thought.

Gramps looked up from the biography he was reading. "Have a good time, sweetheart."

"Thanks, Gramps."

"Wait one minute," Gran said. "Where are you going? Who are you going to be with? What time will you be home? Do you have your phone with you?"

"I'm not going anywhere. I was going to drive around by myself. I can be home by eleven."

"Ten," she corrected.

"Sure. Ten, and yes, I always have my phone."

"How are you going to pay for the gas of *just driving around*?"

I opened my mouth and then closed it. Gas. Maddox had gotten a part-time job to pay for the truck. "I'll ask Miss Alicia if she needs help at the studio."

Gran nodded approvingly. "That's my girl."

I'd been dancing at Miss Alicia's studio since I was four. Lila had gone to another studio until we met in the second grade over our mutual love for Lisa Frank. She'd transferred studios so that we could dance together. We'd done everything together until she moved to St. Catherine's. It sucked, not having her in school. But at the same time, I was glad that she hadn't heard any of the rumors about me. Leigh and Danielle had spent all week tiptoeing around me, and I didn't want that from Lila too. So, I was going to do this on my own.

The sun wouldn't set for a half hour, but it was at least a twenty-minute drive out to the marina. Miss Alicia would have to wait. I'd ask her tomorrow during studio time if she needed help for competition season this spring.

Gran would bring Maddox and me out to Tybee Island

every weekend all summer to get beach time in. Water was my happy place. I'd always been that way. The water calmed me down. But I'd never been on a boat out. That was reserved for people with money, which we never really had.

I pulled the minivan behind the Publix and down a back alley. I craned my neck, hoping that this was the right place to be on Whitemarsh Island. The directions weren't the best. I'd scribbled them down at home, but I hadn't wanted to study the map too long, or Gran might have noticed.

The parking lot was empty, save for a shiny black Range Rover. A smile crossed my face. That had to be Derek's car. The fact that he had a brand-new eighty-something-thousand dollar car while I was driving Gran's old minivan said everything about where we'd come from.

Still, I hopped out of the minivan, rolled my shoulders back, and headed for the dock. I had no idea which one of the boats belonged to Derek, but my gut said it was the biggest one at the end of the dock. I was heading determinedly in that direction when I heard a voice clear behind me.

"Well, well, well."

Derek climbed out of a smaller sailboat. He looked skeptical. As he well should since I was here for nefarious purposes. But damn, he looked good. His whole sailing outfit fit a lot more out here. This time in navy-blue shorts and a white button-up with those same boat shoes. He'd clearly been wearing a hat because there was an indention around his almost curls at his ears.

For a second, all thoughts fled my head. The whole reason for me being here. The moment I'd been waiting for since he'd ruined my reputation and not cared at all. Because it'd been a week and it hadn't blown over. In fact, it might have gotten worse. Now, everyone at school had heard about it, and the girls were being terrible too. Of course, they didn't have sympathy for what I was going through; they'd rather think the worst and shun me. Fun times.

"Hey, Derek," I said with a smile.

I'd worn something that Gran would have never let me out of the house in. I'd changed out of my jeans and hoodie into a miniskirt and tank top. She'd flip her lid, but I had a plan.

"Marley," he said with a head nod. His eyes dropped to my legs and back up. "What are you doing out here?"

"Came to see you."

He crossed his arms. "Yeah? And how did you know that I'd be here?"

"I saw Kathy."

"Hmm... she didn't mention that."

"She might have thought that I was your date."

He laughed. "Yeah, well, I have a date with Krista Kendrick tonight. So, you should probably go."

That name sounded familiar, but I didn't know why.

"She's a St. Catherine's cheerleader. Miss Junior Savannah," he filled in.

I blinked. "Oh."

Shit. Krista was one of those bombshell girls. She was in all the pageants and sometimes came into Miss Alicia's for solo lessons. I was sure she had no idea who I was. But also, clearly, I couldn't compete with the Kristas of the world. My plan was coming unraveled, and I'd just gotten here.

I needed to stall. "That's your boat?"

He hardly blinked at the change of subject. His eyes lit up, and his smile went with it. "Yeah, this is *Sandra*. She's a beauty, and she's all mine."

"Kind of small. I expected..." My eyes drifted back to the massive sailboat.

"Yeah. Well, that one is my dad's. I saved up for three years to get *Sandra* here. I bought her off of a local and do most of the repairs myself."

"You *bought* the boat?"

He grinned at me. "Yeah. I've been working out on the marina since I could walk. The only thing that I've ever really wanted to do is be on the water. Now that I have my own boat, I can take the Intracoastal Waterway up to Charleston and see my cousins. I could take it all the way up to Virginia and down to Florida if I wanted."

I tried to reconcile this Derek with the one I saw when he was with other people. I'd put him squarely in the bad category. But here he was, just a guy with a passion. It was what had drawn him to me when he helped his sister and then talked about Duke versus UNC. I'd never expected him to be more than the charming playboy.

"That sounds amazing," I finally admitted. "I've never been sailing."

"What? It's the best feeling in the entire world. I should take you out sometime." Then, he frowned and glanced back to the marina entrance just as a car door shut. "Just not right now. What are you doing here anyway?"

But I didn't get a chance to tell him.

"Derek!" Krista Kendrick called. She was in a flowy dress and tall wedges. Her hair was down, as if the humidity didn't affect it at all, and a full face of makeup. She stepped onto the dock and scrutinized me. "Who is this?"

"Hey, babe. This is no one. Just a friend."

Krista looked doubtful. "Just a friend," she drawled. "I know you, Derek. You don't have any female friends."

I shot her an innocent, wide-eyed look. "I should be going. Sorry."

"Wait," Krista spat. She looked between us and saw

Derek's reputation and not what was reality. As I'd suspected she would. I didn't even have to say anything. His reputation would do its work for me. "Did you forget about us today?"

"No, of course not," Derek said hastily. He glanced over at me. I smiled sweetly at him, and he narrowed his eyes. "Marley, you should go."

"Right, yeah."

Krista held her hand out to stop me. "Are you double-dipping, Derek? Did you already take her out?"

"What? No."

"Oh my God," she said with a shake of her head. "I ignored all of my friends who said this was a bad idea. I said that you were different with me. But I was wrong, wasn't I?"

"Krista, babe..."

"God, I'm an idiot. We all know who you are, Derek. That you'd do this to *me* is beyond stupid."

I tried to inch around her. "I didn't mean... I'll just get out of here."

"Were you here for a date with him?" she demanded.

"I... no..." I told the truth, stumbling over the words, as if I had no idea what she was talking about.

"Tell her, Marley," Derek demanded.

But I just smiled at him. And it was that moment that he realized what I was doing. Why I'd shown up. It was as if all the pieces slid into place in his mind.

Krista snorted. "Well, Marley... he's all yours."

She turned and stomped back down the dock. Derek followed after her, trying to explain. But how could he explain my presence? His reputation had worked against me... so why shouldn't it work against him too?

I waited with a smile as he tried unsuccessfully to salvage his date. But Krista got back into her car and peeled out of the parking lot without a backward glance. Derek jogged back onto the deck. He looked mad but mostly shocked that I'd gotten him back at his own game.

"What the fuck was that?"

"Oh sorry," I said, batting my eyelashes at him. "Would you like me to go after her and tell her that we didn't sleep together?"

His jaw set. "So, that's what this is about."

"What? Did you think I'd stop caring about all this?"

"It's not my fault that people are talking about you at school."

"It's *your* reputation," I snapped. "You clearly knew how people would see it. You get off scot-free, and I have to suffer the consequences. I decided if you wouldn't do anything about it, then I would."

He shook his head. "You're insane."

I laughed. "No, I'm brilliant."

He tilted his head again, giving me that look that I hadn't been able to decipher at the party. "You could always let me take you sailing."

"What?" I asked, stunned by the offer.

"You could make it up to me," he said with a panty-melting smile.

I blinked. "Have you lost it? I just fucked up your date."

"Yeah. Well, I'm a *make the best of any situation* kind of guy." He patted *Sandra*. "So?"

"You know what? You could make all of this up to me by telling people we didn't hook up."

He sighed. "Are you going to keep showing up here and sabotaging my dates?"

I grinned devilishly. "Yes."

"Then, yes, I'll do it. I don't think it'll change anything, but fine. Are you happy?"

"Yep."

"So... sailing?"

"You think I'd get on that boat with you?"

I checked my watch. Technically, I didn't have to be home until ten, which was unheard of, especially since I'd been grounded. And yeah, I wanted to go out on that boat. I'd never been before, and God, I loved the water.

But one look at his smug face told me exactly why I couldn't. He expected me to say yes. He knew his charm worked on everyone, and then he could get away with murder. I wasn't going to be another one of his girls.

"No thanks," I said and then strode down the dock away from him.

"You're really just going to walk away?" he asked disbelievingly.

"Yep!" I called back. I popped open the door to the minivan. "Have fun out on the water alone, Derek."

"Aww, Minivan, you're breaking my heart."

I waggled my fingers at him. "Get used to it!"

Then I hopped into the van and left him behind.

7

SAVANNAH

PRESENT

"Thank you so much," I said, holding my hand out to the attorney.

"Of course, Miss Nelson," she said. "Mr. Nelson." She shook Maddox's hand next. "I understand that this is a hard time in your life and you want to focus on grieving. I'm glad to take the case. I'll get to work on it, but I'd like to reiterate that this can be a long process. Just bear with me through the worst of it."

"We understand," I said.

Maddox nodded. "Thanks for your help."

"Take my card, and if you ever have any questions, feel free to give me a call or email."

I took it and slid it into my purse before following Maddox out of the office. My stomach rumbled with anxiety. It had been two weeks since Derek had shown up at my house and flipped everything upside down. I'd gotten in contact with an attorney right away, but this was the first available meeting time. I'd been a wreck since then.

"Well, that was fun," he muttered, running a hand back through his curls. They'd grown longer this summer, looking more like when he'd been in high school. Sometimes, I missed Maddox's wild curls.

"Not particularly."

I got into the passenger seat of his Wrangler and tried to keep the tears from falling. If this were a normal school year, I'd be back at Emory, getting ready for my classes this fall. School started Wednesday and instead, I was still in Savannah. It was worse because I'd finally been approved for my sabbatical semester. I'd taken the fall off so that I could spend it with Gran during her sickness. And then she'd passed before I even got here.

I squeezed my eyes shut. I couldn't change any of it, and I needed to be in Savannah to deal with all of this anyway. But it didn't make any of it easier. I just wanted my Gran back.

"Where to?" Maddox asked.

"I need a drink."

"All right. There's a dive bar that I like—"

"No. Not in public," I said automatically. "Just... I don't know. Let's go to the liquor store."

Maddox nodded. "We'll get through it together."

He drove through downtown, nabbing a parking spot directly in front of the nicest local liquor store. Not generally the store I'd drop into, but I had to admit, it had a better selection.

Maddox followed me inside, but we split up as he went for the beer and I headed for the wine. I wanted to get a few bottles. I still had enough brandy at Gran's to make a few sidecars. I'd watched Gran drink them for years and fallen in love with them when she finally let me have one of my own.

I added a few bottles of red and white into my basket

and then went to take a look at the mixers. I turned the corner in the mixer aisle and nearly dropped the basket.

"Holy shit," I hissed. "Ash?"

Ash Talmadge looked up at me, and I nearly swore again. Ash had been Lila's on-again, off-again since high school. They'd called it off this summer, and I hadn't seen him since then. I'd assumed that he was upset, but I hadn't assumed that he would look like... this.

Normally, Ash was carefully buttoned up with short brown hair and piercing blue eyes. He was a wealthy Holy Cross boy who still worked with his father in real estate. The Talmadges owned half of downtown at this point. I'd seen him after he got into a car accident and broke a few ribs, and he'd looked better then than he did now.

His wrinkly polo was unbuttoned with the collar popped with khakis and flip-flops. I'd never seen him in flip-flops. I hadn't been sure he even owned them. He had a little more than a five o'clock shadow. I'd only ever seen him freshly shaven. Then there were the sunglasses... he was wearing inside. Oh, and the entire *shopping cart* full of alcohol.

He stalled abruptly when he saw me. Something flashed across his face, and then he looked away. "Hey, Mars."

"Are you... are you okay?" I asked, closing the distance.

"Fine."

"You don't look fine."

"Thanks. Real nice," he grumbled. "What are you even doing in town?"

"Gran died," I whispered. I hated saying those words.

He looked over at me again and slowly removed his sunglasses. His eyes were bloodshot, and he had dark bruises under them, as if he hadn't been sleeping since Lila left. "I'm sorry. I hadn't heard."

"Yeah. She'd been sick for a while. I thought we had more time."

"Sorry, Mars."

I nodded and choked back tears again. "Thanks. What about you?"

"What about me?"

"You were wearing sunglasses inside," I pointed out. "And you have a cart full of alcohol."

"Been a rough couple months. And I'm throwing a party."

"Yeah?"

"Labor Day out on the yacht."

I remembered quite a few parties that he'd thrown out on the yacht. I was usually invited because of Lila. This was all new territory. And while I was Lila's best friend, I'd been around Ash too long to let him crawl into this shell of himself. I was worried about him.

"That sounds fun."

"Eh," he said noncommittally. "It will be something to do to pass the time rather than being alone."

I winced. Jesus, he was in a terrible place. "Are you sure you shouldn't just go see a therapist instead? What happened with Lila—"

"Stop," he spat. "Don't say her name."

"Sorry," I said quickly. "I didn't mean to..."

He slid the glasses back into place. "I don't want to talk about my *feelings*. I don't want to talk about her. I just want to get drunk. You can come to the party if you don't mention her."

"Ash..."

"Are you coming or not?"

"Yeah," I said finally. "Yeah, I'll be there."

Mostly to keep an eye on him. He was nosediving into

the worst version of himself. I had some experience with that.

Ash wandered off, and Maddox found me a few minutes later.

"Whoa, did you see Ash Talmadge?" He whistled with his hand out like an airplane and then made a crashing sound.

"Well, he's been through shit. He invited me to a yacht party on Monday. Want to go?"

"Nope. We only went before because of Lila."

"Yeah, but I'm worried about him."

"Can't blame the dude."

"No, me neither."

Still, just because I got Lila in the breakup didn't mean that I couldn't check on Ash. I just wouldn't tell her about it.

"Don't you think Derek will be there?" Maddox asked once we were in the car again.

"Fuck. I didn't think about that," I muttered. "Well, I'll be there for Ash. I can avoid him, right?"

"Probably not, but maybe you can tell him to go fuck himself again. He might deserve that," Maddox said, white-knuckling the steering wheel.

I stared out the window. I didn't want to see Derek. Especially after what had happened with the will. But I wouldn't let him run me out of events either. Ash needed someone to help him, and if his Derek wasn't doing it, then I'd try.

8

SAVANNAH

PRESENT

"You're doing what?" Josie asked on the Bluetooth in my car as I drove to the Savannah Yacht Club.

"You heard me."

"But why, Mars?"

"You didn't see him, Josie. He's a wreck."

"Well, yeah. You were there. You know what happened."

"Yeah, and it's kind of our fault."

Josie snorted. "Don't put that on us. They all made their own choices. Ash Talmadge was never good enough for Lila anyway."

I didn't know about that. She'd been happy with him. But all of that was over now. He didn't deserve to be miserable.

"I'm still going."

"Are you going to tell her?"

I shook my head. "No way. Lila doesn't need to deal with his baggage. That's why I am."

"I swear you're a saint, Marley."

I laughed. "Not by half."

"Speaking of people not good enough for my friends, are

you going to see Derek while you're there?" Josie asked as if she were being nonchalant.

I hadn't told either of my friends about what had happened with the will. I needed to get it out there, but I was still so mad that I didn't want it to even exist. And I knew they'd both come running. I wasn't prepared for that.

"Yeah. I think he'll be at the party."

I could practically see her wicked smile. "And he's divorced, right? Officially."

"I don't keep up with him."

"Well, have fun at least. You deserve some fun after Gran."

I cleared my throat. "Love you, but I'm here. I'll call you later and tell you how it went."

"Don't do anything I wouldn't do."

"There's nothing you wouldn't do," I muttered.

She laughed. "I wouldn't hook up with my best friend's ex."

I gagged. "Ew. I couldn't even think that."

"See, there you go. You're good."

I laughed and then hung up. I pulled my bag filled with everything I needed for a day out on the water out of the trunk and walked out onto the dock. Ash's yacht technically belonged to his father, but Ash used it more than his dad. He always had. Ash and Derek had their love of the water in common. I tried not to think of all the times I'd been on the water with Derek as I stepped onto the yacht and found two-dozen mostly naked women on board.

My eyes rounded in surprise. I didn't recognize a single one of them. They were all probably a decade younger than me, giggling with White Claws in one hand and their phones in the other. There was nothing wrong with any of that, but I certainly didn't fit into any of those descriptions.

"Marley!"

I turned to find Amelia Ballentine in a two-piece white suit. She was as stunning as any of the doe-eyed blondes on board. Honestly, I'd never guess she was twenty-eight to my thirty. She still looked exactly the same. Those Ballentine genes were something else. Though I was sure it was a lot of hard work to stay so physically fit. She'd been Miss Georgia and Miss Georgia USA, having competed in both the Miss America and Miss USA pageants.

Amelia pulled me into a hug. "It's so good to see you."

"Hey, Mia," I said, hugging her back. "You too. How have you been?"

"Busy! Working full-time at the boutique and coaching pageants."

"I really should swing by the store. I haven't been since you opened."

"Yes, come by. I'd love for you to try on my new collection." She twirled in a circle. "This is one of my latest."

Amelia had gone to Parsons in NYC for fashion design. She'd worked in high-end fashion after but ultimately come home to open her own shop right here in Savannah. I still found it hard to believe that she'd wanted to leave everything behind. But she seemed happy doing her own thing. She always had.

"I love it. Better than my Target bathing suit."

She laughed as I stripped out of my tank top and shorts.

"Oh, shush. You're adorable."

"You're sweet."

"I'm glad that someone else with a brain is here," Amelia said with an eye roll. "The entire thing reeks of desperation."

My gaze traveled over the lot of women and then found the source of their excitement. Ash Talmadge had appeared shirtless in baby-blue swim trunks and Ray-Bans. He still looked like a hot mess, but he was sure faking it for his adoring crowd.

"Yeah. That's kind of why I'm here. I saw him at the liquor store. He looked..."

"Rough?" she offered. Amelia threw her long, dark hair off of her shoulder. "Of course he does after what happened. What I don't get is why all these girls are throwing themselves at him. He needs time to recover, not whatever *this* is."

I shrugged. "He's encouraging it. You can't blame the women."

"Yeah. Well, at least he has an excuse," she said venomously. Then she shrugged a petite shoulder. "Come on. I secured the best tanning location."

She dragged me away from Ash's shitshow and to the other side of the yacht. I lathered sunscreen on my pasty self and was grateful that there was an umbrella that I could use to shield myself. Otherwise, I'd be a lobster within minutes.

I pulled out a book. I'd brought one for *fun*. Usually I was reading the latest articles from the neuroscience field to try to keep up with my research. But since I had the semester off, I could pick up a fiction novel. I'd settled on Sarah J. Maas's *A Court of Thorns and Roses* because who didn't like hot Fae and a *Beauty and the Beast* retelling?

My brain was deep in the woods with Feyre when a voice cleared to my left. And then cleared again. I glanced up in a daze and found Derek in all of his glory. He was shirtless, his toned chest and stomach on full display. How he managed to still have a full six-pack was beyond me. His pale pink shorts were a few inches shorter than his knees with Rainbows on his feet. He sported Ray-Bans and a smirk that made my brain short-circuit.

"Sidecar?"

I blinked at him in confusion. "What?"

He held a drink out to me. "You still like sidecars, right?"

"Oh." I straightened, putting a cute bookmark that read, *The stars belong to those who read*, inside the book and took the drink. "Yeah, I do. You remembered."

"Yeah," he said with that same great smile.

"Derek, if you ruin this for me, I will cut you," Amelia threatened.

Derek laughed. "Mia, shut it."

"She's the only one here I like. I need a good sunbathing partner."

"I'm mostly in the shade," I reminded her.

"Your legs are in the sun!"

"I won't ruin your tan," Derek muttered.

I took a sip of the drink and nearly groaned. It was perfection. It was the same brandy that Gran always used. For a second, I teared up. All the happy memories soured with the first sweet taste and the note of lemon. I blinked away the tear and took another drink.

"Thanks for the drink."

"You okay?"

"Yeah. Fine. Just tastes like Gran made it."

He shot me a sympathetic look and nodded. "Yeah. I should have thought of that."

"I like it. I don't want to forget her." Then I arched an eyebrow at him. "Or watch her legacy be destroyed."

He winced. "I did try not to take the case."

I rolled my eyes and held a hand up. "Let's not discuss this. If I have to be on this giant boat with you all day, I would rather not bring it up." Then, I opened my book again and tried to get back into the story.

"All right." He ran a hand back through his hair and

looked out on the water. "I'm surprised that you showed up today."

I sighed heavily and put my book aside. Obviously he was not going to let me sit here and read. "As I was telling your sister, I saw Ash at the liquor store, and I'm worried about him."

"Me too."

Derek grabbed a nearby chair and scraped it across the deck to bring it over to where we were sitting. Amelia glared up at him, and he shot her a look that clearly said, *What?* She huffed and lay back down, facedown.

"Why are you even letting him have this stupid party?"

Derek snorted. "As if anyone could make Ash Talmadge do anything."

"True."

"Are you going to tell Lila?"

"No! Why is everyone asking me that? I'm not going to tell her anything. I just don't want him to jump off a building or something."

"Derek! Stop bothering her," Amelia said.

"I'm not bothering her," he snapped back. "I'm trying to see if Delila Greer is going to walk back into his life and ruin everything again."

"She won't," I told him confidently. "And anyway, I'm here for Ash. That's it. I'll help however I can."

Derek nodded as if that was what he wanted to know. He was a dick, but he was loyal to his people. He and Ash had been close since high school but had really become best friends once Ash moved back home. This couldn't be easy for Derek to watch.

"Good," he said with a wink and then strode away into the sea of women.

I watched him walk away with a pang in my chest. As

much as I was mad at Derek, there had always been something between us. Something I hadn't even known existed for many, many years. Being around him, even when I wanted to slap him, just felt... normal.

"Don't go there, Mars," Amelia said softly.

"What?" I said, jerking my attention away.

"I love my brother, but he's as much of a wreck as Ash."

"About the divorce?" I couldn't help but ask.

Derek had been married to another local girl, and it hadn't worked out. As far as I knew, the divorce had been finalized sometime this summer. But as much as Josie joked, I really hadn't been keeping up with him. I'd blocked him on my social media so that I didn't have to see any of it. He made me angry, but we'd been real for however brief of a moment, and I didn't want it in my face.

Amelia laughed. "Hardly. Good riddance. He was pumped when the divorce was settled."

"Oh," I said. "I didn't know what happened."

"She's crazy. That's all you need to know." Amelia flipped over, applying more bronzing lotion all over her lean figure.

"I see."

"And he never got over you."

I laughed heartily and opened my book again. "Yeah right."

Amelia shrugged. "Believe what you want, but he doesn't look at anyone else like he looks at you."

"He took on a case to contest my grandma's will," I told her with more bite than I'd intended. "I don't think he'd have done that if he was still into me."

"I'm a hundred percent sure that was because of our father."

"Yeah, well, it doesn't matter. Derek and I are old news."

But as the day progressed, I wondered if maybe Amelia

was right. Derek brought me sidecars all afternoon until I had to stop drinking because I was getting drunk. Then, he brought me water unprompted. I finished the book in record time and hadn't brought a second with me, like an idiot. So, I spent a lot of time hiding under the umbrella and watching all the women fawn over Ash. There were other guys there, too, but it was as if Ash were some Greek god and not just a damaged rich boy.

I headed inside at some point to get out of the hottest part of the day and found Derek on the other side of the bar, chatting with the bartender and laughing.

"Ah, hey, Minivan," Derek said with a grin. "I was coming up to bring you another drink."

"Don't call me that."

He smirked. "Right. Yeah. Another sidecar."

"You're making them?"

The bartender shrugged. "He insisted."

"I know how you like them."

"Well, thanks."

He passed me the drink and swept a finger over the bridge of my nose. "You're a little pink."

"Story of my life. Forgot a hat."

He pulled off the UNC baseball cap he'd been wearing and plopped it onto my head.

I gagged and passed it back to him. "I'm not that desperate."

He chuckled. "Come on. It's not that bad."

"We both know that Duke is better."

"We both do *not* know that," he said with a shake of his head. Then, he dropped the hat back down. "Leave it. It'll keep you from burning too bad."

I huffed and tugged it lower on my brow. "I'm going to regret this."

He laughed and held up his phone. "Let me get a picture of you in that."

"Oh God, no." I covered my face as he snapped a picture.

He laughed even harder and showed me the series of pictures of me hiding and then sticking my tongue out at him. "This is definitely your new photo for your phone number."

"And when are you going to use that again?"

Derek glanced down at me. "Anytime I want."

I took another sip of my sidecar and a step away. I remembered all the ways that Derek could make me turn to goo and all the ways he could break my heart. I didn't have time or energy for that, especially with the case between us.

"Oh, Derek… do those lines actually work?"

He tipped the hat up to see my pink cheeks. "Sometimes."

"Thanks for the drink," I said, pulling away from that heated look.

He shot me a perfect smile on those pouty lips, and for a second, I was transported back in time. Back when those lips had touched mine and everything in the entire world had been different. A lot had changed since then. But somehow, we were still on opposite sides of everything.

PART II

9

DUKE

OCTOBER 23, 2009

I jogged off of the basketball court in Cameron to loud applause from all the Cameron Crazies. Duke was kicking off this basketball season with Countdown to Craziness, and the dance team had performed their season opener before the guys came out onto the court.

I breathed heavily as I faced the captain to listen to the post-dance pep talk. Hilary launched into an excited recap and then pulled us all together for a picture.

Brinley nudged me and laughed. "You *killed* that aerial sequence."

"You seriously did," Lora said. "I just *wish* that I had your acro skills."

"Girl, your turns!" I chef-kissed my lips. "Both of you! I swear."

Brin hugged me tight and then grabbed Lora. "Bestie's the best," she said as she danced in a circle. "You're still down for going to the frat party after Countdown, yeah?"

"Hell yes!" Lora said.

I nodded as we followed Hilary back into the stands next to the band. "Absolutely."

We cheered the rest of the night through the Blue-White scrimmage, beaming from ear to ear to be back in Cameron. I was a junior at Duke, and the Dancing Devils were the best thing that had ever happened to me. I'd rushed a sorority solely because Brinley was rushing and Lora was already in the sorority. I never in a million years would have thought that I'd be in a sorority, but here I was. Not that sororities at Duke were the same as everywhere else in the South. Definitely not like what Lila had said it was at UGA.

The game finished late, and we all decided to leave on our stage makeup and head to the party. I'd packed a tight black dress and heels. We all stuffed our pom-poms and bags into the back of Lora's car. I didn't have a car on campus, because parking expenses were out of this world. It sucked not being able to get to and from where I needed to go. Luckily, Lora had a Chevy Tahoe that was nearly the size of my old minivan, and her rich Filipino parents didn't mind paying for it. She parked the beast outside of the frat, and we piled out like her kids coming from soccer practice.

"Have you heard from Samar?" Brinley asked. She checked her brown complexion in a mirror and applied another coat of red lipstick.

I grumbled and pulled my phone out of my purse. "He's being unresponsive."

"My desi brother is going to get his ass kicked," Brin said, snapping the mirror closed. "If his mother knew how he was treating you."

"We are not bringing his mother into this," I said hastily.

Brinley and Samar had grown up together in DC, and their families were close, spending Diwali together every year. We'd been dating for just over a year, and while his father and sisters were supportive, his mother was less so. Though he claimed she was like that about everyone.

"I thought he was going to be at Countdown," Lora said, brushing the waist-length black hair back off of her face as we entered the house.

"He was."

But he hadn't shown. He was working in the Chem lab, where we'd met sophomore year. We had the same advisor, and he'd been pissy ever since I had been pushed into a more advanced program than him.

I jotted out yet another text. He hadn't responded to any that I'd sent before the game.

Are you still coming to the party?

When there was no immediate response, I stuffed the phone back in my purse and decided to ignore the issues with Samar.

We grabbed punch from the kitchen. It had been a long time since I'd turned my nose up at crappy punch. Now, I drank cheap liquor all the time. Though I was seriously planning to start liking some better shit when I turned twenty-one next weekend. Maddox was driving up with Josie and Lila for my birthday, and I couldn't wait.

"Watch out. Bekah alert," Lora hissed as the president of the sorority walked by.

Bekah Bridges was every reason that I had never wanted to rush a sorority. I didn't get along with everyone in the organization, but most people I could at least tolerate. Bekah ran the thing like a dictator. She was primly Southern perfection and drove me up the fucking wall.

"Ladies, don't forget who you're representing while you're here," she said with that big, fake smile that made me want to scratch her eyes out.

I put on my best fake enthusiasm. "Oh, bless your heart, Beks. Were we disrespecting the organization?"

She sent me a scathing look. "Marley, one, I know what bless your heart means. I'm from Atlanta. I grew up in a country club." God, didn't we all know that? She talked about it all the time. "And two, I am just *reminding* you. So, keep the snark to yourself. If you even can."

I couldn't. It was my defining trait.

Lora grabbed my arm to keep me from digging myself into a deeper hole. "Isn't your brother here this weekend?"

Bekah's smile brightened, and her eyes moved across the room. "Y'all remember Ramsey?"

We sure as hell did. He was three years older than us. He'd been a senior while we were freshman and head of the frat that Ash Talmadge was now a part of. We'd all swooned over his blond hair, great smile, and even greater ass. He came back every now and then to visit his sister and hang with the fraternity.

My phone buzzed as he and Ash came over with a few other frat brothers that I didn't remember. Ash nodded at me. I nodded back. That was usually the extent of our interaction after the shit that had gone down with Lila.

I checked the screen as they all chatted with Ramsey. Finally, a text from Samar.

Almost there. Was too busy for basketball.

That was another thing. Samar didn't care for Duke basketball. It was blasphemous on campus to even say. I had never been a basketball fan before coming to college, but I sure as hell was now. It helped that I cheered at every home game. No use in bringing up his weird aversion. It would only result in another fight.

I sent him a message.

Okay. See you soon.

Despite the text, it took Samar another half hour to get to the party. He found me in the living room when he arrived. He shot me a confused look when he got a glimpse of my outfit. I straightened out my skirt self-consciously.

"Hey, what took you so long?"

"Nothing," he said. "What are you wearing?"

I glanced down at my dress. "A dress?"

"Since when do you wear things like that?"

"A dress like what?"

He gestured to me as if it explained everything. It was a short dress, but it wasn't anything out of the norm.

"Are you just trying to pick a fight?" I asked with a sigh. "You see me in stuff like this all the time for dance."

"Yeah, but not out. This isn't you." He waved at me, as if to say a dress could change who I was.

I swallowed back tears. This was stupid. All of it was stupid. How many more fights could we have? And about such stupid shit?

"This is just what I'm wearing."

"Whatever. I'm getting a beer."

Then, Samar vanished. I swallowed and stared down at my drink. Brinley appeared then and slung an arm around me.

"What the fuck was that?"

"Don't, Brin," I whispered.

"He can't treat you like that. Let me give him a piece of my mind."

"Can we just get through the night? I don't want to deal with this in front of everyone."

Already, it felt like people were staring.

"When did he become such an asshole though?" she asked.

That I didn't have an answer to.

Lora came over with her current friends with benefits—Vicky—laughing and telling crazy stories, and I tried to forget the fight with Samar. He came back at some point and sulked behind us while we had a good time. It felt like having a target on my back all night. I was half-ready to go before it was even midnight. But I stayed by sheer force of will. I was not going to let him ruin this.

"Holy shit," Brinley said.

Lora whistled low. "Yeah. Who the hell is that?"

Vicky elbowed her. "Babe."

Lora shrugged and held her hands up. "I'm bi, babe. I can appreciate that body."

But when I caught who was standing in the door of the house, I froze in place. "That's Derek Ballentine."

"Who?" Brinley asked.

"And how do you know him?" Lora asked with a wicked grin.

"Yeah," Samar grumbled, "how do you know him?"

"He's... an old friend," I stumbled over the words to describe Derek. *Friend* was the wrong word. Old enemy was more accurate.

"Hey, Derek!" Lora called out.

He turned our direction, and my face went bright red. Because he didn't just look at us, he looked at *me*. And the entire room disappeared as those hazel eyes settled completely and entirely on me. A slow smirk crossed those pouty lips. I could sense Samar stand up, and he might have said something to me, but I didn't hear it. It had been years since I'd seen Derek, and somehow, he'd gotten even more attractive. Taller, stronger, more confident, if that was possible. It was recognizable in the angles of his body and the tilt of his head. The easy grace of his rich-kid clothes. And the way he filled a room just by stepping inside.

Then, before I could utter another word, he strode through the crowd and straight to me. I gaped at him for a heartbeat before his mouth was on mine.

My brain stopped working. Everything settled into a buzz in the background. The world shifted ever so slightly on a different axis.

Derek Ballentine was kissing me.

A part of me had thought that I'd made up how good of a kisser he was. He'd been my first. Of course I would have exaggerated it in my head. But dear God, no. He was just... this good. His lips were soft and supple yet full of command. His hands pushed up into my loose, dark curls, holding my head in place for him to devour me whole.

And I just stood there and forgot reality.

That I hadn't seen him in years. That I had a boyfriend standing a foot away. That none of this made a lick of sense.

Because Derek was kissing me, and I was kissing him back.

And I wanted to.

I wrenched backward. My breathing was irregular, and my hand shot up to my lips. He still had one hand in my hair.

He looked down at me like I was his next meal. "Hey, Minivan."

Then, I heard a muttered, "Fuck this," and Samar slammed into my shoulder as he left the room.

I jerked forward into Derek. He caught me easily. But I shoved against him.

"What the fuck, Derek?"

He laughed as I rushed past him and after my boyfriend. I needed to get my head on straight. I shouldn't have kissed Derek back, but it had all happened so fast. Jesus Christ! What was I even going to tell Samar?

"Samar, wait!" I called, running out of the house after him.

"Save your breath, Marley."

I grabbed his arm, dragging him to a stop in the grass. "That was *not* what it looked like."

"It looked like you kissing some other guy right in front of me!" he shouted at me. "If you want to break up, then just do it. Don't cheat!"

"I didn't. I haven't. I wouldn't! That was not that."

"I watched you kiss him! You wouldn't have done that if you'd never done it before. If you didn't want to."

"I have," I said with a shake of my head and followed him as he trudged down the street. "In high school, Samar. We kissed once at a party forever ago."

"I'm not an idiot, Mars."

"I swear that's all it was. I have no idea why he kissed me. He doesn't even go to Duke. I don't know what he's doing here."

Samar shook his head at me. "Whatever. It's over. You know it's over."

I stopped in my tracks and tried to hold back tears. Yeah, it had been over for a long time, but I hadn't wanted it to end like this. "Yeah," I whispered.

"Then stop following me. You've apparently already moved on."

"Samar..."

"Save your breath," he snapped and then stalked away from me.

I ground my teeth and let him go. I wasn't going to

change his mind. We'd been on the rocks long enough. Derek had put the nail in the coffin. My hands turned into fists. Derek fucking Ballentine.

I rushed back to the house and up the stairs. Derek was standing there, talking to Ash Talmadge, as if *nothing* at all had happened. I walked right up to him and pushed him as hard as I could.

He took one step backward. "Hey, Minivan."

"You absolute asshole!"

Ash ran a hand back through his hair. "Uh, what's going on?"

"How could you do that?" I snapped, ignoring Ash. "My boyfriend just dumped me because of you."

Derek crossed his arms and smirked down at me. "Do you want me to run and tell him we didn't sleep together? Do you think he'd believe me?"

My jaw dropped. "This is about high school?"

Ash took a step back. "I'm going to let you have this one, bro."

Derek patted Ash's shoulder twice. "I got this."

"Don't you dare tell Lila!" I snarled at him.

Ash raised his hands and retreated. "Keep me out of this. I don't even talk to Lila anymore."

I looked back at Derek. "You made a huge mistake."

"Look, payback's a bitch. And anyway... you kissed me back."

I had. Which was the real problem, but I wasn't going to admit it.

"That is beyond the point."

Derek stepped forward, slipping his hand back up into my hair and tilting my face up to his. "And you're still a good kisser."

I slapped him. His head jerked sideways, and he just

laughed. I pulled away from him, all the anger from the breakup turning into fury. "I'll get you back for this. Don't forget what started all of this to begin with."

"Hey, I told people at your school that we didn't hook up, just like you'd asked."

He had. Not that anyone really believed him, like he'd predicted. But the leering and shit had ended. I never knew what he'd said to make it all stop. The Ballentine name had a lot of leverage, so he must have gone to bat for me in some way. I'd appreciated the gesture until tonight.

"And then you had my boyfriend dump me."

He leaned forward with that same damn smirk. "You still kissed me back, Minivan."

"God, I hate you."

"No, you don't."

"And don't call me that!" I said, storming away from him.

"Good seeing you, Minivan."

I clenched my hands into fists and went to find my girls. I needed to leave this party before the adrenaline left and I started crying. The last thing I wanted to explain was Derek. But maybe they'd forget if I talked about Samar. And in the meantime, I'd find a way to get Derek back for this.

10

UNC

FEBRUARY 5, 2010

Olivia stopped me at the door to the master's level Chemistry class we had together. "Hey, Marley, wait up."

I stalled in the doorway to let her catch up, Sarah and Carly right behind her. We fell into step as we left the class and went out onto UNC's campus.

My advisor had gotten me into advanced courses for spring semester junior year and all of senior year. I was doing dual-enrollment for my BA/MA. The only requirement was that some of the classes were shared with UNC. Since it was only a few miles away, that wasn't a problem with most people. I, however, hadn't had a car. Gran had gotten me a small fixer-upper, and I had an assistantship in my Chemistry department to help pay for the parking fees. It didn't make it any weirder that I was taking classes at Chapel Hill.

Olivia pushed her thick-rimmed glasses up the bridge of her pale, freckled nose and smoothed back her stick-straight red hair. "So, we were wondering if you wanted to go out with us after class. We were thinking we'd meet on Franklin," Olivia said with a wink.

I laughed. "Uh, no thanks."

Franklin Street was the main stretch of bars right off of the UNC campus. It was the *it* place to be seen if you went to school here, which I did not.

"Come on, *amiguita*," Carly said. She nudged me with her hip and smiled brightly. Her light-brown skin practically glowed, and her thick, curly, brown hair was tied up tight at the top of her head. "We know you've never been out on Franklin, and it's a rite of passage."

"Yes, but I'm a Duke student," I reminded them.

Sarah wrinkled her nose. "We try not to hold that against you."

I laughed. "Well, this isn't my scene."

"It's not all bad," Olivia said. "I did my undergrad at Colby College up in Maine, so I don't get the whole UNC thing either, but it's still fun."

"Maine," Carly scoffed. "I came from Puerto Rico to North Carolina. Talk about different."

We all laughed as Carly dissolved into rapid Spanish.

Sarah shook her head at the lot of us. "I'm the only UNC undergrad. Born and raised in the Outer Banks, baby. And I am *telling* you that Franklin is better than whatever you have over at Duke." She swished her natural corkscrew curls to the side and smiled wide with her gorgeous, full lips. Sarah was a knockout with onyx skin and a figure that I could only dream about.

"You would say that," I said with a laugh.

"I would," she agreed.

Sometimes it still blew my mind that I was in classes with these girls. That, as a junior, I was getting to take classes with PhD students. People who were actually doing research. It thrilled and terrified me. I'd spent so long surrounded by people who couldn't quite keep up or who, like Samar, got mad when I excelled. I didn't want to lose these friendships over some silly bar scene. It wasn't like I had to cheer UNC on during basketball season.

"Yeah. All right. Just tell me where to meet you."

Olivia whooped. "Yes! Excellent. Let me text you."

I couldn't believe they'd roped me into this. I would never hear the end of it with Brin and Lora. Still, I hustled home for rehearsal, going through the motions. We were in full swing for basketball season with a game yesterday and next week. But at least nothing tonight. Plus, rehearsal was only an hour to go over our dance for the game. Then, I rushed into the shower and prayed my curls would be dry in time to meet them on Franklin.

As expected, Brinley scoffed when I told her that I already had plans. "Franklin? It's one thing to take classes there. Are they going to turn you into a Carolina girl? Are you going to start wearing baby blue?"

"Don't blaspheme," I said with a grin. "How do I look?"

"Cute, but no..." Brinley dived into her closet and came back out with a black miniskirt and white tank. "Wear this."

"It's thirty degrees outside."

"Wear a jacket," she said with an arched eyebrow. "You haven't dated since Samar. Maybe these new girls can find you a hottie to hook up with since you don't care for anything Lora or I throw your way."

I wrinkled my nose. "Whatever. I don't have to date. I'm busy."

Brinley rolled her eyes. "Just wear the outfit."

I shimmied into the tiny skirt and shrugged. She was right. I did look hot. Even if it wasn't what I normally wore. It had been months since Samar. Maybe it was time to find someone else. There was never a good time with everything I had going on, but I did miss sex.

"Fine. I'll wear this."

She snorted. "Yes, girl. Have fun but not too much fun. We'll miss you."

"You could come."

Brin held her hand up. "Don't even suggest it."

I laughed and hugged her before heading out back to Chapel Hill. I managed to find parking in a lot a few blocks behind Franklin and headed to the aptly named Library. It looked like any other college bar with a dance floor full of sweating college students. I found the girls near the bar, and we did a round of shots before joining the throng. They claimed they wanted me to have the "full experience." So, we jumped from one shitty bar to the next, and I hated to admit it, but I was having fun. A lot of fun. It was different than Duke, and I'd never tell my friends, but it was just as good of a time.

"Let's go to He's Not," Olivia yelled over the music at whatever current bar we were in. "My friend is there."

"Your 'friend,' " Carly said with air quotes. "You mean, *jevo*."

I arched an eyebrow. "What does that mean?"

"Fuck buddy," Sarah said with a laugh. "Context clues, friend."

"Shut up!" Olivia said, turning beet red. "He's *really* hot."

"Well, let's go meet him," Carly said with a wink. "I hope he has hot friends."

"Seconded!" I said, raising my hand.

We all laughed and left the sweaty bar behind. We trekked down Franklin and through a back alley that led to the famous He's Not while the girls regaled me with the origin story of its name as we walked. Apparently, Michael

Jordan used to go to the bar when he played for UNC. People would constantly call the place, trying to find out if he was there, and they had to say so many times, "He's not here," that the name just stuck.

"Did you hear the story about the UNC girl who dated that senator?" Sarah asked once we stepped into the bar.

I nodded. "Oh my God, I did. It was on the news. She was a reporter here, and they hooked up?"

"Yeah. Mega scandal. I was friends with one of her friends," Sarah confessed.

"Seriously? Did she ever tell you what really happened?"

Sarah shrugged. "Victoria is Victoria. If you knew her, you'd know," she said with a laugh. "We had some good times though. All I know is that I don't blame the reporter, Liz, one bit. Brady Maxwell is hot as sin."

"Oh," Carly gushed. "Are you talking about the senator? Us Puerto Ricans deserve the right to vote anyway, but let me tell you, I wish that I could just so I could vote for him. Hot, smart, and dating a UNC student? Sign me up."

We all burst into laughter, and I was still laughing as Olivia turned around to introduce us to her little *friends with benefits* situation.

"This is who I was telling you about," Olivia gushed.

And standing next to her was Derek Ballentine.

"Marley?" he asked in exasperation.

"Hey, Derek," I said with a slow smile as payback blossomed invitingly in my mind.

"You two know each other?" Olivia asked, pushing her glasses back up again in a sign that I knew from our few weeks in class meant she was uncertain.

"Oh, we go way back," I said, looking down and then up at him from under my lashes.

His jaw set. "Can I talk to you in private for a minute?"

Olivia looked up at him in alarm. "What for?"

He smiled at her, trying to go for reassuring and missing the mark. "It'll just be a minute, babe."

He kissed her cheek, ignoring her distress. Then, he grabbed my arm and practically dragged me away from my friends.

"Ouch, you're hurting me," I snapped at him.

He released me immediately. "Sorry, but what the fuck are you doing here? And how do you know Olivia? And don't you fucking think about ruining this."

I rubbed my arm. It hadn't been that hard, but I might as well milk it. "I'm here because the girls invited me out."

"How? You go to Duke."

"Some of the graduate-level classes have students on both campuses," I explained.

"But you're a *junior*."

I rolled my eyes at him. "I'm getting my bachelor's and master's at the same time."

"In neuroscience?"

"Yes. Some of us are smart and don't need a fifth year," I grumbled.

He smirked. "I'm taking a fifth year for basketball eligibility, not because of academics. And anyway, none of this is important. Just... don't do whatever that wicked head of yours is thinking right now."

"What would that be, Derek?" I asked.

"You know exactly what I mean."

"Oh, what? Like kiss you in front of your new girlfriend?" He glared at me. "Should I tell her we're not sleeping together? Would she believe me?"

He huffed. "This feud has gone on long enough."

"I thought it was over in high school," I reminded him. "You're the one who fucked up *my* relationship." I glanced over his shoulder and saw Carly and Sarah trying to console a clearly upset Olivia. I liked her and didn't want to hurt her. "Anyway, you're doing more damage just by talking to me."

He looked back and saw Olivia's concern. "Just stay out of it."

I held my hands up. "You're digging your own grave."

Derek just walked back to the group. He slung an arm around Olivia, who perked up when his attention was back on her. Sarah and Carly were being over the top to try to get around the awkwardness. Derek's friends left to get shots for everyone.

"So, how do you two know each other?" I asked Olivia after she downed a tequila shot with a grimace. I declined a drink to try and sober up enough to drive back to Durham and opted for water instead.

Olivia's cheeks heated again, and she looked up at Derek. "We met in class."

I glanced between them, saw the smug look on Derek's face, and knew. I just *knew*. "Oh God, are you his TA?"

"What?" Olivia gasped. Then, she leaned into me. "How did you know that?"

"Olivia!" Sarah cried.

Carly grimaced. "Seriously? You could get kicked out of the program."

"It's fine!" Olivia said. "I swear..."

Derek shook his head. "Literally, how did you know?"

I shrugged. "Educated guess. I know you."

"And *how* do you know each other again?" Olivia asked.

"Derek," I offered, holding my hand out to let him explain.

He narrowed his eyes at me. "We know each other from high school."

"Didn't you go to an all-boys private school?"

"Oh yeah, he's a *Holy Cross boy*," I said like it was an insult. Which... when we'd said it at the public school, it was.

"No one says it like that," Derek said. "They how we said St. Catherine's girls."

"They said it that way about you," I teased.

Olivia cleared her throat as Derek seethed. "So, how did you meet if you went to different schools?"

"We met at a Halloween party. No, wait, it was a football game first."

"Marley's friend dated my friend."

"Okayyy," Olivia said, drawing out the word.

Olivia looked wounded by the whole thing, which I hated. I really liked her. Derek hadn't known Samar when he kissed me. He'd just seen revenge. I didn't want to hurt Olivia. So, I backed off. Derek would probably sink this one himself. I was honestly surprised that she would do something so reckless as to date a student. Even one as attractive and charismatic as Derek.

The night wound down quickly after that. It was already near bar close. I was glad that I'd stopped drinking when I did so that I could drive home. The rest of the girls were sloshy. Sarah was making out with one of Derek's friends. Carly was dancing with another. It was my time to bail. I said my good-byes and headed back to the parking lot, getting on the phone with Brin as I walked so I wouldn't be alone.

"So, how was it?"

"Fun until I ran into Derek."

Brin gasped. "The guy who kissed you when you were dating Samar?"

"Yep."

"Oh my God. Did you kiss him again?"

"He's seeing one of my friends."

"Bummer. He's hot."

I laughed. Oh, Brin. Priorities.

Then, my phone beeped as another call came through. I didn't recognize the number, but it had a 912 area code, which meant it was someone from Savannah.

"Hey, Brin, I have another call. Let me call you back."

"Okay. Stay safe. Love you."

I clicked over and answered, "Hello?"

"Where are you?"

I froze outside of the parking lot to the sound of Derek's voice in my ear. "Derek?"

"Yes. Where are you?"

"I'm in a parking lot?"

"Where?"

"I don't go to UNC. I have no idea." I glanced at the nearest street sign and told him where I was.

"Don't move. I'll meet you there."

"What? Why?" I asked, but he'd already hung up the phone. "And how did you get my number?" I muttered to myself.

Derek had never called me. I hadn't even known that he had my number. I'd certainly never given it to him. Plus, I had no idea why he was coming to see me. I'd backed off so as not to hurt Olivia. He couldn't blame me this time.

He appeared under the streetlight. He wore khakis and a Carolina-blue polo with a navy three-quarter zip pulled over top. I huddled in my jacket, shivering from the cold. I should have started the heater in the car while I waited.

"There you are," he said with half of a smile. He wasn't pleased.

"What happened?"

"Why do you think something happened?"

I shrugged. "I can read your expression."

"Olivia broke it off."

"Ah," I said softly. "Sorry."

"Are you?"

"I mean… not really. She could lose her entire life for this. It doesn't seem like a risk worth taking."

He huffed. "And you don't think you had anything to do with this?"

I held my hands up. "Hey, I didn't tell her anything she didn't already know."

"This has to stop." He slid his hands into his pockets. "We can't keep doing this."

"I wouldn't be doing this, but *you* did it to me, Derek."

He ground his teeth together and nodded. "Fine. Look, let's bet on it."

I laughed. "Bet on *what*?"

"This. Us. When UNC beats Duke in basketball this weekend, you'll stop ruining my relationships."

"And when Duke wins, you'll what? Stop ruining mine? As far as I'm concerned, you've done a lot worse in all of this."

"I was actually into Olivia, you know?"

"No, I didn't know. You acted the way you do with everyone else."

"And how is that?" he demanded.

"Expendable," I spat. "You're not even really mad that it ended. You're only mad that I had something to do with it."

"That's not true."

"If you were actually upset, you would be following *her* home to beg her to reconsider, but you're not."

He stilled at that comment. As if he'd never had anyone dissect him before. I didn't know when I'd become the expert on Derek, but I'd had enough time to think about all the girls he had gone through in high school and the way he treated everyone, including me. I'd been determined to be the one girl who didn't fall for his stupid tricks after that kiss. And he'd treated Olivia the same as all the rest.

"Fine. If Duke wins, then I won't get back at you for what happened with Olivia," he told me and held out his hand.

"Fine." Then, I put my hand in his and shook. "Good luck next week, Derek. You're going to need it."

11

SAVANNAH

PRESENT

The doorbell rang at Gran's. Maddox had a key, and there was no one else I wanted to see. We were thankfully past the point of strangers showing up, claiming to be friends with Gran and handing me dinner or dessert. They all wanted to talk about how much they loved her. I didn't have the bandwidth for one more *sorry for your loss*.

I peered through the peephole and gasped, wrenching the door open. "Lila, what are you doing here?"

My best friend rushed inside and wrapped her arms tight around me. "Surprise!"

"I mean, I love the surprise, but it's football season."

Lila worked as a physical therapist and trainer for the Falcons. Every fall was a complete shitshow. I usually saw her on her bye week and then not again until Christmas or even after New Year's. The fact that she was here on my front step in the middle of September was baffling.

"Maddox called," she offered sheepishly.

"What? Why?"

"He said that you're a wreck and need some girl time. I

took two days off to come down. I have to be back for the game this weekend, but I wanted to be here for you. I love you."

"I'm glad you're here, but I'm fine."

"Uh-huh," Lila said. "He said you've seen Derek."

I wrinkled my nose. "That little snitch."

"Hey, I'm not opposed, but I know how he hurt you in the past."

"Plus, he's Ash's best friend?"

She grimaced and fiddled with her nails. "How's he doing?"

"How would you be doing?"

She bit her lip and nodded. "Right. Well, my fault. I guess I don't have a right to wonder how he's doing."

"You loved him forever. It's not surprising, Lila."

"Anyway," she said with a sigh, "I'm not here about me or Ash. I'm here for you."

"How's Cole doing with you down here alone?"

"He's fine," she said with a wave of her hand. "We're happy. But you're not. Now, get in my car. We're going to get Leopold's."

I could never say no to Leopold's. So, I grabbed my purse and followed her outside. We drove downtown, getting a coveted parking spot on Broughton, directly across from the ice cream parlor. Unsurprisingly, there was already a huge line, even in the middle of the week during school. It was outrageous but worth it. We chatted about unimportant things, like how Miss Alicia was finally talking about retiring. She'd had the studio since she was in her twenties, and we were all surprised she still ran it, let alone still *teaching*.

When I had my mint chocolate chip cone and Lila had one with strawberry and cookie dough, we headed up Abercorn toward Reynolds Square. We stood in front of Pink House and licked the ice cream in the shade.

"You know I've never eaten there," I said.

Lila laughed. "How have you never been to Pink House? It's iconic."

"I never moved back like you did. It just never happened. I feel like it's too hyped for me now."

"You would think that. It's delicious. Maybe Derek can take you," she said with a wink.

I snorted. "Don't even, Delilah Grace."

"How are you really doing with everything? Gran?"

"I don't know." I sighed heavily. "Sad. I miss her. She was my go-to person. I have you and Josie—when she's not busy—but it's not the same. I used to call her and tell her everything that happened to me. She'd always have the best, most unorthodox advice. You know, she once told me that the most important lesson to learn was to get back at someone who thought they could take advantage of you."

Lila burst into laughter. "Oh, Gran. That sounds just like her. I miss her laugh. She had that big, hearty laugh when she found something really funny."

"Me too. Or all the silly nicknames she gave us."

"Chickadee," Lila said. "That was my favorite."

"Yes."

"She was a great woman with a long, beautiful life."

"She left a lasting impression."

Lila arched an eyebrow. "When were you going to tell me about the will?"

I groaned. "Did Maddox tell you?"

"That your mom and aunt are contesting it? Yes. How horrible!"

"Yeah, it's bullshit. I spoke with an attorney and the executor of the will. We have to get evidence to disprove whatever BS my mom comes up with for her reasoning. Then, go to court and wish for the best."

"And Derek is their attorney?"

I nodded. "His dad made him do it."

"Huh."

"He's going for partner, I guess."

"Does his dad know that you two..."

"He met me once, but it was in college. I don't know how much he remembers. *You* didn't even know."

She narrowed her eyes at me. "You'll never live that down either."

I chuckled. "Yeah, yeah. I'm the worst. But a lot of it is just a waiting game."

"Have you asked Derek about the will?"

I shook my head. "I don't want to talk about it with him."

"He can't give you the scoop?"

"No way. You know how he is."

"Yeah, I guess I do." She put an arm around me as we continued toward Bay Street. "Well, I'm sure you're going to win. Gran wanted you to have the house. That's all that matters."

"I hope you're right."

We walked out onto Bay when I jerked to a stop. Stepping out of an open doorway was none other than Derek Ballentine. He froze as the door to Ballentine Law closed shut behind him. I'd completely forgotten that this was where the practice was. I'd only ever been here once before.

"Marley," he said evenly. His gaze shifted to Lila, and he narrowed his eyes. "Delilah."

"Hey, Derek," she said with a smile.

"What are you doing here?"

"Checking on Marley."

He looked around as if Ash Talmadge might jump out at any second. "Just Marley?"

"Yes," she said flatly.

"It's fine," I said, jumping in. "She's here for me."

He nodded. "All right." Then, his gaze swept to mine, and something shifted there. "Can I talk to you a minute?" He looked to Lila and back. "In private?"

"Uh..."

"It's fine," Lila said easily. "I'll wait here."

"Sorry," I said to her and then stepped aside with Derek. "What?"

"What is she doing here?"

"I told you already."

"She's not going to see Ash?"

"No!" I ground out. "Jesus, she's not stupid. If you just want to talk about that, then I'm going to go back to my friend."

He reached out for my arm. I looked down at it in surprise. "That's not why. Look, were you serious about helping with Ash?"

I blinked at the change of subject. "Yeah."

"His birthday is next week, and I wanted to get him out of the house but not something like... the yacht. Want to come with us?"

I met his gaze head-on, trying to find the Derek-sized play in all of this. But he seemed genuinely concerned for his friend. And I was equally concerned about Ash.

So, I finally nodded. "Sure. I'll come out."

He grinned, and my body melted at that look. "Great. I'll text you the info."

I stepped back quickly. "Sounds good. See you around."

Then, I hastened back to Lila.

She arched an eyebrow at me. "What was that about? The case?"

"Ash's birthday."

Lila bit her lip. "Oh. Right. That's next weekend."

"Yeah."

"Well, we're not here about my worries. Let's wander around and talk about Gran. River Street?"

"Definitely," I agreed.

I followed my friend down the steep steps and reminisced. So many people had wanted to talk about missing her. It was another thing entirely to *remember* her. That made it worse and also somehow better. It was just what I needed.

12

UNC

FEBRUARY 10, 2010

Sarah looked at me in exasperation. "Girl, what are you wearing?"

Olivia and Carly looked equally uncomfortable.

"Seriously?" Olivia asked.

I looked down at my outfit—a Blue Devils T-shirt, Dancing Devil shorts, and a blue Duke D logo on my cheek. "What?"

"When you said that you wanted us to get you a ticket to the Duke-UNC game, we knew that you were going to *cheer* for Duke," Sarah said. "We didn't think you'd dress like the enemy in the student section."

"You're going to get so much shit," Olivia said.

I shrugged. "Who cares? Technically, I am a UNC student as well. Sort of. Unofficially."

Carly rolled her eyes. "You'd better hope we win, or I don't know if we'll be able to get you out of the Dean Dome alive."

"How did you get an extra ticket anyway? We can never get them at Duke," I said with a wink. "Someone offered me ten thousand dollars for my floor pass last year. Just some stranger on the street. It was crazy."

"Whoa," Carly whispered.

"I pulled some strings," Sarah said. "My dad knows some of the coaches from when he went to UNC. He was able to weasel out *one* extra ticket. And then you blaspheme in Duke attire."

I laughed and followed the girls through the line and into the Dean Dome. The stadium was much bigger than Cameron, nearly twenty-two thousand to Duke's nine thousand. But I thought Cameron had more charm while the Dean Dome was much more modern and fancy. I got a seat in the bleachers, ignoring the incredulous stares from Tar Heels fans.

"*Amiguita*, you enjoy it," Carly said with a head shake. "You're twisted."

I was a pot-stirrer to the core. No one could shake my love of Duke. Not after years of TIP and a full-ride scholarship to the university. UNC hadn't offered me anything like that.

The crowd went wild as the UNC basketball team came out and made a lap on the court. Each starter was announced. I ignored them to find Derek in the lineup. He wasn't a starter for UNC, but he was a constant sub for the defense. He was completely in the zone when I found him in his white-and-Carolina-blue home uniform. Ballentine was written in block letters across the back. I'd seen him in uniform before, but it was different on his home turf.

I'd always been attracted to Derek. It was just his mouth that got in the way. Here with an entire stadium cheering him on, everything felt inexplicably different. His charm was next level. The smiles to the camera and crowd undeniably alluring. He cast a spell on the stands that day, and I was captured with the rest of them.

Even as I watched and cheered for Duke to take him down. I had a bet on the line. I couldn't lose focus. Not even to Derek. Especially Derek.

"He's amazing tonight," Olivia said longingly.

And she was right. Derek had been subbed in with ten minutes left in the second half, and he was playing like his life was on the line. Which made me chuckle to think about. Was he playing like this to beat me? Could he see our bet in the faces of all of the Duke players?

"He is," I agreed.

Olivia and I hadn't talked about her breaking it off with Derek. I could see that she wasn't over him. I hardly blamed her either. It hadn't ended because she wasn't interested. It had ended because she had made a stupid decision and she was smart enough to recognize it before it blew up in her face.

I'd thought that she'd be weird with me after it all, but she was the same bouncy, joyful Olivia as always. She could have hated me for being the one to point out that dating a student wasn't just irresponsible but also potentially life-altering. They hadn't even been that careful if they wanted it to be a secret. The entire school knew who he was. He was currently doing the thing they all loved him for.

But then something shifted. Derek was pulled out of the game at the two-minute warning. He argued with the coach, but he wasn't having any of it and sent Derek to the bench. He flopped down, clearly boiling over with anger. Then, the game went to shit.

It hadn't really been in UNC's favor, but it had been close. And when the buzzer rang, Duke was up by ten. I screamed my head off as angry UNC students filed out around me. My friends hid their faces in disappointment and pretended like they didn't know me. That was fine. We'd won. *I'd* won.

I filed out of the Dean Dome with my friends, reading over the texts from Brinley and Lora. Duke was partying all night to celebrate defeating our rival. I sent them a picture of me walking out of the stadium in my Duke outfit. A riot of laughter followed in our messages.

"I'll see y'all next week in class," I called to my friends.

Sarah sighed. "Could you be a little less excited?"

"Would you be if you were in my place?"

Carly playfully nudged Sarah. "Of course not. But that doesn't make it easier."

"It was a good game. It wasn't even a blowout." Though beating UNC by ten *was* a bit of a blowout in our long rivalry.

"They shouldn't have taken Derek out," Olivia groused. "He was on fire."

"Ah, *pobrecita*. Let's get you home," she said with a laugh. "Good night, Marley!"

I waved them off as I headed to Derek's house. He lived off of campus in a house that his dad had purchased for him. It was kind of ridiculous, but he'd let me park in one of the extra spots, so I didn't have to pay for parking. For that, I was grateful.

I followed the mass exodus from the game and out past Franklin to Derek's house. I shot him a text when I was almost there.

Guess that settles that.

Are you close to my place?

Yeah.

I'll be there in a few minutes. My roommate should already be back. Wait for me.

I rolled my eyes. We'd bet. He'd lost. He wasn't going to be able to weasel his way out of this one. But when I got to his house, I had no other option but to go inside. Someone had blocked me into Derek's driveway. I wouldn't be leaving until that person came back or we towed them.

So, I knocked on the door, and a lanky Black guy in full UNC garb answered.

"Wrong house," he said and then nearly shut the door in my face.

I laughed and put my hand out. "Wait, I'm Derek's friend. He told me to come inside and wait for him. My car is blocked in." I pointed to my tiny little Civic.

"Well, that explains the extra car. Derek didn't mention it." His eyes narrowed at my attire, but he opened the door and let me inside. "How the hell does he know a Duke fan?"

"We went to high school together. Well, sort of."

"You're a St. Catherine's girl?" he asked with an arched eyebrow.

"That would be a no. I went to public school. We crossed paths a few times. I'm Marley."

I held my hand out, and he took it.

His mouth popped open. "Ohhh."

I tilted my head. "What?"

"I've heard about you."

My cheeks heated. "I don't even want to know what Derek said. I'm sure it's not true."

He laughed. "I'm Kenny, by the way. And I bet some of it's true. He's never mentioned the same girl this much in exasperation. Whatever you're doing to keep him on his toes, keep it up." He headed toward the kitchen. "Beer?"

"Nah, I have to drive back."

He guffawed. "Not anytime soon. Everyone will be out on Franklin, drowning their sorrows over the loss. You aren't leaving until after midnight."

"Ugh," I groaned. "Then sure. Whatever you have is fine."

"My kind of girl," he said, reaching into the fridge and pulling out two beers.

He passed me one, and we sank into the couch to watch postseason coverage of the game. It was another hour before Derek finally showed up. Kenny and I had gone through a few beers each and started a game of Egyptian Ratscrew to pass the time. I currently had eighty percent of the deck of cards in my hands. Kenny was holding on to the game by a jack and queen.

He threw down the jack, confident that he'd win something valuable at least. Another jack came up out of my hand, and I dashed out, slapping the cards faster than he could even get his hand out.

"Noooo," he cried dramatically. "Fuck, Mars. How are you so good at this game?"

"I have a twin brother," I told him, taking his last hope of winning.

Derek glanced between us in confusion. His hair was still wet from the shower. His postgame UNC attire was all Nike gear. "Sorry that took longer than I thought."

"I got blocked in," I told him.

"Saw that." He scratched his head. "What's going on?"

"Egyptian Ratscrew, man," Kenny said with a shake of his head. "I thought it was a game of chance. She has proven me wrong. She's kicking my ass."

"That sounds right." Derek dropped his backpack at the door and went for his own beer.

"Grab me one of those while you're at it," Kenny said. Derek handed him one and took a long slug of his. "Also, you didn't tell me your girl was a genius."

Derek sputtered around the beer, "What?"

My cheeks heated again. "We're not—"

"Right. *Right*," Kenny said. "Mars was telling me all about this BA/MA program she's in. She said she'd help me survive Organic Chemistry."

"That's nice of you. Mars?" Derek tripped over the name.

"My friends call me Mars."

"I've only ever heard him call you Minivan as a nickname," Kenny said with a laugh. "I don't get it."

"I drove a minivan in high school. Derek likes to make fun of me."

"Derek, you're such a dick," Kenny said. He forfeited the rest of the deck. "I give up. Checkmate or whatever." He glanced between us and then stood. "I'm going to see if Kristy's gotten back to me."

Then, he made himself scarce. I shuffled the deck the way Gramps had taught me. They waterfalled beautifully into place. I did it a few more times so that I didn't have to look back up into Derek's face. The way he'd been looking at me since he'd walked back inside his surprisingly large two-story home was unnerving. The last time he'd looked at me like that, he'd stuck his tongue down my throat in high school.

"Kenny's nice," I said.

"Yeah. He's a cool guy." He ran a hand back through his hair and then dropped into Kenny's abandoned seat. "Best two out of three?"

"What?"

"The bet. Best two out of three?"

"We only have one more game against each other."

"Regular season game. We'll probably play each other in the postseason."

My gaze drifted up to his eyes, which were almost blue against the Carolina blue of his jacket. Something hiccupped in my stomach at the sight. We were sitting close together. All I had to do was shift, and something could happen.

Derek must have realized the same thing. His eyes drifted down to my lips and back up. His hand came to rest on the card deck... over my hand. My pulse jumped in my throat, and time slowed. We could close the distance. We could give in to this, like we had that one time all those years ago.

But no. That wasn't what I wanted. I didn't want to be another girl who fell at his feet. Kenny had just said that I was the only girl who kept him on his toes. He'd said it as a compliment. If I was going to have anything with Derek, it seemed safer to be the one he argued with rather than the one he threw away, like all the others.

So, I pulled my hand back and the cards with me. "I guess I can give you another chance," I said with a smirk. "You're going to have to step up your game, Ballentine."

His eyes met mine again as he drew his hand back to himself. "I can do that."

And for a second, I wasn't sure if we were talking about basketball at all.

13

DUKE

MARCH 6, 2010

The final game of regular season was always exciting and sad. We were all ready to beat UNC and make our way into March Madness, but it also meant that Lora would be graduating in one month. Brinley and I had already signed a lease for our senior year together, but it wouldn't be the same without the final member of our trio. It would be like me and Lila without Josie, which we'd actually had to deal with most of our lives and always missed her.

Lora stood at the front of the row with Hilary today, our two graduating seniors. Brin and I were directly behind them. We'd be taking over next year as captain and cocaptain.

And while all of that was on my mind, Derek Ballentine walked out onto the court inside Cameron to a rousing round of, "Hey, Derek. You suck!" from the student section.

I laughed along with everyone else, as they did it to every single UNC player as they were announced. Normally, we just yelled their name, almost welcoming, but no, for

UNC, we had to let them know what we thought about them. Not that any of them reacted to it.

"That's your Derek?" Brin asked as we settled into our first set of cheers.

I didn't quibble with the phrasing. "Yep."

"Is it bad to say that he's even hotter in uniform?"

No. No, it was not.

The game started off like any other rivalry—dirty. Tempers were hot. Adrenaline was high. Neither wanted to give an inch. But it was undeniable that Duke was the better team this year. We hadn't lost a home game all season, and in the first half, we were up by double digits. I'd never seen anything like it. After three years in a row of losses to UNC here in Cameron, we'd all braced for the worst. Watched some of the UNC guys flash four fingers as they walked in like they were going to conquer our home one more time. But this year, it wasn't in the cards.

In fact, it ended up being a *blowout.* Like, never in a million years had I thought we'd beat UNC by *thirty* points when Derek and I started this bet. Cameron Crazies were literally losing their minds, screaming as the buzzer rang for the end of the game. I hugged Brin, who was crying tears of joy.

The band started playing again, and we cheered and cheered until we were finally dismissed. Most of Cameron had emptied out, but a group of dedicated fans had stuck it out through all of the cheers.

I followed Hilary and Lora out of the stands, still bubbling with joy, when I heard my name.

Brin touched my arm and said, "I'll wait for you."

I got out of line and stepped back toward the court. There was a face that I hadn't seen in a few years. "Amelia?"

"Marley, hey!" Amelia said. She ducked under the divider and pulled me into a hug.

Despite Amelia being Derek's sister, we actually got along. She'd taken lessons from Miss Alicia for pageant choreography for a few years. Lila and I had hung out with her, and she was cool despite the pageants and being a St. Catherine's girl and… Derek's sister. I never brought up seeing Derek throw Chuck Henderson against a wall when he was into Amelia. She never brought up Derek at all.

"What a game, huh?" I asked her.

She sighed and pulled the UNC hat off of her head. "It was brutal. Derek is going to be pissed *forever* that it was his last regular season game."

"Can't blame him."

She laughed. "For real. What are you doing tonight? Out celebrating? I'm in from New York through the weekend. We should get drinks or something."

"You could come out with us tonight," I offered.

"Will I get shit for being a UNC fan?"

I shrugged. "Probably."

"Let me tell my dad and Kathy. They flew me out for the game."

"Sure. No problem. Meet me out front after?

"Done!"

I hugged her again and then ran back to Brinley. We headed back to Wilson and grabbed our bags from the gym. I promised to meet Brinley and Lora back at our place before heading out in my black-and-Blue Devils-blue cheer two-piece to find Amelia. Everything had cleared out already, so it was easy to locate her standing with her dad and Kathy.

Kathy about lost it when she saw me. "Marley?"

"Hey, Kathy."

She pulled me into a hug. "It is so good to see you. It's been a few years. Look at you on the sidelines."

Derek's dad held his hand out, his deep drawl prominent as he said, "Apparently, I'm the only one who doesn't know you. I'm Doug."

"Marley," I said, shaking his hand.

"She danced at Alicia's studio," Amelia filled him in.

"I see it's paid off if you're dancing for Duke."

I flushed at the praise. "Thank you, sir." My drawl coming out slightly to match his. It always did that around other Southerners.

"She got a full ride!" Amelia added.

"In academics," I said quickly.

"Sharp girl," he said with a head nod. Doug straightened up, and his smile brightened. "Hey! There he is. Good game, son."

I startled at the words out of his mouth. I didn't know why, but I'd always assumed that Doug Ballentine was sort of an asshole. He had a new, pretty, young wife. He'd insisted on Derek going to UNC. He'd always seemed the type. But he was congratulating Derek on *that* game? He must have been all right.

"Thanks, Dad," Derek said. He'd changed into a regular jacket and khakis to come outside. Ditched all of his UNC gear to talk to his family. He'd probably be a target otherwise. He hugged his dad and then Kathy and Amelia. "It wasn't my best."

"You went out there and tried. Today wasn't the day. You'll still dominate in the postseason," Doug said confidently.

Derek smiled at his family and then turned to face me. "Hey."

"Derek, you remember Marley? She danced circles around me in high school. Her friend dated Ash Talmadge."

For a second, all the air was sucked out of the world as he looked at me. As he was *introduced* to me by his sister. Amelia must not have heard the rumors about me in high school. She didn't know about me and Derek. I waited on bated breath to see how he'd play this.

But before he could say anything, Kathy laughed. "Of course he remembers her—they dated."

Amelia nearly choked on the water bottle she'd just taken a sip from. "What?"

"No," I said quickly. "Um, no, we didn't date. We were just friends."

Everyone looked at me dubiously. Maybe they also all knew that Derek didn't have female friends.

"Yeah," Derek agreed. "Just friends. We've seen each other around."

"Oh," Amelia said with a furrowed brow. "Well, that's cool. Marley asked if I could go out with her tonight." She looked at her dad. "Is that okay, Daddy?"

"Sure, sweet pea. Just don't be late for your flight home tomorrow."

"I won't."

She kissed her dad's cheek. They all hugged, and then Doug and Kathy headed back to their hotel, leaving the three of us alone.

Derek ran a hand back through his wet hair. "I'm supposed to take the bus back with the team. So, I should head out."

"You could come out with us later," Amelia offered.

He chuckled. "Nah. I'm too recognizable on this campus."

"He's right. It might be dangerous."

"I'll go home and meet you in the morning for breakfast, Mia."

Amelia sighed and nodded. "Okay."

Derek tipped his head to the side. "Can I talk to you a minute?"

I glanced at Amelia. Her head was buried in her phone, as if she'd known this was coming. Well, she must have known Derek's moves.

"Sure."

We stepped away from his sister and back toward the darker alcove between Cameron and Wilson. It had been a late game. I was tired, but I wasn't at the same time. I had a jittery energy from our win. Derek clearly had the opposite reaction.

"Does this mean I won?" I teased.

He looked down at me with that half-smile on his face. "Whoever gets further in March Madness?"

I laughed. "You really can't handle losing, can you?"

"I can handle losing." He paused and considered it. "A basketball game. I can lose at basketball. I won't lose against you."

"And why not?"

"Because somehow, you'll find a way to ruin my next relationship."

I snorted. "I didn't ruin the last one. And anyway, does Derek Ballentine do relationships?"

His half-smile turned full blown at the question. "What do you think?"

"I think everyone bores you," I answered honestly before I could stop myself.

"Yeah?"

"Except me, of course."

He took a step closer. "You're right. You don't bore me."

I swallowed. “Which is why you don’t want to lose to me.”

“You’re right,” he said evenly. “That is not what I want to do with you.”

I had no response to that. None. No quick comeback. Nothing at all. I stared up into his gorgeous face and knew that things were getting wholly and truly complicated. Because I was supposed to hate him. I was supposed to be disgusted by his behavior and tired of all the shit he’d caused me. I wasn’t supposed to be thinking about the shape of his lips and the way the light caught the curls in his hair or the heat coming off of him in this March evening. Or wondering what it would be like to give in to this instead of fighting it.

He tipped my chin up to look at him. “Marley…”

“You should probably get back to the team,” I said, not trusting myself to say anything else.

He released me with a sigh. I wasn’t playing into any of the games he was used to. I could see it in that moment that he had no idea what to make of me.

“Probably. March Madness?”

I nodded. “I’ll make a bracket. Winner takes all.”

His grin was devilish at those words. “I accept.”

Then, he disappeared back into the stadium.

I released my breath. Shit. I was in way too deep.

Amelia cleared her throat. “You ready?”

“Yeah,” I said, stepping back toward her. “Let’s go.”

“So…” Amelia said, glancing my way. “You’re dating my brother?”

“Definitely no.”

“He’s into you.”

“I think it’s just a conquest thing. I’m the one thing he can’t have.”

She shook her head. "No. I know Derek. I've never seen him look at anyone else like that."

I laughed because I just couldn't fathom how that could be true. "Come on, Amelia."

She shrugged. "Believe what you want, but find me a hot guy to make out with tonight, yeah?"

"That is much easier than discussing your brother," I said as we headed out.

No Derek in sight. No confusing looks or mixed messages. We'd see how March Madness went and figure out what was going on between us then.

14

DUKE

APRIL 5, 2010

Lora tipped her drink toward me. She'd been drunk for the last hour, and the game hadn't even started. "So, tell me again... what happens if you win this bet?"

I leaned against the couch in Ash Talmadge's off-campus house. Unsurprisingly, his parents had gotten him a place in Durham for college in the same way that Derek's parents had, and he was throwing a national championship party. Because Duke was in the national championship.

"Technically, I've already won."

UNC had fizzled out in the tournament, and Duke was about to clinch the title for the fourth time. Neither of us had called in for the end of the bet, even when UNC lost. It was as if we were both holding our breath to see how far this would all go.

"Yeah, but still..."

"She gets to get back at him for what he did... or something, right?" Brinley asked. "It's a feud."

I nodded. "We've been feuding since high school. He

keeps fucking up my relationships, and I keep messing up his. So, now, we're in a holding pattern."

"Okay," Lora said, tipping her cup forward and nearly pouring her drink out. "Hear me out. What if you just hooked up instead?"

I snorted.

Brinley cackled. "I said the same thing. But she swears that it's platonic."

"Yeah right," Lora said. "You want him bad."

I flushed at the comment. I did. I didn't know what had happened over the last couple months. But Derek and I had started texting, and we hadn't stopped. Not just about the bet. Actually, we never talked about it anymore. He was gone a lot for the tournament, and he sent pictures from wherever he ended up. What had gone from a feud and bet had morphed into something that I could hardly deny to my friends, let alone myself.

And then Derek walked into the house. Ash called his name, and they shook hands, laughing and heading to the kitchen to tap the keg. But for one split second, Derek turned away from Ash and glanced into the living room, as if he were looking for something. He found me, and his smile brightened. He'd been looking for *me.* My cheeks heated at that one glance. Then, he was gone.

"Girllll," Lora drawled. "If you don't fuck that, I'm going to."

Brinley and I both burst into laughter. Lora wasn't even going to make it through the game. I'd also been drinking steadily since I'd gotten here, but I didn't want to get too drunk. I wanted to remember the game. And whatever might happen after.

Derek and Ash came back out of the kitchen with a

bunch of Ash's frat brothers. For the first time, I realized what Derek's shirt said.

"You didn't!" I said.

He arched an eyebrow. "What?" He pulled his shirt out for me to see. "You don't like it?"

Duke was playing Butler in the national championship, and the bastard had gotten a *Butler* shirt to wear to the party. Such an asshole instigator.

"Where did you even get that?"

"Bought it online." Derek sank into the open space next to me. Our knees and hips touched. I shivered slightly.

"I can't believe you."

"Had to support the correct team at a Duke party," he said with a lazy smirk.

"You're a dick," Ash said with a laugh. "Why do I put up with you?"

"Because you've known me your entire life?"

"Yeah, yeah."

"So, Derek," Lora said, batting her eyelashes at him, "what's your plan after graduation?"

"Ahhh," Ash said dramatically. He punched Derek in the shoulder. "Tell them."

I looked at him expectantly. We hadn't talked about the future. He was graduating in May. But we hadn't discussed what would come next. As if we'd called a time-out on the clock moving forward.

"I got into Harvard Law," Derek told them.

"Whoa," Lora said.

"Like it's hard?" Brinley joked. "That's amazing."

Then, he looked down at me, and I brightened for him, even as a slight panic formed in my chest.

"Congrats. Going to be just like your dad?"

He frowned. "Yeah. I guess so. Always thought I'd take over the law firm one day."

And for a second, a chasm split between us. It had always been there, but it was another reminder of how different we were. I had big dreams, but I always worried about how to afford them and what was going to happen. He, on the other hand, was a legacy at Harvard Law. He would work for his dad right after graduation. Things were always so easy for Derek.

"Your dad's an attorney too?" Brin asked.

He nodded, looking away from me. "Yeah. He owns his own practice in downtown Savannah."

"Best in town," Ash said.

I fell silent as everyone discussed their own hopeful plans for when they graduated. Lora would be off to DC, working for a lobbying firm. Ash wanted to move back home and help run the family business, which was essentially owning the entire town. Brin wanted to travel for a year and maybe look into international business. When it got to me, I told them what I'd been saying for years.

"I want to find a cure for dementia. So, probably a PhD in neuroscience and decide from there. Become a professor or work in the private sector."

Everyone stared at me long enough that I flushed.

"That's ambitious," Ash said.

"Our girl is going to save the world," Lora crowed.

I laughed just as the game got started, and the focus was pulled from me. Everyone zeroed in on the TV, but Derek was still looking at me.

He touched my leg and leaned in close. "Is this about your grandpa?"

I gulped and nodded. I'd told him over one of our chats about my Gramps' declining health. It ran in his family, and his memory had been getting progressively worse. It was only a matter of time before it took him too. I hated thinking about it.

"They're lucky to have you," he said gently.

I looked up into his gaze and found him sincere. "Thank you."

He nodded and went back to the game, but he didn't move his hand from my leg. He stroked slow, methodical circles into my exposed skin. My breath hitched at the feel of him touching me and the heat spreading up my legs. It made concentrating on the game difficult.

At halftime, he got up to get a drink for us both, and I thought that might be the end. But he settled right back to where he'd been sitting. He passed me my drink, and then his hand returned right to where it had been before. Maybe an inch higher. I shifted my legs together, trying to reduce the growing heat in my core, and he glanced over at me with a knowing look on his face. I could barely meet that gaze. Damn him. I was turned on... and he *knew*.

But he didn't say anything about it. Just left his hand on my leg throughout the rest of the game. Thankfully, no one *else* said anything about him touching me either. This was all new, and I didn't know how he'd react to it. I didn't know how *I'd* react to someone pointing it out. Because I didn't want him to stop touching me... and I didn't know how I felt about that either.

Duke won at the last second, and everyone in the room jumped up to cheer. Even Derek got into it, though when I looked at him, he just shook his head at me.

The party swelled and swelled. I lost Brin and Lora in the mass of people. Suddenly, it was just me and Derek in a sea of unfamiliar faces. I was tipsy from alcohol and drunk on the adrenaline of our win.

So, when Derek tipped my face up to his and pressed his mouth to mine, I didn't pull back. I didn't even consider it. I kissed him back. My fingers dug into the material of his stupid Butler shirt, and my body arched into him. His hands came around my back, holding me tight. I'd known he was tall and big. He was a college basketball player after all. But I'd never felt so *small* as when I was in his arms. As if I had been made to fit right into him.

He pulled back slightly. My eyes were still closed, and I slowly, lazily opened them to look up at him.

"I believe this means you won."

"I guess it does," I said, dazed.

He moved a stray curl from my face, and I leaned into him again.

He bent down and brushed his mouth against the shell of my ear. "It's kind of loud in here."

I shivered at that one touch. I knew what I wanted, and I was drunk enough to ask for it. "My place isn't far."

He took my hand without another word and drew me out of the party. I texted Brin to let her know that I was leaving. She probably wouldn't see it until later, but it didn't really matter. I wanted to let her know that I was safe.

Duke was on fire—both figuratively and literally—as we headed to my place. I was glad to have Derek at my side as we walked through the madness. I wouldn't have felt safe otherwise.

Derek reached down for my hand and threaded our fingers together. I gulped and looked down at where we were connected and then back up at him. This felt surreal. How could this be happening? This was Derek Ballentine. He'd been my enemy for so long that it was disorienting how fast everything had shifted.

I opened the door to my place and let Derek inside. "Do you want a drink?"

He shrugged. "Sure."

I went into the kitchen, reaching inside and drawing out two beers. When I turned around, he was there, taking them out of my hands and setting them down. I opened my mouth to say… who knew what. But before I got a word out, he had me pressed back against the fridge. His hands ran down my sides, and all my thoughts fled as his lips tipped forward against mine.

This wasn't like any of the other kisses we'd had before this. Derek was claiming me. He wasn't hurried. He was completely sure of himself in this moment. He knew what he wanted, and I was it.

"You're so short," he murmured against my lips.

His hands traveled down my ass and to the backs of my legs. He effortlessly hoisted me up, as if I weighed nothing at all. Then, he deposited me on the kitchen counter, pushing his weight between my legs. I wrapped my arms around his neck, as I was suddenly *almost* on his level.

"That's better," he growled.

He ran fingers down my bare legs and then up, up, up and under the hem of my skirt. His lips were back on mine, dizzy and disorienting. I wanted more, and yet everything was moving at lightning speed. Hands on my inner thighs, his pelvis pressed forward against mine, out lips wet and perfectly in sync.

I could feel the hard length of him even through layers of clothing, and everything in my mind went blank. I didn't know quite when it had happened, but I could deny this no longer. I'd kept him on his toes so long that I'd done nothing but deny myself what I wanted. I didn't want to deny anything anymore.

"Mars," he breathed. His finger rested on the lace of my thong. He trailed the line of it experimentally.

My head dipped backward. "Oh God."

"You like that?" he asked, deep and breathy.

"Yes," I gasped as he touched the apex of my thighs and ran back and forth over my clit.

"You're already wet for me."

My cheeks colored at the words, but he wasn't wrong. His teasing all evening had left me wet, and now, with his mouth on mine and his dick pressed against me and that finger trailing along my clit… I was positively soaked.

"Derek, please," I groaned.

He grinned devilishly. "Oh, I like that." He kissed down my neck, and I tilted my head for more. "Say my name again."

"Derek," I all but whispered.

"Again."

He slipped under the material of my thong, and he dragged a slicked finger over my clit.

"Fuck," I gasped. "Derek, oh God."

He nipped at my collarbone and then withdrew. I whimpered at the loss of him, but he just hoisted me up off of the counter. His hands on my bare ass as he carried me out of the kitchen. Our drinks forgotten.

I pointed him in the direction of my bedroom, and he toed the door open before dropping me back on my bed. Then, he sank to his knees before me, drawing my thong over my hips and discarding them onto the floor.

"What are you…" I managed to get out before he descended onto my clit, sucking and licking me. I gasped, my hands fisting into the comforter. "Derek!"

He pushed my legs open, spreading me wider for him. I bucked off the bed at the first touch of his fingers at my opening. He spread my lips apart and then trailed lazily through the wetness at my sensitive core. Expletives left my mouth at his practiced touch. Then, without notice, he sank two fingers deep inside of me, plunging in and making me cry out in pleasure. All the while, his mouth was still attached to my clit, building everything to a crescendo.

Suddenly, everything went cataclysmic. My body seized and then exploded in waves as I came at the behest of his mouth. I shuddered all over, covering my face with my hands. I came down from the high to find him still on his knees, just watching me. He slowly pulled both hands away from my face and pressed a kiss to my lips.

"That was hot."

I laughed, too tipsy to even care. "I never thought you would call me hot."

"That's because you're beautiful," he said, kissing me again, slow and unhurried.

I was all flustered from that comment. Hot was one thing. Beautiful was... I didn't know. It didn't sound like a word Derek ever used.

"We need to get you out of this ridiculous shirt," I said, pushing the Butler shirt up to reveal the six-pack underneath.

As he drew it up over his abs, I gaped. Was it a six-pack or more of an eight-pack? Because, holy shit, he was all muscle. Straight muscle. Arms and chest and abs, and I ran my hands over every inch of him.

"You're huge," I muttered without a thought in my head.

He chuckled, and I could see the dirty thought form without saying a word.

"Oh my God, that isn't what I meant."

"Isn't it?" he asked with a wink.

He took my hand and pressed it down farther and

farther, over those miraculous abs to the waistband of his pants until my hand rested over his dick. I took it in my hand through the material of his shorts. He groaned and grasped my hips, dragging me closer to him on the bed. It only made me grip him harder as I felt the full length of him. My eyes widened the entire way. Because *shit*. He *was* huge.

"Derek," I breathed, wanton.

Neither of us could move fast enough. A bubble had been popped at the thirsty way I said his name. I yanked off the rest of my clothes, and he stripped out of his shorts. A condom appeared from his wallet, and then he rolled it into place. He crawled over me on the bed, all six foot five of him towering over me. My breath caught at the first feel of him pressed against my opening. He took his time easing into me, and at that final push, where he seated himself fully within me, we both released harsh breaths.

His hazel eyes met mine. A half-smile cracked on his face, and then he was kissing me with fervor. I clutched at his back, wanting him closer. So much closer. He complied by pulling out and then slamming back inside of me. It jerked me upward at the force of the momentum, and I didn't care for a damn minute. I just wanted more. I'd denied myself this for so long. Ignored every single part of me that said I didn't want him. I didn't want this. And now, we were here, and I could feel every single lie break down and dissolve into nothing.

I wanted Derek Ballentine. I wanted him more than anyone else in my entire existence. And here, right now, was the climax of a long-held desire. It didn't seem like I was the only one. He responded to every single little squeak and moan out of my mouth with vigor. Attentive to my every move, as if he could read my mind.

He grasped my leg and braced it against his shoulder, diving even deeper inside. I gasped as everything shot through my body. I was so close. So fucking close.

"Mars," he ground out, raw and earnest.

"God, yes," I said.

His finger slipped down to my clit, and he rubbed me in circles as he pushed in. "Come with me."

And I did, letting loose all at once at the command in his voice and the overload of his hands and dick and mouth. Everything coalesced into one earth-shattering orgasm that left me speechless and seeing stars on the ceiling. Derek thrust a few more times, his body tensing around the buildup. Then, he grunted and came hard and fast inside of me. He dropped forward over me. We were both panting, our bodies slick with sweat.

He got up briefly and tossed the condom before falling back onto my naked body.

"Derek," I breathed, running my fingers through the slight curl in his dark hair.

"Hmm?" he said groggily.

"Does that make you my prize?"

"I guess it does." He chuckled against my chest, and then his lips moved over my sticky skin. Kissing my neck, chest, and then down to my breasts. Taking one nipple into his mouth while massaging the other breast.

I was entirely spent and yet somehow still aroused by his touch.

"We just finished. You're going to get me all hot again," I teased.

His eyes lit up at my words, and he moved to the other breast. I squirmed under him. He braced a hand against my hip, holding me in place.

"If I'm the prize, then I should make sure you get off a

few more times, right?" he asked with a naughty glint in his eyes.

I gaped at him. "I just came twice."

But then there were no words as he sucked a nipple into his mouth while his hand traveled south again. There was only gasping and crying out and coming. There was only round two and round three and collapsing into bed, exhausted and spent and never wanting the morning to come.

15

DUKE

APRIL 6, 2010

The next morning dawned bright and early. I yawned, throwing my arm across my eyes to hide from the sun coming in from the window. I wasn't ready to be alive today. My body ached in a way I'd never experienced. Every shift brought memories of his scratchy face against my chest and my legs shaking from exertion and the ache between my thighs. I'd have trouble walking for days, and I was looking forward to every memory.

I rolled over to say that much to Derek and found an empty bed. I blinked into the light, trying to clear my eyes. No Derek. That was weird.

I grabbed my phone off of the nightstand, having no recollection of how it had gotten there. There were no messages from Derek. I scrolled back a few days and the dozens of texts we'd sent back and forth. And yet there was nothing today?

I crawled out of bed and threw on shorts and a tank top and stumbled out of my bedroom. The lights were all off. Brinley was probably going to sleep until at least noon. I hadn't even heard her come in last night. So, maybe she'd sleep in until noon elsewhere. But there was no Derek.

My stomach flipped. I stepped back into my room and looked around. All of his clothes were gone. There was nothing of him in my room except a few discarded condoms. I was going to be sick.

The rational side of my brain said that I needed to calm down. It could be nothing. He could have had an emergency. Or practice. Or something. I didn't know what it could have been that he wouldn't even tell me about, but fuck.

I jotted out a text to him, typing and deleting the words out of fear enough times before settling on something neutral.

Had a good time last night. Where'd you run off to?

I waited for him to respond. For the three dots to show up that said he was replying. But he never did. A whole hour passed and nothing.

Fuck.

My fingers shook as I realized what had happened. He'd gotten what he wanted from me... the one girl who always turned him down. I'd stopped being a challenge, and he'd bailed. What else could it be?

Finally, anger won. I dialed his number. I didn't think he was going to answer anyway. But to my surprise, he picked up the phone.

"Hello?"

"Derek," I said softly. Thinking about all the times I'd yelled his name out last night.

"Hey, Marley."

"I, uh... just woke up. I thought you'd still be here. Did you go get breakfast?"

"Nah, I went home."

His voice was different. It wasn't the guy who had been here, worshipping my body last night. He was so closed off. I didn't understand.

"Oh," I said lamely. "Okay. I thought… I don't know. I didn't think you'd just ditch."

He chuckled softly. "What did you think this was, Marley?"

I winced at the words. My stomach dipping at the way he'd said it. He was essentially asking me if I was an idiot. I wasn't an idiot. I knew who he was. I'd just… thought he was different with me. Probably like every stupid girl before me.

"I don't know," I said honestly. I tried to reach for that hard girl who could laugh at his idiocy and bravado. But I wasn't her right now. I was hurt. I was vulnerable. Two things I hated and never wanted to be again. Yet here I was.

"It was fun," he said slowly.

"Stop," I said, closing my eyes. "Just stop."

Where had the guy from last night gone? What had I done? How had we ruined this so completely?

"Okay. I don't know what to tell you."

"Do you always self-sabotage like this? I thought we had something, Derek."

"I'm leaving in a month," he said evenly. "It's not like we were going to date. You said yourself that I don't do relationships. So, we had fun. It doesn't have to be more than that."

It didn't have to be more than that, but it had been. I'd started to like him. I'd thought that I was different. How wrong I'd been.

"Sure," I said icily, holding back tears. "Right. I get it."

I hung up on him because if he said one more thing that broke my heart, I'd dissolve completely. I dropped down onto my bed and then immediately jumped back up. I yanked the comforter and sheets off of the bed until it was bare to the mattress and then curled them up into a ball. I'd have to wash it all before I could sleep in it again without smelling sex. The whole room was still perfumed with it.

I wouldn't cry. I didn't want to. Like an idiot, I kept checking my phone to see if I'd get a text from Derek that explained his behavior. But what did he have to explain? This was who he was. I had known that, and I'd slept with him last night anyway.

Tears came to my eyes, and I squeezed them shut to stop them. No. I would *not* let him take a part of me. After all these years of anger, I didn't think that I could hate him any more. But no... I had been wrong. Because I hated him now more than ever.

I dialed Gran's number without thinking. She answered on the first ring.

"Chickadee, congratulations! Gramps and I watched your national championship win last night."

Then, I burst into tears.

"Oh, oh, sweetheart, what's wrong?" she asked, so calm and concerned. "Are you okay?"

"I made a mistake," I sobbed into the phone. "I made a huge mistake."

"That's okay. You're allowed to make mistakes. Tell me what happened."

I hiccupped. "I... remember that guy in high school that I kissed at the Halloween party? We had a big feud?"

"The Ballentine boy?"

"Yes. He goes to UNC, and we've had a bet the last couple months over the games."

"I see," she said uncertainly.

"And it got heated. Last night, we..." I swiped at my eyes to try to stop the tears. "We slept together."

"Ah," Gran said.

"And he bailed this morning without a word."

"Have you spoken with him?"

"Yeah. He was a dick."

"Language, Marley Sue."

"He ghosted me and then treated me like I was the idiot for not realizing, Gran! He was a *dick*. I made a huge mistake. I never should have given in."

"Okay, breathe. Just breathe. And listen to me. You didn't make a mistake. You liked this young man?"

"Yes," I whispered.

"And you believed he felt the same?"

I nodded. "Yes."

"And you're not pregnant?"

I laughed in horror. "No, Gran! I'm not pregnant. Oh my God!"

"There. Then, you're okay. Your heart will hurt for what could have been, but it wasn't a mistake. The only mistake made was on him walking away from my brilliant girl."

I sniffled and let the tears dry up. "Thanks, Gran. I love you."

"I love you too."

We spoke for a few more minutes until I could carry on a conversation without crying more. I felt better and not better at all. All I knew was that I'd have to put Derek behind me. Nothing good could come from having feelings for him. I knew who he was. I wouldn't soon forget it.

16

SAVANNAH

PRESENT

"I can't believe that you agreed to go out with Derek again," Maddox said from Gran's old chair.

"Me neither," I admitted.

"He's the enemy."

"Yep."

"How do you reconcile what he's doing to us with seeing him?"

I shrugged and adjusted my dress in the mirror. "I try not to think about it mostly. They were going to contest the will either way. The fact that Derek is representing them is frustrating, but it would have been someone even if it wasn't him."

"I guess," he admitted.

"You could come out with us. Bring that girl you're seeing."

He tensed. "I'm not seeing anyone."

"From what I hear, you've been seeing a lot of someones."

He arched an eyebrow. "So?"

"Got a bit of a playboy reputation, little brother."

"You're thirty-seven minutes older, Mars," he groaned.

"Still counts."

"Do you really want to talk about my sex life?"

I pointed at him. "Fair. No. Gross."

He laughed. "Have fun with your ex."

I rolled my eyes at him. "This is about Ash."

"Don't have fun with Lila's ex," he said with a smirk.

I smacked him upside the head and called the Uber to take me downtown. I'd just been picked up when my phone rang. Derek's name popped on the screen, and I tensed, wondering what he could want. I was already on the way to see him against my better sense.

"Hey," I said when I answered.

"Change of plans. Game is still on. Meet us at Dub's."

"What game? Duke has a bye week," I said with a grin.

He huffed. "The only team that matters, obviously —UNC."

"How's it going?"

He didn't say anything for a few seconds, which said all I needed to know. "Tense. Just get here, Mars."

Then, he hung up the phone. I giggled at him. The game must have been going really poorly for him to slip up and call me Mars. I hadn't heard that name from him in years.

I leaned forward and asked the Uber to change the destination to Dub's Pub on River Street. It was a large sports bar with pool tables and ping-pong tables, which were primarily used for beer pong. It'd been a few years since I'd been there, but nothing had changed. I found Derek, Amelia, and Ash seated at the bar. Derek was yelling at the screen. Amelia had her hands over her eyes and was shaking her head.

"What did I miss?" I asked as I approached them.

Ash had a shit-eating grin on his face. "Mars, you have to check this out."

I glanced at the screen and then began to cackle. "Oh. My. God. Is UNC losing to App State?"

"Shut it," Derek growled.

But I couldn't stop laughing. Not that UNC or Duke were particularly good at football. We were both basketball schools through and through, but Appalachian State was a crap team. They'd pulled an upset over Michigan when I was in college, but they'd moved back into obscurity since then.

"We can still pull it out," Amelia said with a wince. She peeked back up at the screen. "We're almost set up for a field goal."

Ash kicked back at the bar and threw peanuts into his mouth. He was enjoying this, which was a sharp contrast to how I'd seen him every other time. But hey, we both loved to watch UNC lose.

"Come on," Derek shouted.

I took the seat next to Ash and watched the field goal get set up. "Ten bucks he misses," I said to him.

Ash nodded.

Derek glared at me. "Watch your mouth."

I couldn't keep the grin from my face. "You're losing to App State."

He rolled his eyes and went back to praying. I could actually feel them hold their breath as UNC got the last-second field goal off that would tie up the game and send them into overtime. I'd been joking when I said he would miss. I hadn't expected App State to block it.

I gasped. "Oh fuck."

Derek's head hit the bar with a loud groan. Amelia's jaw fell. Ash tried not to look too smug.

“Should we go get drinks elsewhere?” Ash asked, patting Amelia on the back.

“I need one,” she said. “That was…”

“Terrible,” Derek groaned. “There goes the whole season.”

“Didn’t you lose last weekend too?” I asked.

Derek threw his hands out. “We beat South Carolina. I don’t get it.”

“You’ll probably still be bowl eligible,” Ash said like a consolation prize.

“Clemson is going to wipe the floor with us next week,” Amelia said as she hopped off the chair. “I don’t even want to watch.”

“But we will,” Derek said, following us out, “because we’re masochists until basketball season.”

“Admit it,” I said with a laugh. “You’re masochists during basketball season too.”

“Hey, didn’t Alabama beat you forty-two to three in *your* opener?” Derek asked.

“Shh, we’re talking about your defeat to an unranked App State right now.”

“It was pretty beautiful,” Ash said. “You wanted to cheer me up, and look, that made my birthday.”

Derek shot him a look. “So glad that my defeat could bring you such joy.”

“Thanks, man.”

Ash stepped forward with Amelia, and I fell into step with Derek as we took the stairs up to Bay Street and walked toward City Market. Ash dragged us into bar after bar, and it became increasingly evident that Ash Talmadge knew every bartender. He got free birthday shots at them all. He was clearly a regular.

“How often do you come out?” I asked him when we

stepped into Rouge Water and the tall blonde offered us another round of shots.

Derek passed his extra to Ash because he planned to drive home.

"Often enough."

I glanced at Derek, and he shrugged. "Like every weekend or every night?"

"What does it matter?"

Because you're a wreck, was what I wanted to say. But didn't he deserve to wallow for a while? It had been three and a half months though. He needed to find a way to move on. And not just by getting under someone else.

"I know that look, Mars," Ash said, leaning back against the bar. He didn't even slur.

Meanwhile, I was having trouble standing from all the shots. Amelia was a beast because, somehow, she still seemed fine.

"Spit it out."

"It's your birthday. I'll be nice."

Ash snorted. "Since when does that matter?"

"Hey, I've been nice to you before!"

He nodded, his eyes going briefly distant. "Right. Yeah."

Ash turned back to the bartender to order another shot. I grimaced. I hadn't even brought up Lila, but clearly, it had made him think of her.

"Come dance with me," Ash said to Amelia and dragged her out into the middle of the dive bar. Other people were sort of dancing, but it wasn't the kind of place to dance.

"Good job," Derek muttered. He turned to the bartender. "Can we get a few waters?"

"Maybe I'm not the right person for this job. I don't have many memories of Ash outside of college that don't include my best friend."

"Ah yes, she who shall not be named." Derek handed me a water, and I took it gratefully. "It's fine. This is better than what he originally wanted to do for his birthday, which is all that matters."

"What did he have planned?"

"It was a tie between sit at home alone and drink until he passed out or go out alone, drink until he nearly passed out, and take home some stranger."

I cringed. "Gross."

"I'd rather have him here with us. Less time to think."

"Agreed." I watched him dance with Amelia. He was definitely drunk, and the boy still managed to have good rhythm. It was kind of impressive. "He's not going to try to hook up with Amelia now, is he?"

"I don't think he's that stupid."

I remembered the one time I'd seen Derek throw a guy against a wall for touching his sister. But that had been years ago. He couldn't *still* be that protective, could he?

"What? You wouldn't want Ash and Amelia together?"

"I wouldn't care if they were together. But I would beat the shit out of him if he tried a single fucking thing with my sister when his mind was still stuck on Lila."

"That seems... fair."

I didn't think Amelia was interested in a dejected Ash Talmadge anyway. She was too smart, beautiful, and successful to settle for second best to anyone.

I finished my water and relented when Ash ordered us more drinks. Amelia and Derek decided against anything more. I thought Ash was going to reject Amelia's idea to pop into Lulu's next door for her delectable chocolate desserts, but he just shrugged, and we all stepped inside.

"Chocolate martinis?" I asked Ash.

He laughed. "That's not exactly my style."

"Who cares? It's your birthday. I'll drink one too," I said, my Southern drawl coming out the drunker I got.

Ash shook his head at me and then held two fingers up to the waiter. "Two chocolate martinis, two chocolate chip cheesecakes, and a strawberry suspension cake."

"Derek, you must get pictures of me and Ash drinking chocolate martinis."

"Whoa," Ash said. "Not that far, Mars."

Amelia laughed. "It's your birthday!"

When the drinks came, Ash posed with me, pinkies out and all. The drinks were to *die* for. Maybe better than the cake, which was two layers of chocolate cake sandwiching a layer of strawberries and cream, but never better than their cheesecake. We ate every last scrap of dessert to celebrate Ash getting another year older. And by the end of it, we were both too drunk to do much more than stumble around.

"I'll get an Uber." I pulled my phone out and immediately dropped it. I giggled and bent to pick it up. I nearly fell over, but Derek got an arm around me just in time. He picked up my phone, which was miraculously not cracked, and slid it back into my purse.

"I'll drive you," he said.

Amelia nodded. "Good idea. I'm going to walk Ash. It's not far."

"No way. I'll drop you off too."

"I'm a hundred percent fine." She did a twirl to prove it. "I'll catch an Uber from his place."

"Text me when you're home," he said like the protective older brother he was.

She laughed. "Will do, *Dad*."

Derek hadn't released me, and I was pretty sure I'd fall over if he did. That last martini must have been potent.

"Derek," I said as we headed toward the parking garage.

"Yeah?"

"I think I'm drunk."

He laughed. "You've been drunk for a while."

"How'd you know?"

"Your Southern accent came out."

I glared at him. "I don't have an accent."

"Yeah, and I don't like UNC."

"I got rid of it," I said. I'd purposely spent a lot of time getting rid of the accent that defined me as other. By the time I'd left Duke, no one would have even guessed I'd grown up in the South.

"Well, when you're drunk, it always comes back out." His gaze shifted to me. "I love your accent."

I flushed. "Oh."

He stopped in front of a sleek, brand-new black BMW. "This is me."

"Of course it is," I said, drawling the words and proving his point.

He popped open the passenger side with a laugh and helped me into the seat. Then, he got into the driver's seat, pulled out onto MLK, and headed toward Gran's house. I tipped my head in his direction, leaning my elbow onto the console between us.

"Why are you driving me home?"

He arched an eyebrow. "Because you're drunk. I don't trust an Uber to get you home."

I dropped my head on my hand and fluttered my eyelashes at him. "That is very gentlemanly of you."

"You know tonight was as much about you as Ash."

I blinked, trying to clear my fuzzy head. "What do you mean?"

"He's not the only one who is going through something. I know you're sad about Gran."

I swallowed and tried not to let memories crush me. Gran would have liked this car. She'd always loved Lulu's chocolate chip cheesecake. She would want me to be happy. Not here and sad and dealing with all of this.

"Yeah," I finally whispered and sat back in my seat.

"So, I'm glad we got you out. You looked like you had a good time." He peeked over at me. "Did you have a good time?"

"The best. I liked watching UNC lose."

He barely suppressed a smile. "Of course you did."

A few minutes later, he pulled over in front of Gran's house. I looked up at the big, empty house and sighed. Maddox's Wrangler wasn't here, which meant he'd gone home. So, that meant I had to go inside all alone.

I put my hand on Derek's arm. "Thanks for driving me."

"Of course."

My eyes traveled from his hazel eyes and down to his lips. I was drunk, and this was a bad idea. And my brain couldn't quite put the two together all at the same time.

Because without thinking, I crossed the divide and pressed my mouth to his. For a second, he did nothing. He sat there in apparent shock. Then, he moved with all the careful assurance of Derek Ballentine. His hands slid up into my hair, and he dragged me closer. We kissed with practiced ease. Chocolate still lingered between us, and it was sweet and decadent.

Everything superheated at that touch. Desire pooling in my core, sending fire down my spine. I wanted to crawl across the car and get our bodies closer together. To feel every inch of skin against skin. To feel *him*.

Then, slowly, ever so slowly, Derek pulled back and looked down at me. "Marley, I—"

"Do you want to come inside?" I interrupted.

He stiffened, and his eyes swept my body, landing on my lips and then back up to my eyes. I could see the struggle. The one that said he wanted what I was offering as badly as I did right now.

Finally, he pulled back. "I don't think that's a good idea."

I jerked back into my seat, heat hitting my cheeks. "Oh."

"You're drunk, and I don't want to take advantage of you. I don't want you to regret anything in the morning."

"Oh how things have changed," I muttered and unbuckled my seat belt.

"Mars," he groaned.

"It's fine."

He grabbed my arm before I could get out of his shiny, new Beamer. "Don't be mad at me."

"You're right. This is a bad idea. Thanks for reminding me."

He groaned and unbuckled his seat belt, following me out of the car. "Marley, you can barely walk. How can you be this mad at me when you're struggling to get inside?"

"Being mad at you is easy," I told him, too drunk to think clearly.

He grabbed the keys out of my hand and opened the door. Then, he took my face in his hands and kissed me softly. My eyes were still closed when he planted a tiny kiss on my nose and dropped the keys back into my hand.

"Don't hate me in the morning when you sober up."

Then, he turned and walked back to his car. I watched him, my body all needy and my brain all confused.

When had Derek Ballentine become a gentleman?

PART III

17

HARVARD

OCTOBER 27, 2012

"Is he still singing?" Misty groaned, flopping back on her bed in the off-campus apartment we'd scrounged up from housing.

"He is." I peered out my window and saw the hot guy I'd dated for, like, a whole month, trying to win me back by pulling a move from an '80s movie and singing to me from the street. I found it desperate and annoying, just like him. He might have been hot, but he wasn't worth my time. That was becoming more and more blatantly obvious.

"Let's go out and get drunk instead. I heard there's a Halloween grad party tonight."

There had been a grad party every night since I'd gotten to Harvard for my PhD a year earlier. I was once again on full scholarship for my PhD in neuroscience, working as a research assistant for the most distinguished professor. It was a lot of work and more than rewarding. Plus, Misty was in my program, and we'd instantly bonded, deciding to move in together for our second year.

"I have to be in the lab in the morning," I complained.

"But it's your birthday weekend!'

"And we celebrated last night and last weekend when my brother was in town."

Misty stuck out her bottom lip. "Hurricane Sandy will be here on Monday. We need to celebrate before it hits." I was still wavering, but she continued, "Do you want to listen to *that* all night or go to a party?"

"Point taken."

It wasn't hard to convince me to go out. I had a Halloween costume ready, and I wasn't going to get to wear it *on* Halloween with a hurricane blowing up the east coast. So, I'd just wear it tonight. It was cliché, but I'd gone with a French maid. My skirt barely covered my ass. My breasts barely fit into the square top. My waist was microscopic since I'd worked my ass off my first year here. Misty had thigh-high tights that I paired with black high heels. She wore a Playboy bunny costume complete with ears and a tail.

We took the back way out to bypass my ex and headed over to the party. Half the people weren't wearing a costume at all. Either too cool or too nerdy to get dressed up. But my birthday was so close to Halloween that I'd always loved it. It had been a part of my life for so long that I couldn't imagine it any other way.

"So, how did you find out about this party?" I asked, taking the punch out of her hand and downing half of the contents in one big gulp.

"Hear me out. A friend of a friend said they talked to their friend who knows someone in the law school."

I eyed her dubiously. "The law school?"

"Yeah. I don't know. Just that this was the grad party to go to on Halloween weekend."

"Uh-huh."

My gaze swept the room.

When I'd gotten the full ride at Harvard, I'd been hesitant. I knew only one other person who was at Harvard right now, and he was quite literally the last person that I wanted to see. But I looked up the numbers. There were more than twenty *thousand* grad students on Harvard's campus. What was the likelihood that I'd run into him here? A year later, and I still hadn't seen him, but I hadn't gone to any law school parties either. If Misty had told me that was where we were going, I probably would have declined. Or at least found another party that would have been equally fun and not given me the problem of running into… him.

"Why do you suddenly look like a deer caught in headlights?" Misty asked. "Is the drink shitty?"

"Uh, yeah," I said quickly. "The drink is shitty." I finished it in another gulp. "I need a second, and then we should go dance."

That was the hardest transition to Harvard—no dance. I still sometimes took classes at a local studio, but it wasn't the same. Not by a long shot.

Misty crossed her arms. "You're a shit liar."

I laughed. "That is very true. So, I have this old friend. Erm, flame? I don't know. This guy I used to know is in the law school."

"Old friend you used to fuck?" Misty asked with a grin.

"Sort of," I said uncertainly. "Anyway, with my luck, I'll probably run into him."

"All the better! You can get over Mr. Serenade You Out Your Window!"

"No!" I said quickly. Then, more calmly, "No. Uh, no. That's not what I'm interested in."

"Okay," Misty said, holding her hands up. "Avoid old flame. Got it."

Despite my anxiety, we ended up having a great time.

We drank until I knew I was going to regret it in the morning and danced in our heels until I wanted to claw them off my feet. The law party had *plenty* of hot, available guys who were more than happy to lavish us PhDs with attention.

It was fun.

"Neuroscience?" the guy asked.

He'd told me his name, but I'd already forgotten it. He had me leaned up against a wall outside. He was cute with floppy blond hair and brown eyes. He was dressed like Captain America. He didn't quite fit the bill, but who cared?

"Yeah. I'm researching dementia."

"That's brilliant," he said with a grin.

Oh, and he had an accent. Australian. Swoon. Made up for the not-quite Captain America. In fact, it made it all the funnier. Or maybe that was the alcohol.

Then, he was kissing me. One minute, my major. Next minute, making out.

He was an okay kisser. Not my worst. Not my best. But considering this was the entire reason I was out tonight, I decided not to complain. I didn't need to marry this Australian Captain America. Just have a little fun.

Suddenly, the guy was ripped away from me. I protested, and he cursed violently.

"What the hell, mate?" he snapped.

And then I saw who was standing over him—*towering* over him. My blood went cold. Fuck.

"Derek!" I yelled. "What the fuck are you doing?"

He shoved the other guy away. "Go."

Derek had a good six or seven inches on him and a hundred pounds of muscle. He went.

"Are you out of your fucking mind?"

He turned the full force of his attention on me. I didn't

back down. Not an inch. I was drunk enough for my anger to want to blow.

"Hey, Minivan," he said easily, as if no time had passed at all. That same perfectly pouty smirk on his lips. That same *eat you alive* look. The same hint of desire.

"Go fuck yourself."

I pushed past him, but only made it a few steps before Derek wrapped a hand around my arm and pulled me to a stop. I swatted at him, but he didn't let go.

"You're drunk. That guy is a *creep*. What were you thinking?" he demanded.

"That guy was *nice*."

"He's a 1L, and he's come on to half of the school. He's not nice. He's one step away from sexual assault."

I gaped at him. "Then turn him in."

"With what proof and what witnesses, Marley? As much as I'd love to do that, no one wants to jeopardize their position in law school to come forward. Most of us watch him and scare him away. When I saw him with you..." He looked ready to put his hand through the wall. The last time I'd seen him look like that, he'd had Chuck Henderson against a wall because he'd touched Amelia. And now, he was protecting me.

I shook him off. "Thanks, but I don't need your help."

"You clearly do."

"I don't get you. Is this another part of our old feud?"

"No," he spat out. "You won. That's over. This was keeping you from making a terrible mistake."

I looked him up and down. "Too late."

His jaw clenched at the words, but I was already out of there. Of course, it would be the night I really wanted to kick back that I finally saw him here. On Halloween weekend, just like in high school.

I found Misty inside. "I'm heading out. You can stay."

"You're walking home alone?"

"I'll call a cab or something."

Misty bit her lip uncertainly and then looked to the hot guy she was talking to. "Text me when you get back."

"Will do."

I didn't look back as I left the house, dialing a cab company to come pick me up. We lived within walking distance of the house, but it was the middle of the night. Even if that Australian guy hadn't been a creep, I wasn't stupid enough to go off on my own. But it sucked because the company said a half hour. Jesus Christ. I could walk home and back in that time.

Then, I saw Derek head out of the house and straight toward me. I huffed in irritation. Great. Just fucking great.

"Are you walking home alone?" he asked.

"Cab."

"Alone?"

"Derek, I am not a fragile little flower. I can take care of myself. Go back inside and bother someone else."

"Why are you leaving so early? You don't have to run out because I'm here."

"I'm not." *Lie*. "I have to be at the lab at eight a.m. to help with the hurricane prep. Not everything is about you."

"Come on, Mars."

"Come on what?" I demanded, finally turning to look at him. "How did you think this was going to happen?"

"Well, I didn't think I'd see you again. I didn't realize that you were at Harvard."

"You can be here, but I can't?"

"I didn't say that."

"It was implied."

He clenched his hands into fists and then took a big

breath and released it. "It wasn't implied. I know how smart you are. You deserve to be here as much as anyone, maybe more than most. I just didn't know."

"You made sure of that too." Then, I turned back to face away from him.

Just seeing him again made the pain fresh. How stupid I'd been to think he'd change for me. When he wouldn't change for anyone else. For thinking it would be different. But it was never different. He was always the same.

"I'm sorry," he finally said.

My head snapped to the side. "What did you say?"

"I said that I'm sorry. I'm sorry for what happened and how it all went down and the things that I said."

I blinked at him. "What?"

"Mars, I'm sorry."

"Derek Ballentine is actually *apologizing*?"

"Yeah, I am. I was a fucking idiot."

"You were," I said warily.

"I left. I was cruel and stupid. I don't know why I did or said the things that I did and said."

"Yes, you do," I said. "You did them because that's who you are. You told me not to forget it, and I haven't."

"That's fair. I get it." He ran a hand back through his hair. "I thought I was over it... over you. Then, I saw you kissing someone else, and I just I lost it. I don't know what came over me, but the idea of you with another person drove me out of my mind."

I crossed my arms over my chest. "So, was he a creep, or were you out of your mind?"

"Yes. Both."

"I don't know what you want me to say, Derek."

"Nothing. I don't know." And he actually looked flummoxed. As if this had never happened to him before.

Which it likely hadn't, knowing him. "Let me walk you home."

"I already called a cab."

"Cancel."

I glared at him. "Why? What would be the point?"

"Because I miss you." He shot me a small grin, not the full-blown cocky smirk that he always wore. This was something else. I wasn't sure I'd ever seen it on him before. This was hesitant but hopeful.

I sighed. I was mad at him. Still mad at him for what had happened. But that smile had made me stupid one too many times. "Fine. I'd rather walk."

I shot the driver a text to cancel the trip and then headed off toward my place. Derek jogged after me, falling into step at my side. We were silent most of the way there. He gave me his jacket when I began to shiver in the cold.

"Cambridge sure isn't Savannah, huh?" he asked as he draped it across my shoulders.

"No, it isn't. Not like North Carolina either."

I wanted to resist it, but what was the point? I was actually cold. He was being nice. He'd apologized. Something I'd never thought he would do.

"At least here, I can sail," Derek said.

"You're sailing?"

"Yeah. I bought a boat in the harbor to take out on weekends."

I rolled my eyes. "Of course you did."

"I could take you out."

"By this time, you should know that those lines don't work on me."

He stuffed his hands into the pockets of his khakis and said softly, "It wasn't a line."

I lapsed back into silence until we reached my place.

"This is me." I glanced around and found no man with a guitar. "We are in the clear."

"What do you mean?"

"Oh, I was casually seeing this guy, and after I ended it, he brought his guitar and sat outside my window, playing songs he had written about me."

"Wow," Derek said with a snicker.

"Yeah. It was desperate. My roommate and I snuck out the back to avoid him, and *now*, I'm standing here with you. What a night."

"Hopefully, it made the night better," he said with that characteristic smirk.

I rolled my eyes. "There it is. You can't help yourself, can you?"

"Not with you."

"I'm not interested," I told him. "I know better now."

"It won't be like before."

"You say that now."

Derek stepped forward, brushing a stray curl from my cheek. "What do I have to do to prove you wrong?"

I backed out of his touch. "Nothing. I don't want you to do anything."

"Okay."

"I'm serious."

He smiled, and I forced down the sudden urge to kiss him. Because he was still the most gorgeous person I'd ever met in my entire life. And my body remembered exactly how he could use that mouth in a variety of delightful ways. Unfortunately, my heart knew what it felt like when it was broken. I didn't really want that to happen a second time.

"Good night, Derek."

"Night, Minivan."

I glared. "Maybe start by not calling me that."

He laughed and called after me, "Any other requests?"

"No!"

But he stood outside of my door and smiled at me as if it were a challenge. I'd offered him one way in. He would certainly take it. I didn't know what I would do if... when he did.

18

HARVARD

FALL SEMESTER 2012

At seven thirty the next morning, there was a knock on the door. Misty had come in at close to four, and I'd slept like shit. I wasn't expecting visitors, but I was supposed to be at the lab by eight. So, I was awake, however much I wished that I weren't.

"Coming," I grumbled blearily.

I pulled the door open and found Derek in the doorway, wearing a rain jacket and holding coffee and a bag of bagels. He looked far too chipper for the early hour.

"Morning, Mars."

"What are you doing here?" I leaned on the doorframe.

"You said you had to be at the lab at eight. I thought you could use breakfast." He held up the coffee mug. "Coffee?"

I narrowed my eyes. "Okay. But why are *you* here?"

"I also have to be at the Law Library at the ass crack of dawn. I thought I'd walk you. I don't live far from here."

"What is this?"

"What is what?"

"Derek..."

"It's breakfast. How much more innocuous can it get?"

His hazel eyes had shifted to green against the green of his button-up. His hair had grown out some and fell forward into his eyes, curling at the edges. "Walk with me?"

I huffed and grabbed my jacket and an umbrella. "Only because there's coffee."

He grinned. "Fair."

I shrugged into my jacket and took the drink from him protectively. After a good long sip of it, I shuddered at the taste but drank more anyway.

"I didn't know how you liked it."

"Like this," I said. "Hot and full of caffeine."

He chuckled. "Same."

"Ugh, I hate this weather. My birthday week isn't supposed to be this cold *or* rainy."

"This is exceptionally rainy," he agreed as we headed out in the beginning of the storm. "Though, my birthday is always this cold."

"When's your birthday?"

"December 17."

"Brr," I said. "I just want it to still be fall. This *living in the North* thing is not for me."

"You get used to it."

"Never," I said to him like he was a traitor.

He laughed harder at me. "How long is your program anyway?"

"I don't know. Usually five years for the PhD. Some people get out in four, and some people get out in seven. All kind of up to the person." I glanced up at him and saw him looking determinedly forward. "This is your last year?"

"Yep," he said. "3L year."

"And then what?"

The last time I'd talked to Derek, he'd been leaving too.

Just another reason not to ever let myself get attached to him.

"Not sure. There are a few options. The last two summers, I interned with a firm in New York City. My buddy Camden hooked me up, and I worked corporate law for the hotel chain that his family owns."

I blinked at him. "You have a friend who owns a hotel chain in New York City?"

"Yeah. He was at school here. Percy Hotels?"

"Jesus Christ," I gasped. "That's huge, Derek. You'd be set for life. They're swanky."

He shrugged. "Yeah. I mean, it was fun, but I didn't love it."

"So, the other option is going home?"

"Yeah. Obviously, I have a spot in my father's firm," he said stiffly. "But my advisor has dropped hints that he wouldn't mind keeping me on for another year after I pass the Bar."

"Is that normal?"

He shook his head. "Not really. Legal research and such. It's really dry, but we get along, and I enjoy it. I never thought I'd say that, but I do."

"Makes all the difference."

"Yeah. I guess you get the research side, don't you?"

"That I do," I said with a small smile. I was starting to feel more human after devouring the coffee. We reached my lab building and hurried inside out of the rain. Derek shook out his wet hair and I dropped the umbrella.

"So, is there a bagel for me?"

"There is," he agreed, offering me the bag. "I got a variety. Wasn't sure of your preference."

"I like lox on everything," I said, taking out the everything bagel and biting into it.

"Noted."

I glanced up at him. He seemed happy that his plan seemed to be working. I needed to stop this immediately. "That wasn't an invitation for more breakfasts like this."

"Why not? If we both have to be up early…"

"Derek, you know this is never happening again, right?"

He took another sip of his coffee. "Okay."

"I'm serious."

"You look serious."

He smiled down at me, and I forced myself to meet that gaze levelly.

"We can be friends, but that's it."

"Friends," he said softly.

I nodded. "Yep. I am officially friend-zoning you."

He snorted and drank more of his coffee. "We'll see."

"Yeah, we will," I said as if it were a challenge.

I remembered too late that Derek loved a good challenge. And I'd just issued one that he wouldn't back down from. His smile only widened.

I gulped. "Thanks for breakfast."

"What time are you done?"

"I don't know. It's a short day. Maybe two. Need to get home before Sandy hits."

"Cool. See you then." Then, he started to walk away.

"Wait! Derek," I groaned. "That wasn't an invitation."

He walked backward so that he could look at me. "Have fun at work, Mars." He winked, drawing the hood of his jacket back over his hair.

I tried not to smile but failed. He was insufferable. But I didn't mind the groveling… even if it wasn't going to get him anywhere.

* * *

Derek kept it up. I was shocked, but he had shown up right when my shift ended, and he came back bright and early after the hurricane passed through with coffee and bagels. Lox on an everything bagel, to be exact. He got my schedule from Misty—the traitor—and showed up to walk me home when he didn't have class. He snuck me into the Law Library to work on my papers in peace. He charmed Misty, as if it were difficult, but somehow also my friends, Kyle, Matt, and Courtney. The five of us had come into the program together, and Derek had inserted himself into the group as if he were a neuroscience PhD. It was absurd. And somehow wonderful. Damn him.

In these few weeks, I had seen more of Derek than all the moments we'd had together over the length of our long acquaintance.

"So," Derek said, walking me out of the lab on the first day of Thanksgiving break.

"So?" I stretched my arms high and yawned. I'd been burning the midnight oil too often.

"Misty told me y'all are having a Friendsgiving Thursday."

"Yeah?"

"And she invited me."

"Oh," I said softly. I looked down at my feet and back up to him. I'd seen him nearly every day since Halloween. Of course my friends would invite him to our Friendsgiving if he was going to be in town. Still, it felt like a step, and I didn't know why it did. It wasn't like it was one with Kyle or Matt. "That's fine."

He stared at me for a second, speechless. "I thought it would be a lot harder to convince you."

"Why? We're friends, right?"

"Right," he said slowly.

"It's not like you're my date. Misty invited you."

He stuffed his hands into his Arc'teryx winter jacket. "Right."

"Josie and Maddox are coming."

"Josie... as in Josephine Reynolds?"

I nodded. "Yep. She told me she was going to be in Boston for something for the show."

Josie had gotten a major break in college. She'd gone to SCAD and gotten picked up by a director to star in a new show, *Academy*, where she was a lead girl at a supernatural school. It had broken records in its first season. The second season was airing right now.

"I sometimes forget that you're friends with her."

"She was at that Halloween party of yours when we first met."

"No shit?" he said with a laugh. "Go figure. And your brother?"

"Yeah. He was going to bring his girlfriend, but she couldn't get the day after Thanksgiving off. So, it's just us."

"Interesting."

"Anyway, it'll be a good time, and if you don't have plans, then you should come. Just bring a dish with you."

He looked like he wanted to ask something else but then let it drop. I didn't ask what he was thinking. I'd learned quickly that I didn't always want to know what the answer was. Most of the time, it involved moving back out of the friend zone I'd squarely put him in. He might be trying to get out of it, but I wasn't budging.

* * *

When Josie showed up a few days later, she nearly knocked me over with her enthusiasm. "Marley!"

I laughed and squeezed her tight. "Hey, Josie. I missed you."

"I missed you too!" Josie pulled back to look me over. "So, tell me everything. Boys?"

"Nope. No boys. Mostly work."

"Ugh, lame. Come to LA and have fun with me sometime," she said with a hip check. "All work and no play makes Marley a dull girl."

"I think you and Lila have enough boy troubles for the lot of us."

Josie brushed her beautiful, supermodel black waves off her shoulder. "I am not having troubles. I'm in a perfectly great relationship right now."

"With your costar," I murmured under my breath.

"Hey! There's nothing wrong with that. It's why our chemistry is great!"

"If you say so." I arched an eyebrow at her. "And where is the inimitable Martin Harper?"

She waved her hand in a distinctly Josie way. "Busy. We have plans for Christmas." Her eyes twinkled with delight.

I was glad she was happy even if I thought dating her costar was a recipe for disaster. But once Josie got it in her head, that was that.

"Look who arrived," Maddox said, coming out of my bedroom shirtless. His hair was still wet from the shower, and he tugged a T-shirt on.

Josie stood there, frozen for a second. Her eyes roaming my brother. There'd always been *something* between them, but I'd figured it was one-sided. Maddox's obsession with my best friend had never been a secret, but Josie's teasing and disinterest were also infamous. She didn't look uninterested now.

"Hey, Maddox," she said with a soft smile.

Maddox crossed his arms. My brother had clearly started working out. He'd left behind the skinny rocker look, thankfully. "The superstar has graced us with her presence." There was venom in his voice.

Maddox hadn't said anything when I told him Josie was coming, but I hadn't thought anything about it. I glanced between them. Something had *definitely* gone down, and I didn't want to be in the middle of it.

"Anyway!" I said loudly, breaking the tension. "I'm going to check on the turkey. People should be here shortly. Josie, you can dump your stuff in my room. We'll figure out the sleeping situation later."

"Sure," she said and breezed past Maddox without a word.

Misty and I hustled the rest of the afternoon to get food ready. Maddox made Gran's biscuit recipe. They smelled divine even if they weren't exactly right. They were a taste of home, and that was what mattered. Misty thought it was strange that I was fussing about pecan pie and sweet tea. As if she didn't know where I'd grown up.

Matt and Kyle showed up with Courtney, carrying green bean casserole, dressing, and mashed potatoes. The table was set and everything nearly done when our last guest knocked on the door. Misty nudged me with a pointed grin, and I left the kitchen to answer.

Derek stood there in a navy-blue suit coat and khakis, complete with a bow tie. His hazel eyes were almost amber in the light, and he smiled brightly for me with an aluminum foil–covered dish in his hands.

"Hey," I said. I was glad that I'd changed into a dress a

half hour ago, so I didn't look quite like the mess I'd been all day.

"Happy Thanksgiving," he said. "You look great."

I flushed and then tried to swallow it all down. I didn't care what Derek thought I looked like. I pulled the door wide and he walked inside. "Thanks. What did you bring?"

"I called Kathy, and she walked me through her baked mac and cheese."

"Oh God, you're a godsend. I was just complaining that we didn't have any. Misty thought I was crazy."

Derek settled the dish into the open space on the table. "Why?"

"Mac and cheese isn't Thanksgiving fare."

Josie, Maddox, Derek, and I all looked at her like she was out of her mind.

"Come to the South more often," I said with a laugh.

Derek glanced at the table with a smirk. "Man, this looks just like home. The last two Thanksgivings, I suffered through Northern food. No biscuits or pecan pie or sweet tea."

"I know what I'm doing, obviously," I said.

Maddox stepped forward and shook Derek's hand. "Hey, man."

As they did the guys thing, I headed back to the kitchen to check on the turkey, and Josie followed.

"So..." Josie said, leaning against the counter as I carved the turkey up.

"Yeah?"

"That's Derek Ballentine."

"I know who it is."

"What secrets have you been keeping from me?"

"None," I said defensively.

She laughed. "He's *so* into you, Mars. Are y'all sleeping together?"

"No!" I said quickly.

Josie crossed her arms and waited expectantly.

"Well, not anymore."

"I knew it!" she cried.

"It was one night in college, and he ditched me afterward. I'm never going through that again. So, we're just friends."

"You can be friends with someone you had sex with?" She screwed up her face in confusion.

"I'm not you."

"What does Lila think about this?"

I frowned and avoided her gaze. "Uh..."

"Oh shit! This is serious. Lila doesn't know?"

I shook my head guiltily. "I wanted to tell her. I wanted to tell you too. But I was too embarrassed. I was such an idiot for getting sucked in by him."

"So? It's *us*," Josie said. "Think about what Lila went through. She'd totally understand."

"Yeah. I didn't want to think about it. And anyway, it's not happening with him again."

Josie peeked her head out into the living room. "He's making friends with your brother. He's clearly charmed your roommate and friends. He's dressed like a Southern gentleman on Thanksgiving. Why *wouldn't* you?"

I stuffed turkey into her hands. "Because I'm not you or Lila. It's not going to happen. He showed me who he was, and I plan to believe him the first time."

"People can change, Mars," Josie said gently. "I have."

"You're not Derek."

"Okay," Josie said with a shrug. "If you say so."

"Just... don't tell Lila."

Josie shook her head at me. "Fine, but you owe me one."

I hated owing Josie anything. She'd definitely collect eventually. Still, I sighed and nodded. "Fine."

* * *

I stood outside of my lab, trying not to freeze my ass off. It was snowing, and Derek was late. I jogged in place to keep my body temperature up. Which was how Derek found me as he walked up to the lab.

"Sorry. I got hung up," he said.

"My eyelashes have frozen, but it's fine."

He laughed at me and didn't say anything. We walked back to my apartment. The sun had already gone down, and the temperatures were dipping well below freezing tonight. It was our last day on campus before winter break, and I couldn't have been happier to be going back to Savannah.

My stomach twisted with excitement as I opened the door to my place. I'd been keeping a secret for two weeks, and it was finally time.

"Misty isn't home?" Derek asked as he stepped out of the cold. He flicked on the light to the living room.

Everyone jumped out of their hiding spots and yelled, "Surprise!"

A Happy Birthday sign hung over the living room. All of our friends were in attendance—neuroscience and law students all mingled together.

Derek's jaw dropped. He looked at me in shock. "You did this?"

"Yes! Happy birthday!"

Without a second thought, he picked me up and twirled me in a circle. I laughed until he set me down. Our bodies dragged together, slow and heated. His head was dipped down toward me, and I hastily stumbled backward out of his arms as everyone else came forward to wish him a happy birthday. I was glad to be out of his spotlight to get the cake out of the fridge.

We spent the rest of the night drinking cheap beer, eating the cake Misty and I had made, and watching basketball. Slowly, people dwindled out of the party, stumbling home through the snow, until it was just me and Derek in my living room. Misty was seeing Kyle now, and they'd disappeared into her bedroom some time ago. The lights were low. Derek and I sat on the same couch, as we'd been in most of the night. I could have leaned into him so easily, but I stayed rigid.

"This was a nice party," he said.

"I'm glad you liked it. I thought it would be a fun way to send everyone off for the holidays too."

"It was."

I looked down at my fingernails. I'd been chewing on them lately, and they were down to the quick. "You never said what you were doing for the holidays. Lila said that Ash is having a New Year's party on his yacht. I guess they're talking again."

"He mentioned that," Derek said.

"Good idea or bad idea?"

He shrugged. "Ash isn't exactly sane when it comes to Lila, is he?"

"No, and vice versa."

"So… are you coming?"

His eyes found mine again. He searched for something there, like I would give him the answers to the universe. "Do *you* want me to be there?"

"I was just asking if you were coming."

"No," he said slowly. "My parents are taking us to Paris for the holiday."

Paris. Sometimes, I forgot that Derek came from money, and then other times, he went to Paris for Christmas, like it was normal.

"Oh."

"Marley," he said, brushing his hand against mine. I stiffened as he turned my hand over and drew figure eights into my palm. "Do you want me to be there?"

"What? And miss Paris?"

"You could come with us then."

I laughed softly, very aware that he was touching me and I should be stopping him. "I can't come to Paris, Derek. That's absurd."

"Why are you denying this?"

I tried to pull away, but he slid our fingers together. We fit perfectly, as if it was always meant to be. I'd forgotten how easy we were together.

"Because I remember how you threw me away last time," I said softly.

"I'm not that guy."

"I want to believe you," I told him truthfully.

"But you don't."

I shook my head and withdrew my hand. "I don't."

So, I watched him walk away, out of my apartment. I didn't expect to see or hear from him again. He'd been putting in the effort, and I still didn't trust him. He'd go off to Paris and have a great time. I wanted him to. But I wouldn't deny that it hurt to consider...

19

HARVARD

SPRING SEMESTER 2013

Winter break hadn't been as revitalizing as I'd thought it would be. It had been fun to get away with Lila on Ash's yacht, and to hear from Josie that she'd fucking *eloped* with her costar at Christmas. She hadn't even invited us! But my Gramps' health was failing. Gran had finally moved him into a nursing home for dementia. It seemed like all my years of research would be for naught since I couldn't seem to do anything for the one person I wanted to help.

When I got back to Harvard, I tried not to think about it. Misty wasn't showing up until tomorrow. I hadn't heard from Derek. He'd sent a text on New Year's Eve, but that was it. I figured that was all I'd hear from him anyway. I'd turned him down at his birthday. He'd probably been off, having a wonderful holiday with loads of Parisian women.

I hated to admit, even to myself, that it made me sick to think about. I didn't want Derek off with other women. But it made no sense because I didn't want him here with me either. Well, I *wanted* him, but I didn't trust him.

There was nothing to do but obsess about it or get it out

of my head. So, I took a scalding hot shower, spending an inordinately long amount of time with conditioner in my hair, scrunching it to perfection. I had *a lot* of hair and curls that were sometimes a mix of waves. To make it look as good as I wanted took time that I usually didn't have. So, I added gel and a curl cream before spending the next hour diffusing the locks so they gleamed. Perfect curls that hit me mid-back. My curls had never been this long. Of course it would be on a night when I had nowhere to be and nothing to do.

Then, the doorbell rang.

I was still in my underwear since blow-drying was hot business, even in a Cambridge winter. I pulled on sweats and a Duke sweatshirt and then yanked the door open. Derek stood at my door, half-covered in snow.

"Derek," I said with surprise in my voice.

"Hey, Mars."

His smile made my insides melt. I'd missed him. I'd *really* missed him. Fuck.

"Come in."

He dusted most of the snow off of his jacket and then came inside. He hung his jacket on a hook at the door. I laughed softly when I saw that he had a UNC basketball shirt underneath it all. He so rarely went casual, and of course, it would be when we were wearing opposing teams.

"Nice shirt," I joked.

He laughed. "Yeah, you too."

"When did you get back?"

"Just now," he said, running a hand back through his hair. "I came right over."

"Oh," I whispered and then turned toward the kitchen to hide my blush. "Do you want a drink? I have everything for sidecars."

"You sure love that drink."

"Gran had me drinking them at a tender age."

"Show me how you make them," he said and followed me into the kitchen.

"All right. It's not hard or anything. It's just brandy... well, cognac, but use whatever you have. I only have Hennessy. Gran has this bottle of Pierre Ferrand that she sometimes uses, and dear God, it's divine. But if you don't have two hundred dollars to throw around on a bottle, Hennessy it is. Then Cointreau, which is an orange liqueur. Triple sec is fine if you don't have the good stuff." I winked at him. He always had the good stuff. "Squeeze of lemon. I like to sugar the rim." I shook everything together and poured us each a sidecar.

He took a sip and startled. "This is delicious."

"I know, right? It's basically the only drink I can make," I said with a laugh.

We took our sidecars back into the living room. He'd already drained half of his, as if he needed the liquid courage before he turned to me.

"I got you a Christmas present."

"You did?" I froze. "I didn't get you anything."

He waved it away and retrieved a long, thin box from his jacket. "I got this in Paris." He passed it to me, and I held it in my hand uncertainly.

"You got me a present from Paris?"

"Yes."

"Thank you," I said softly. "You didn't have to get me anything."

"No, but I wanted to. I thought about you the whole time. I was in a shop with Amelia. She was getting a purse, and I saw this, and it just... it made me think of you."

Well, with that introduction, my stomach was flopping

around. He'd been thinking about me. He'd seen something that reminded him of me. What the hell was in this box?

I slowly slid the top off of the box. Nestled among a poof of tissue paper was the most delicate silk scarf I'd ever seen in my life. I withdrew the beautiful creation, and it unraveled into a perfect square, which was when I could finally see what it looked like. The border was white and the interior a black, white, and red design that was almost but not quite the galaxy. It wasn't *space* in a way that was gauche, but rather, it had been transformed into something stunning, a true work of art.

"Wow," I breathed. "It's beautiful. This made you think of me?"

He grinned. "To Mars and back."

I laughed because I couldn't help it. All of my years of being Mars, and I'd never been the planet until this stunning piece of silk was between my fingers.

I wrapped it around my neck once and let the ends drape over my collarbone. "I love it."

"Good. I worried that you might not keep it."

"You picked it out for me. And it's probably the prettiest thing I've ever owned."

He smoothed down one side of the scarf, leaning toward me as he did it. My body hummed. I could practically taste his mouth on mine. So much of me wanted that, but the hesitancy kept me from moving forward. I didn't want this to be ruined. Our friendship... our more, I wanted it to stay safe. I didn't want it to end.

So, he removed his fingers from the scarf and returned to his drink, and I didn't stop him. Even as my heart pounded in my chest.

* * *

Even though class had been cancelled for the first time in thirty-four years for the hurricane, class was cancelled again only a few months later for an unpredictable *blizzard*. My lab was closed. Everything was completely shut down. The roads were impassable from all the snow, and more was scheduled to come down for the rest of today and tomorrow. I'd lived through a Massachusetts winter. I'd thought I understood snowfall. But it was nothing compared to what hit early February.

Misty had ditched the city before the worst of it hit, driving home to Connecticut to stay in her parents' house. Derek didn't like that I would be home alone and offered me his guest room. I felt dumb accepting, as it was just some snow, but I also didn't want to be alone.

So, I packed a bag to ride out the storm, wondering all the time if I was making the right choice, and then headed across campus to his place. By the time I got there, snow was coming down in fat drifts, easily pushing me with the bitter, cold wind.

"It's freezing out there," I said, shivering.

"Wait, wait," Derek said. "Don't get undressed."

"Well, I never thought I'd hear *that* out of your mouth."

For a second, he was speechless. Then, that insufferable smirk returned. He took a step toward me, and all the air left the room. "I mean, we can stay in if you have other things on your mind."

I coughed, flustered. "No. That's not what I meant."

He flipped a loose curl from under my beanie. "You sure?" he practically purred.

I wasn't. Not at all. "Uh, positive."

"My mind is successfully in the gutter. We should probably go back out before I let it wander too far."

I swallowed at the heat in his voice. Then blinked. "Wait, back out?"

"Yeah. You have two choices: we could walk down to Cambridge Common or up to Danehy Park."

"In *this* weather?"

His eyes lit up. "Precisely."

He gestured behind me. I turned to see what he was getting at.

"You want to go *sledding*?"

"Perfect weather."

"It's a blizzard."

"Come on, Mars. Live a little with me."

I huffed. It was way too cold out there for this Southern girl. The weather channel had said to expect two *feet* of snow. But it wasn't quite that bad yet. Maybe it'd be fun.

"Fine."

I slid my hands back into my gloves, zipped up my coat, and pulled my hood back up. "You are going to owe me hot chocolate after this."

"Done."

Then, like a kid in a candy store, he hoisted up the sleds and dashed out of the house. Cambridge Common was closer than the park but had smaller hills. I'd never been sledding before in my entire life. So, I was all for the smaller hills, but Derek's law school friends had headed up to the park, and so that was where we went.

By the time I was on top of the hill with nothing but a piece of plastic between me and the ground, I was deeply regretting my decision. "I don't know if I can do this, Derek."

He laughed. "You'll do great!"

I'd watched him go down with intense trepidation, but he'd whooped loudly and run—*literally run*—back up the hill to go again.

"Um, you can take my turn."

"Come on, Mars," he coached. "Conquer your fear. You can do this, and it's so much fun."

"Okay, okay," I said more to myself than him. "I can do this."

"Ready?"

I wasn't. He pushed me down the hill anyway. I screamed as I plummeted toward the bottom, and the group of law students cheered. I couldn't close my eyes even if I wanted to. They were watering as the cold bit into them.

Eventually, I slowed and came to a stop, flopping forward into the snow. Derek's battle cry behind me was the only way that I knew he'd taken the other sled down after me. He collapsed into the snow next to me, a wide, excited smile on his face. I'd never seen him so giddy before.

"You okay?" he asked.

I grinned at him. "Let's do it again."

He laughed and helped me to my feet. "That's my girl."

I opened my mouth to object, but he'd already hoisted both sleds into his arms and was carrying them toward the hill. I had no choice but to follow.

We took the sleds down the slopes until I couldn't feel my extremities anymore and my teeth were chattering. Derek finally relented. We said good-bye to his friends and then trekked back through Cambridge to his apartment.

We both changed into sweats, and he made hot chocolate, as promised. I snuggled under a blanket, trying to regain feeling in my toes. He handed me my drink and turned on the TV to *Jurassic Park*. He got under the blanket next to me, and without a word, he pulled me in close to him. I should have objected, but I didn't. He was *warm*.

"I'm using you for body heat," I told him as I fitted my head against his shoulder.

"Feel free."

We stayed like that until I was warm enough that I could have moved, but I still didn't.

"Hey, Mars," he said, turning the volume down on the television.

"Yeah?"

"How do you feel about New York?"

I tilted my head up to look at him. "I don't have feelings about New York. I've never been."

"Really?" he asked. "Do you want to go?"

"Doesn't everyone?"

"How about spring break?"

"What do you mean?"

"Come with me to New York for spring break." I tried to sit up, but his arm was still around me, and he just smiled as I listed back into him. "I want you to go with me."

"Derek, I don't know," I said, looking down. "Why are you even going?"

"I have an interview."

"Oh," I whispered.

"Why do you sound so sad?"

My gaze met his again. "You're going to leave at the end of the semester."

"Maybe. That makes you sad?"

"It shouldn't, but... yes," I admitted softly.

"New York isn't that far away."

"No."

But my fears were deeply rooted. They were a result of him ditching me all those years ago. He didn't seem like the same guy who had done that to me. He'd put in all the effort to win me over. And dammit, it was working. Only for him to leave again.

"Can we cross that bridge when we get there?" he asked.

"Just come with me to New York. You've never been. I'm staying with a buddy. He won't care if you come with."

"You're sure?"

Derek chuckled. "Yes. He has *plenty* of room."

"Okay," I said quietly.

He didn't push for more. He just held me against him with such tender ease. "Don't think about it, Mars. Just be here with me."

"I don't want it to get complicated," I told him.

"Then don't make it complicated."

20

SAVANNAH

PRESENT

Everything was a fog the next morning after Ash's birthday.

How much had I had to drink? I'd stopped counting when I hit double digits. Plus, the chocolate martini to top it all off. I didn't know the last time I'd had that much to drink in one night, and my body sure wasn't twenty-one anymore. The hangover was significantly worse.

I stumbled through Gran's house, searching for some Tylenol and wishing desperately for a Gatorade or Pedialyte to fix this. It wasn't until the Tylenol had gone down and I was stepping out of a shower that I remembered the rest of the night.

"Oh no," I moaned. "Oh no, no, no, no, no."

I'd kissed Derek.

Fuck, fuck, fuck.

Maddox had been right. I shouldn't have gone out with him. He was single. I was single. There was nothing wrong. Except that *everything* was wrong with kissing him. Because I already knew how this would end, and still, my drunk brain had taken one look at the man I'd always wanted and said *fuck it*.

Fuck you, *Brain*.

He'd turned me down, thank God. As humiliating as that thought was, I was glad that he'd done it. We'd both be pissed this morning if it had gone further than that kiss.

And worse… I probably needed to apologize for how I'd reacted. Today was the fucking worst.

With a sigh, I dialed his number. He might be in church, if he still went. Catholic and all.

But after a few rings, he answered, his voice hesitant, "Marley?"

"Hey, Derek," I said, resisting another sigh.

"How are you feeling this morning?"

"Hungover."

"Yes, I imagine so."

"I… actually wanted to apologize," I said with a wince.

"Nothing to apologize for."

That wasn't true. We both knew it.

"I shouldn't have acted the way that I did."

"I didn't mind the kiss, if that's what you mean." Genuine laughter came back into his voice. He was teasing me.

"I bet you didn't. But… considering we are in, uh, a legal case"—God, I sounded dumb—"we should probably keep things professional. I crossed a line."

"Right. Legal case. Professional. I get it."

I cursed myself. "I could make it up to you with breakfast though."

He was silent for a minute. "I'm about to walk out the door for church."

"Oh yeah." So, I'd been right. "I caught you at the right time then."

"Yeah. I could meet you after?"

I swallowed. It was a bad idea. I didn't know why I'd suggested it. Keep it professional, but come to breakfast with me?! Except that against all the odds and for all the ways he'd hurt me, I wanted to see him. Which should have been the main reason that I shouldn't.

"Sure. Clary's?"

"I'll see you there."

* * *

I was glad for the extra time to get ready. My hangover wasn't completely gone by the time I made it into Clary's Cafe, which had been in its downtown location in Savannah since the 1930s, but at least the headache was gone. I'd put on a simple green sundress and taken the time to diffuse my curls. They were just past shoulder-length right now and took considerably less time to dry than they had when I was in college.

Derek came straight from church, which meant three-piece suit and bow tie. I floundered for a second at the sight of him. Jesus Christ, the man could pull off a suit. I looked like a girl playing dress-up next to him. I should have thought about that.

But he smiled when he saw me. "You look great."

"I... well..." I brushed my hands down the sundress. "Thanks. You do too. I feel underdressed."

He laughed. "We're at Clary's. I'm *over*dressed."

True. But damn.

The hostess seated us a few minutes later. I ordered the biscuits and gravy. They were the closest I'd found to Grans' recipe. Derek got corned beef hash and a coffee. We managed small talk until the food arrived. It wasn't actually something we were any good at. We'd spent too much time together to survive on *the weather's nice*.

"So, what's your plan while you're here?" he asked.

"I don't have one. Besides stopping you from winning your case."

He snorted. "Yeah, besides that."

"I'm serious."

"I know you are."

"I still can't believe you took that case."

He set his fork down and looked at me baldly. "I told my father I couldn't do it because we'd been involved. And he said to me that if I didn't take the case because I'd slept with the person, then I'd never have any cases in Savannah."

I blinked, horrified. "He *said* that?"

"Yes."

"Jesus, Derek."

"He can be a dick when he wants to be."

"Yeah, but he knows me. We met."

Derek shrugged. "I don't think he remembers. Or maybe he doesn't care because he wanted me to take it."

"Seems crazy but okay."

"I'm happy to keep business and personal separate," he said, meeting my gaze. "If you are."

That seemed impossible especially where my mother was concerned.

"We've never been good at that."

He smiled, leaning forward in the space between us. "I'm glad that you're in town. I want to see more of you."

"Derek, you're representing my mom."

"I know."

"You know how I feel about her."

"I do." He sighed. "I didn't know I'd be dealing with you directly in anything, Mars. I thought I'd primarily be working with the executor of the will. Maybe Maddox since he still lives in town."

"And that makes it better?"

"I'm just doing my job," he said defensively.

I sighed and returned to my food. "I know. I know you are. We're not here to discuss that anyway. I wanted to make up for last night. That was stupid of me. I shouldn't have gotten drunk like that and... all the rest. Thank you for taking care of me. For being a gentleman."

"Always, Mars," he said slowly. "But you could make it up to me by going out on the water with me."

I arched an eyebrow. "I thought breakfast was making up for it."

"Come sailing with me, Marley."

And dammit, I said yes.

21

NEW YORK CITY

MARCH 9, 2013

New York City was loud.

It shouldn't have been that different than Boston, but somehow, it *was*. And I never wanted to leave.

It had taken a miracle for me to get my entire spring break off. The lab had only wanted to give me the first weekend, but Derek had insisted we'd be gone the whole time. I never took time off, and so I'd asked for what I wanted, and they'd granted it, albeit begrudgingly. Now, I was here with him, and things were unreal.

Derek's interview had been this morning. I'd been all alone in his friend's house, which was actually an enormous two-story *penthouse* on top of Percy Towers.

I hadn't yet met Camden Percy, but the house was larger than life. I'd never seen this much luxury in my life. Not even Derek's house back home was this fancy. I'd been tempted to look up the Percy net worth and just decided it was probably in the nine- or ten-digit range.

I'd tried not to gape as we took the private elevator up to the top floor. He had a *private* elevator. My mind was boggled. I wasn't sure how many guest bedrooms he had, but I'd taken a separate one from Derek. We were some undefined thing that I was terrified to see come crashing down. As much as he'd said that I shouldn't complicate things, I couldn't stop the fear that this was going to all fall apart again. So, we hadn't taken another step forward. As much as I was sure it was killing him.

It took me longer than normal to get dressed to go out. I'd second-guessed what to bring with me. Misty and I weren't the same size, but she'd rummaged through her sister's closet and brought me back some designer labels. I'd felt ridiculous, accepting them, but apparently, Misty knew the Camden Percys of the world.

When I stepped out of the bedroom with my hair down in waves, my makeup fresh, bright red lipstick painting my lips, and a black designer dress with a square neck that made my boobs look amazing—if I did say so myself—Derek's response was enough to make the effort worth it. His eyes widened to saucers, and he gaped for a few seconds.

"Wow, Marley," he said finally.

I laughed. "Yeah?"

"Yeah. Wow."

At the last second, I'd grabbed the scarf Derek had gotten me for Christmas and brought it with me. It was still cold in the city, and something would be better than nothing.

"Final touches," I said with a grin as I wound it around my neck.

He smirked. "It's perfect."

We headed to the first floor of the penthouse, and I got my first look at the incomparable Camden Percy. He was hot in a controlled possible Mafia boss sort of way. Derek was all Southern charm. No matter how much time he spent at

Harvard, that was who he was. Camden was raw power. It radiated off of him. His eyes and hair as dark as night, he wore a power suit that even *I*—who knew nothing of fashion—could tell had been custom-tailored, holding a crystal glass of scotch. He was intimidating and maybe a little bit terrifying.

I straightened my shoulders and held my hand out. "Nice to finally meet you."

He slipped his hand into mine and shook once. "You too. Ballentine speaks highly of you." His eyes darted to the scarf. "This season, if I'm not mistaken?"

"Uh, yes?" It came out like a question.

He glanced at Derek, offering him his hand. "Your doing, I presume."

Derek laughed. "I have good taste."

"That's why I like you." Camden drained his drink and then nodded to the elevator. "Come on. Party is waiting."

The party ended up being at Club 360, a nightclub on the top of Percy Tower. It was a rooftop bar overlooking the entirety of New York City. A bar was stretched along one side with VIP booths against the opposite wall. The dance floor took up the majority of the space in the middle.

Amelia Ballentine was waiting for us at the entrance. She was radiant in a shimmery black-and-silver number. She was skinnier than I'd ever seen her before in my life. And it was only accentuated by her long ponytail high on the top of her head and the red-bottomed high heels on her feet. She looked imperious and oh-so New York City fashion.

Camden's eyebrows rose at the sight of her. I didn't blame him. Or her when she caught sight of him. Camden made his introduction, and she met him with a Ballentine smirk on her lips.

"Amelia!" I said, crushing her to me as I got past Camden. "I'm so glad we could meet up."

"You're at Club 360. I practically begged Derek to let me come along," she said into my ear.

"How's Parsons?"

"Almost done."

"And then what?"

She shrugged. "I've had a ton of interviews with designers. We'll see where it takes me!"

I loved her optimism. It was definitely born from knowing that no matter what happened, she'd land on her feet.

She fingered the scarf at my neck and winked at Derek. "I have impeccable taste, no? Hermès, darling."

I blinked at her. Even I had heard of Hermès. In fact, we'd passed their shiny window display on Madison Avenue earlier today.

I turned slowly to face Derek. "How much did this scarf cost?"

He laughed softly. "More than a dollar."

"More like five hundred," Amelia said.

My eyes widened in horror. "I've been wearing it into the lab!"

Derek tried to hold back his mirth. "And that's what I like about you."

Camden just eyed our display and gestured for us to follow him inside.

A man in a suit approached him as soon as we entered, and he escorted us to the only remaining empty booth. "Your table, Mr. Percy. If there's anything else I can do for you, let me know."

"Thank you," Camden said, slipping him cash and striding into the booth.

A bartender stepped up immediately and began pouring drinks for the table. Derek ordered me a sidecar before I could get a word in, and then tequila shots were on the table. We downed a round before more people appeared, crashing into the booth. I didn't remember any of their names, just that they were all beautiful.

I stood on my tiptoes and said into Derek's ear, "Do they breed people differently here?"

He snorted. "I felt the same way when I first got here."

I took a sip from my sidecar and watched everything happening all around us. I was on a rooftop bar in Manhattan in a private booth with the *owner*. This was *so* not my life. And yet it was fun to pretend. Camden's best friend, Court, seemed friendlier than most, talking me up for an hour and dragging me out onto the dance floor.

I could feel Derek's eyes on us, and then suddenly, he was there, cutting in as the music continued its jam. Court began dancing with one of the other women who had taken over the booth, nonplussed by Derek's intervention. Camden appeared a few minutes later with Amelia.

For a split second, the entire room seemed to still as another group of people entered. Every one of them more beautiful than the next. But the woman at the center, she could have been a venomous Snow White. Tall with pale legs for literal days. Her dark hair and makeup professionally done. Her lips the deepest, darkest red, nearly matching the blood-colored dress. She had her hand on a man who looked so much like Court that I almost did a double take. They nearly could have been twins.

"Wow," I whispered. "Who is *that*?"

Camden stood at my side when I said it and replied darkly, "*That* is Katherine Van Pelt."

"Is she a model?" I asked.

"Yes," Amelia gushed.

"The resident ice queen of the Upper East Side," Camden spat out.

"I watched her walk at Fashion Week this year. She was stunning," Amelia said. Her eyes were wide with envy and maybe a little hero worship.

"And the guy with her? Court's... brother?"

Camden's frown deepened. "Penn Kensington. He goes to Harvard for his PhD as well," he said, his voice like ice.

"You're friends, I see," I said with a laugh.

"More like enemies."

He turned his back on the supermodel and her friends, dragging Amelia back into the dance. It was hard to tear my eyes away from the lot of them. They moved together like the fucking Cullens. In a way, that probably would have made me feel inadequate if I had cared what people thought about me.

Once the tension in the room burst like a bubble, everyone went back to dancing. The crew held court opposite Camden and his friends, and after another sidecar, I forgot to care. Just let Derek grind against me on the dance floor. I leaned back against his chest, my ass pressed his pelvis. He dragged my arms up over my head, still moving with me. I'd had no idea that he was a good dancer. We'd never danced before. Certainly nothing like this. Where we were both hot and sticky. Our bodies pushed together, a simulation of everything we hadn't been doing over the last couple months. And now, with him tight against me, it was all I could think about.

I'd had no reason to trust Derek when we got together in college. I'd known exactly who he was. But since Halloween, he'd shown me a different version of himself. He'd made the effort. We'd been friends. Was I stupid for wanting more? Or stupid for resisting? I couldn't take it back if I chose wrong.

His lips brushed against my ear. "Mars." I shivered as he flicked his tongue against the lobe. "Your body feels incredible." His words heated me through. He grasped my hips, drawing me harder against him before pushing his hands down the front of my dress and across my legs. "You want this."

And he was right. He could drag one finger between my legs to find out just how bad I wanted it.

His voice was demanding and sensual. "Tell me you don't want this, and I'll stop."

"Derek," I groaned.

"Because I can't lie anymore."

I whirled in his arms, looking up into those hazel eyes filled with lust. His arms came back around me, settling on my ass. My own hands looped into the curl of his hair at the base of his neck.

Some part of me said to let go, to not worry about repercussions, but I'd been so careful. So fucking careful the last couple months to not give my heart over to this man. He had the power to break me, and I didn't want to be the dumb girl who got hurt again. Fool me once, shame on you; fool me twice, shame on me.

"Why?" I asked, my voice cracking.

His brow furrowed. "Why what?"

"Why did you leave the first time?" I asked the question that had been haunting me all these years. "Why?"

"I already told you."

"No, you didn't. You said you were an idiot. You said that it was a mistake and you missed me. Those are excuses, not a reason. We'd had a great time, and then you were gone. You practically called me stupid for thinking it was more."

He sighed and nodded. "You're right. I did those things but not why you think. It's going to sound stupid."

"How so?"

"Because I liked you."

I blinked at him. "That's not—"

He held up a hand. "I liked you, Marley. Not just liked you. I was falling head over heels. I'd never felt that way about anyone before in my entire life. I dated. I'd been with other people. Girls never mattered to me. Then, here you were, crashing into my life over a feud, and I couldn't get you out of my mind."

"But..." I began helplessly.

"So, I ran scared." I met those hazel eyes and saw the sincerity there. "I didn't want to be tied down. I thought that if I acted like an asshole, then you'd let me go. It wasn't until I saw you again at Halloween that I realized how incredibly fucked I was." His hand came to cup my jaw. "No one else is you, Mars. No one else will ever be you."

My world tipped at those words. I'd thought that he treated me just like every other girl. And here he was saying the opposite. My brain and body couldn't seem to process the information.

"How do I know you won't run scared again?"

"I'm still here, aren't I? I made a mistake, but I'm not scared of this with you anymore, Marley." He pressed one soft kiss to my lips. "I'm not going anywhere."

Something sparked in my chest at those words. Something I'd been holding back all this time. Too afraid of the pain he'd caused me to see it too clearly. I'd wanted his body and enjoyed his friendship and felt something budding. But I was way past that now. I was in deep with him. And I didn't want to come back from the precipice. I wanted to jump again. Only the unknown had been holding me back. The unknown was gone.

I raised onto my tiptoes and crushed our mouths together. He kissed me like he'd been waiting his entire life to do so. It was rough and passionate and full of pent-up need.

Derek took my hand without another word and pulled me toward the exit. He texted Amelia to let her know that we were leaving. She sent back a wink emoji. Derek laughed as we took the elevator down to the penthouse. We had two rooms, but Derek drew me into his, kicking the door closed behind him and thudding my back against it.

I gasped, and his mouth covered mine. Months. It had been months of want and need. Months of waiting. Months where I was certain this would never, ever happen again. Not ever.

But he'd stuck by me. He'd waited. He'd been patient. He'd proven himself.

And now, we couldn't scramble out of our clothes fast enough. There would be time to take things slow and reacquaint ourselves with the other's body, but that wasn't happening tonight.

My hands went to his waistband, unbuttoning his pants and shoving them off of his hips. He hoisted up my dress, and reached for my underwear. I gasped as the material ripped in his hands.

"Derek!"

He grinned devilishly. "I'm impatient."

But I couldn't even be mad. Not when he gripped me by the backs of the thighs and slammed me into the door a second time. We were both impatient. A yawning need taking over all of our movements. I grasped for his cock in the dark, drawing him to me. He touched the tip against my opening.

"I should..." he fumbled.

"I'm on birth control."

"You're sure?"

"Derek, please," I whispered.

He didn't need to be told twice. He plunged forward, taking me hard and fast up against the door of his bedroom. His cock hit deep inside of me as he braced me up with his strong arms.

"More," I gasped.

"Fuck," was his only response.

He carried me across the room, laying me out flat in the bed. I stretched my arms out toward him, and he obliged by sliding back inside of me. We both groaned as we fit together.

"God, your pussy is so fucking wet." He pulled out and slammed back into me. "So wet and tight for me."

I pulled him down to me. Our lips meeting roughly. "More," I begged.

"Needy little thing," he teased. "Tell me what you want."

"You, Derek. I want all of you."

"I'm all yours. All yours."

He grasped my hand in his, forcing it up over my head and then did the same with the other. Then, he drove into me with abandon. I saw stars as everything burst around me into oblivion. I came uncontrollably. A cry escaping my lips as my pussy clenched in tight pulses around his cock. He drove home one more time, hitting so deep that another gasp escaped my lips.

He finished in long shuddering movements. Then, he finally released my hands and kissed my swollen lips. "I missed you, Mars."

"You've ruined me," I said with a half-smile on my lips.

"Good," he said, all cocky.

"And I thought my first kiss was the life-ruiner. The sex is..."

"Your first kiss?" He kissed along my jaw. "What do you mean?"

I flushed under his attention. I'd never planned to tell him this.

"Oh, now, I have to know. Tell me." He kissed across my collarbone and to my neck. I squirmed under him, but he didn't give an inch. "Come on. You can't dangle something like that out there."

I sighed. "You were my first kiss."

He pulled back to stare at me. Clearly, that was not the answer he'd expected. "On Halloween?"

I nodded.

"I didn't know that."

"I didn't exactly advertise it."

"No wonder you were so mad at me."

I laughed. "You make it so easy."

He pressed another firm kiss to my lips. "Can't say I'm upset I was your first. I want all the rest of your firsts."

"I might allow that."

My eyes slid shut as he held me tight in his arms. It was the most relaxed I'd been in years. Everything had been so pent-up and tense. Now, here in his arms, with nothing to do but enjoy myself, I found myself slipping toward sleep.

"Derek," I whispered in the silence.

"Hmm?"

"Don't leave in the morning."

He sighed softly. "I'm never leaving you again."

22

NEW YORK CITY

MARCH 10, 2013

My internal clock woke me earlier than necessary. But all that eight a.m. lab work had gotten my body used to waking up at dawn. I stretched my arm overhead as I slowly came back to myself. An arm banded across my middle. Slow, heavy breathing filled the quiet room. My eyes adjusted to the dimness, and I made out the sleeping form of Derek Ballentine.

Not only had he not left in the morning, but he was still sleeping. I'd never seen him look quite so peaceful before. His hair had fallen forward in his face. It was messy from a night full of sex. His lips were slightly parted. I scooted in closer, pushing my body against his and lying on his pillow. His grasp around me tightened.

I gently dragged a finger across his bottom lip, up his jaw, around the shell of his ear.

Derek was here. He was... mine.

I bit my lip. After all this time, after being *so* careful, I'd fallen for him all over again. Maybe I'd never really gotten over him. But having him here again felt impossible. Yet it was real.

His eyes fluttered open. He pressed a kiss to my forehead. "Morning. What time is it?"

"Early."

"Mmm," he groaned, tugging me even harder against him. He rested his chin on the top of my head. "Sleep, my little planet."

I snickered. "Your little planet?"

"Mars." He cracked open one eye and smirked at me. "It's better than how you react to Minivan."

I huffed. "I'm coming around to Minivan when *you* say it."

He rolled over so that I was crushed underneath him. "Oh yeah?"

"Does it make you that happy?"

"You make me happy."

I ducked my chin at the words, a flush coating my cheeks. "Stop."

He laughed and pressed a kiss to my lips. "I love when you blush."

"It happens far too frequently."

"But somehow not when I'm talking about how wet your pussy is."

I blushed even harder and tried to hide my face. "Derek!"

"Or is that only when I'm inside of you?"

"Shh!" I crushed my lips against his again to get him to shut up. But he just laughed against me.

"Oh, I like this side of you," he said with that cocky smirk.

"You know, I've always thought you were gorgeous," I admitted. "Then, you open that mouth of yours."

"And it makes it better?" he teased.

He rolled us back over so that, suddenly, I was straddling

him. Our hips perfectly aligned. His hands on my hips, grinding me downward.

"Always worse," I gasped out at the feel of him. "You are *trouble*."

"Well yes." His hands moved up my bare sides, under my breasts, and then back down my stomach. "You don't seem to mind my brand of trouble at all."

"I mind."

He arched an eyebrow at me. "Back to the point. You think I'm gorgeous?"

I huffed and leaned forward, patting his head twice. "Your poor ego. I should have thought about how to keep it from getting any more inflated."

"I noticed you first," he admitted. His hands stilled on my body. He stared up at me as if I were a vision.

"Yes, yes, I was a cheerleader, and you invited us to your party."

"No," he said immediately. "We'd never invited the public school cheerleaders to our parties. The guys thought I was *crazy* for saying we should go over to see y'all."

"So?"

"So, I saw you and wanted you there. I wanted you. You had this spark."

"I was a challenge," I said with an eye roll.

"No, before you were a challenge, you were a beautiful mystery that I wanted to solve." He brought my face down to his and kissed me. "*Then*, you were a challenge."

I laughed against his mouth. "You're the worst. You know that, right?"

"Ah, but it makes you keep coming back."

"Psh! You keep *finding* me."

"Same thing."

I rolled my eyes at him. "So, what's the plan today?"

"Whatever you want to do. Interview is over." He winked at me. "We could stay inside all day."

"As tempting as that is..." I said. And it *was* tempting. Derek, shirtless and staring up at me with desire, would always be tempting. "I want to see more of the city."

He thrust upward again, and I closed my eyes as I heated straight through.

"Maybe we could just skip breakfast?"

I laughed. "You make a very convincing case."

It was at this point that my phone began to ring loudly.

Derek groaned and tried to keep me in place. "Don't answer it."

"Only a few people can bypass my silent setting," I told him, sliding off of his lap. "Probably Lila."

"Ah, Delilah Greer, always ruining my fun."

I laughed at him. "You're silly."

I picked up the phone and frowned. It was Gran.

"What?" he asked, sitting up on his elbow.

I answered the phone immediately, "Hey, Gran."

"Marley, chickadee," Gran said with a sniffle. She sounded like she'd been crying.

"Are you okay? What's wrong?"

Derek arched an eyebrow and leaned forward, as if he could somehow help whatever was coming next. He mouthed, *What's going on?*

I shook my head at him. I didn't know yet.

"Oh, honey, I'm so sorry to call you so early."

"It's fine. You can call whenever. You know that."

"It's Gramps," she whispered. Something wheezed in her chest, and then the tears came again. "He... he passed in his sleep. He's with the angels now."

I sank back into the bed. All the wind rushed out of my sails. My heart stopped beating. Everything went deathly quiet. I didn't have words to respond to my Gran. I had no idea what to say to that.

My Gramps was dead. The man who had taught me to drive. Who had loved to garden and fix cars and do the *New York Times* crossword every weekend. The man who had been at every one of my dance recitals. Who had cheered for me at every competition. Who had known that I was going to go bigger and better long before I did. He was just... gone.

The only father I'd ever known. The only man in my life. A constant rock. I'd known at Christmas that he wasn't doing well. I'd gone to see him at the home with Gran. He recognized me despite the dementia running through his mind and muddling everything up. He was shockingly lucid. Even the doctors had thought so. How could he go from that to this in a few short months?

"Marley?" Gran must have repeated. "Are you still there?"

"Yes," I gasped out. My voice cracked on the word, and tears welled in my eyes.

"I'm so sorry to tell you this. I know that you're in New York with that boy of yours." She didn't even sound disapproving. Though she had been cautious when I told her about it on the phone. "I don't know how we'll get you down here for the funeral. I have some money saved, but most of it is tied up."

"I'll figure it out. When is the funeral?"

Derek jumped at that word. His eyes going soft around the edges. His hand settled over mine. I squeezed his once and swallowed back the tears.

"We can wait until you're here if we can scrape together enough to get you home again so soon."

Christmas had cost a small fortune. I couldn't expect her

to do this. I'd have to use up the rest of my savings for the flight.

"I can do it, Gran."

She gave me some more reassurances over the phone, and then we ended the call. The minute Derek's arms came around me, I burst into tears. I sobbed until I had no more tears and was practically hyperventilating. Still, he kept me tight to him, running his fingers through my hair and being the constant presence that I needed.

"How much did you hear?"

"Enough," he told me gently.

"I... I have to get back to Savannah. I'm sorry."

"Hey, don't apologize to me. This is way more important."

I broke away from him and swiped at the tears on my cheeks. "I need to look up flights and..."

"Hey," he said, catching a stray tear as his thumb brushed across my cheek. "Let me handle it. You don't need to do anything. Just get back into bed for a bit or take a shower."

"Derek... I can't... I can't let you do that."

He kissed my forehead again. "Let me take care of you, Mars. This is something that I can do."

I wanted to object. Derek had more money than God, but that didn't mean I was okay with him using any of it on me. But there was something so sincere in his eyes. Something so commanding in that touch. Something I'd never seen in him as he tucked me back into the bed and went for his laptop.

A half hour later, I had a flight back to Savannah the next morning. He didn't tell me how much it cost, only that he'd booked one for himself too.

"You're coming with me?"

He grinned as he sat on the bed next to me. "You think I'm letting you go down there to deal with it all alone?"

"I don't know."

"I will be there as much or as little as you want, Minivan," he said endearingly. "But either way, I'll be there."

I nestled against him as the tears fell again. It was exactly what I needed. I'd never known I could get it from Derek, and I fell for him all the more in that moment.

23

SAVANNAH

PRESENT

Sailing couldn't happen right away. Something had come up with Derek's cousins in Charleston, and he'd driven up there to help Daron, Marina, and Tye out. I didn't ask specifics, but it hadn't sounded good. Something about someone trying to purchase their company. His cousins owned Hartage Boating, and it was their entire life. Anything that threatened the company would be cause for great emotional turmoil.

He'd gotten back in last night and already messaged me to see if I was free this weekend. Enough time had passed that I was definitely second-guessing whether or not I should go out with him. What good would come out of this?

I needed a professional opinion before I decided.

"You're doing *what* with Derek?" Josie gasped.

I laughed as I walked through Forsyth Park. It was empty for the middle of the day on a weekday.

"He asked me to go sailing with him."

"And you said?"

"Well, I said yes, but we had to push it back, and now, I'm not sure."

Josie's huff was evident. "You girls and these Holy Cross boys."

"It's been a long time since he was a Holy Cross boy, Josie."

"Yeah, yeah. I just love you and don't want to see you get hurt again."

"Me neither." I kicked a small rock off into the grass.

"But do you like him?"

"Of course I like him."

"He hurt you."

I headed off down a path that led back to Gran's house. I'd never get used to calling it mine. "I remember."

"So, do you want to go through that again?"

"No. I don't want to be stupid about this, but I've dated around. It's not like I've been alone. I just haven't found the right guy."

"And that makes Derek the right guy?"

"Probably not," I said with a laugh. "What do you think?"

Josie sighed dramatically. "Go sailing."

"Really?" I gasped. "I for sure thought you would tell me to skip it."

"I'm not saying you should marry the guy. But some good sex might help."

I cackled, drawing attention from a passing jogger. I waved apologetically. "We did always have good sex."

"Be careful with your heart. Second chances aren't always what they're cracked up to be."

Didn't I know it?

"Love you, Josie. When are you coming into town?"

"Hopefully for your birthday! Pencil me in for around Halloween."

"Sounds good. And, Josie? Thanks."

"Always here for you, Mars."

We said our good-byes by the time I made it back to the house. I had my phone out, preparing a text to Derek when I froze in place. The front door was wide open. I'd closed it. And locked it. I knew that I had.

Fear gripped me. What the hell did I do? Did I call the police to report a break-in? Go inside?

I stopped at the front of the property and shot off texts to both Maddox and Derek, letting them know what was going on. Derek responded instantly.

Don't go inside. Wait for me. I'm on my way.

My heart fluttered at the response. I was scared of what I might find inside, but it made me feel better that he'd drop anything to take care of me. As he always had before.

I hovered over the phone number for the police. I didn't know if it was an emergency. I didn't want to call them here for no reason.

I was about to make the call anyway when I heard voices from inside. Not in anger or yelling or anything out of the ordinary. Just calm voices. And worse, I recognized one.

My blood froze over as I stomped across the yard and up the steps. "Mom?" I shouted.

She appeared then out of Gran's kitchen, holding up an old teapot. I recognized it as an heirloom that had been passed down for generations. One that I loved very dearly.

"Oh, Marley, I didn't know you'd be in today," she said as if it were completely normal for her to be in the house. She'd even dressed herself up. She wore a knee-length black skirt and shiny pink shirt. She looked half-presentable, if I didn't know she was completely rotten on the inside.

"What are you doing here?" I snarled.

"What do you mean?"

"This isn't your property. I don't even know how you have a key. You shouldn't be here."

A second woman stepped out of the kitchen. She was also dressed sharply in a black suit with a blue blouse. She smiled sweetly at me. "You must be the daughter."

"Who are you?"

She stepped forward and offered her hand. "I'm Regina McGregor. Your mom has hired me to help appraise the house and the belongings within. Let me tell you that I am so sad for your grandmother's passing, but don't worry. You're in safe hands."

I saw red. My eyes snapped to my mom. "You did *what*?"

"Don't overreact, Marley Sue," she said, saccharine sweet.

"Get the fuck out of my house."

Regina startled. "But we've only just begun."

"What lie did she spin for you? This isn't her house. It doesn't belong to her. Gran left it for me and my brother. She didn't get a dime. Not a single *cent* from the woman she never treated like a mother. So, no, you can't be in here, appraising *my* belongings."

Regina gaped. "I... I wasn't aware. Hannah said that she had been given the property and there was some legal dispute."

My mother's face soured at my outburst. "Marley, you are going to have to come to terms with reality."

"Reality? You're the one suing *me*, your own daughter. You're not going to get the house or anything in it. Not a single thing as far as I'm concerned."

Regina held her hands up, clearly floundering between the two of us. "I'll just wait outside. We can start things again at a later date, Hannah. There's plenty of time."

Then, she crossed Gran's house and went to step outside, but in her way was all six foot five of Derek Ballentine.

"What are you doing here?" he asked, low and venomous. His eyes found mine in the room, unhurt and in one piece. He released a breath. Then, he saw my mother standing a foot behind me. "Ms. Christianson?"

"Derek," she said coolly. "What are you doing here?"

Her eyes snapped between us, as if trying to decipher something she couldn't quite put her finger on. I minutely shook my head once. He shouldn't give my mother the ammunition she needed.

"I was in the area. I saw the door open as I drove by."

"I see," she said. "We were having the property appraised."

I stiffened all over at those words, and he must have sensed it because his voice hardened when he replied, "As your attorney, I would encourage you to step away from the matter. We can speak about evidence for the trial, but you shouldn't be... entering a property that doesn't currently belong to you."

"Fine." My mom huffed and dropped the teapot into my hand. It bobbled as I grabbed for it, nearly losing the priceless thing. I clutched it to my chest as she passed by without a word.

Derek waited for my mom and Regina to vacate the premises before turning back to me. He was still formal, considering they were so close. "We'll close this behind us. Sorry for all of this, Miss Nelson."

"Thank you," I breathed. My eyes were wide to show how much I appreciated it.

He nodded his head. "Just glad that I... happened to be in the area." He winked at me.

I held back my snicker. "Saturday?"

A smile broke through his polished veneer. "You've got it."

Then, he pulled the door closed behind him and was gone. I crumpled onto the floor, holding Gran's teapot close to my chest. A sob escaped my lips, and tears fell all over again. I hated my mother so much. So, so much. What a horrid woman. I needed to get the locks changed, but I didn't even know if I could do that while we waited for all of this to be fixed. I'd have to call my attorney and ask.

A few minutes later, Maddox burst into the house. "Marley?" I was still on the floor. He skidded forward, dropping to the floor next to me. "What happened?"

"Our *mother* happened," I growled.

I divulged all that she had done in a long-winded panic.

His own fury clouded his vision, and he said the only thing that needed to be said, "We're going to fucking *win*."

24

SAVANNAH

MARCH 11, 2013

We landed in the Savannah humidity the next afternoon. The air hit me in the face, and I nearly cried again, thinking about all the days out in this weather with Gramps. The news kept hitting me fresh. It was still too real. And at the same time, completely unfathomable.

"Who's picking us up?" I asked, brushing aside the tears again. I'd put the entire trip into his hands. I hadn't even considered who could get us at the airport.

"Dad offered to send a driver."

"In *Savannah*?"

"Well, yeah."

"I could have called Maddox."

"While you're all grieving? No."

He seemed so adamant that I just went with it.

Derek recognized a man in the crowd. They shook hands, and then we were escorted into the back of a black Mercedes. It'd have made me feel vaguely important if I didn't feel utterly ridiculous.

"Here you are, sir," the driver said when he pulled up in front of Gran's house.

"Wait here for me while I get Marley inside."

"Of course, sir."

Derek popped open the door and held his hand out for me.

I took it gratefully but said, "You don't have to do any of this."

"I know." He threaded our fingers together. "But I want to."

"I'll find a way to pay you back."

"Don't even think about it."

I headed up the stairs to the front of Gran's house. Just being home made me so much more solid. Like this was where I was supposed to be. My bones belonged here. Savannah was smaller than Durham and Cambridge by a long shot. It wasn't big or glamorous, but it was home.

I knocked once on the front door and then let myself inside. "Gran?"

"Marley, you made it." Gran scooped me up in her arms. She smelled like earth and fresh bread and a hint of the lavender perfume she'd been wearing for years. "I'm so glad that you could get here so quickly."

"Don't thank me. Thank Derek."

He was still standing in the doorway. Half in, half out, as if he were intruding.

"Well, come in, young man. I've heard an awful lot about you."

"I don't know whether that's good or bad," he said with a short laugh.

Gran just pulled him into an unexpected hug. "Whatever happened before hardly matters now. You brought my Marley home." She patted him on the back twice. "Now, close the door and come inside. You're more than welcome to share a meal with us. We're having fried chicken and okra. The sweet tea is better than whatever you've been drinking. Maddox should be here any minute. He's so busy with that damn job."

Derek glanced back outside at the car, waved the driver off, and then carefully stepped inside. "What's Maddox doing these days?"

Gran headed for the kitchen. "Something with computers."

"Graphic design and animation," I filled in for him.

"Ah, that's what he said at Thanksgiving."

"Right," I said, forgetting momentarily that he'd hung out with Maddox when he visited me last semester. "He started his own company, Mad Son Productions."

"Ah, clever. Maddox Nelson. Mad Son."

"Yeah. It's so him," I said with a shrug. "He got him an in with Pixar."

"That must be exciting."

I nodded. "Yeah, he's actually doing phenomenal. Not that he talks about it much."

Another knock sounded on the door, and then Maddox burst into the house. "Made it." A small shih tzu mix yapped at his heels. "Easy, Walt. Jesus, I'm going to let you go."

Maddox removed the leash from Walt's collar, and the dog zoomed around the living room like he belonged there. I laughed at his zoomies, but it was Derek who bent down to pet the tiny, ferocious predator. Walt took a liking to him immediately, jumping up into his lap and trying to lick Derek's face off.

"Walt, come on," Maddox said in exasperation.

Maddox's girlfriend, Teena, shook her head as she stepped inside. "That dog is trouble."

"Yeah," Maddox said with a sigh. "Sunny loves him at least."

Sunny was Lila's dachshund. Lila had been living with Maddox since she started PT school in August, and it was a miracle that their two little dogs got along.

"No, Lila?" I asked Maddox.

Maddox shook his head. "She had something at school. She said that she'll definitely be there for the funeral and to tell you she was sorry."

"It's okay," I said, waving it away. "It's all so unexpected."

Maddox glanced over at Derek, who had picked up Walt and was cradling the dog in his arms like a baby. Walt looked up at him with hero worship. It was adorable. "Didn't know you were bringing anyone with you."

"Sort of last minute," I choked out.

"Yeah," Maddox said, scratching the back of his head. He held his hand out to Derek, who set Walt down to shake. "Good to see you again, man."

"Same. Though not the best circumstances."

Teena was introduced to Derek, and then everyone was ushered into the dining room. For a few blissful moments, everything felt normal. Gran's cooking was as spectacular as always. Derek and I both had second helpings. We couldn't find good Southern cooking in Boston. Maddox and Gran playfully argued about his career. Teena talked about the baking projects she'd been working on and how she wanted to get Gran's buttermilk pie recipe. It was almost like at any second, Gramps would walk in from the backyard. He'd wash his dirt-covered hands in the mudroom before stepping into Gran's clean kitchen. She'd joke about how he always brought the entire garden inside with him. After dinner, they'd dance to the tinny tunes playing through the radio they'd had since the '60s.

But there was no Gramps. No gardening or jokes or dancing. I soaked up the time with my family, but we were missing a person, and each of us felt it distinctly with his empty chair at the head of the table.

Then, just after we cleared the plates and Gran was serving up dessert—her favorite Coca-Cola cake—a knock came from the door.

"I'll get it," Gran said. "Probably another friend bringing us food."

I grimaced. People meant well. I was sure it was thoughtful, but having the reminder of Gramps' death over and over again didn't help anything but to dig the knife in deeper.

Then, I heard the voices from the other room. My eyes snapped to Maddox's. For a second, we were little kids again, able to read each other's minds like only twins were capable of doing. Without a word, we both shoved our chairs back and headed for the kitchen door.

"What's going on?" Teena asked.

"Stay here," Maddox said roughly.

I didn't look at Derek, but I could sense his confusion. This was the last thing I'd wanted him to see when he took me home. There was one thing that I hid from nearly everyone in my life—my mother.

"Hannah, now isn't the time," Gran said with a sigh.

"This shouldn't take too long," my mom said, pushing past Gran and into the house.

She caught sight of me and Maddox stepping out of the kitchen and frowned. She was as stunning as ever, maybe more so. She'd had some work done since the last time I'd seen her. I only knew that it had happened because I'd memorized the face of the woman who had abandoned us. Her breasts were larger. Her smile plumper. Her forehead didn't move. For someone whose entire existence depended on that unmistakable beauty, she had taken very good care of it. I used to think she looked like a supermodel, but I'd seen some of those too recently to think it this time. She looked like a pale imitation of that effortless beauty. A Southern caricature with big, dark hair and too-tight clothes.

"Kids," she said with a sly smile.

Neither of us spoke. I felt Maddox touch my spine, the way he had when we were kids and Mom showed up unexpectantly. A constant reassurance.

"Hannah," Gran repeated more sternly.

"Oh, stuff it," Mom said with an eye roll. "You called me, remember?"

"Yes," she said, losing her edge. "I called you to let you know your father had passed away. I believed that you'd want that information."

She laughed, hoarse and dismissive. "That man isn't my father."

Gran colored. "Hannah Marie!"

"I was the disappointment, *Mom*," she said with bitterness. "Remember? Knocked up too early. He told me to get rid of them."

I winced. That didn't sound like Gramps at all.

"He was mad, and he was wrong. He admitted it. We've had this conversation before. Bringing it up now in front of the kids is just cruel."

"Of course *I'm* the cruel one when he was the one who wanted me to abort them."

My fury pounded through me. "He's the one who raised us. Not you."

Maddox tensed next to me.

"Marley Sue," Gran said with a shake of her head.

"That's enough, everyone. It's been a long, trying day. If you want something, Hannah, just spit it out."

The kitchen door creaked behind us. I winced slightly, knowing that Derek and Teena must have seen and heard everything that had happened. Mom glanced in that direction, and her eyes widened. Derek came to stand on my other side. His presence warm and comforting next to me. Between him and Maddox, I felt… safe.

"I think you should go," he said slowly.

I put my arm out to stop him. "It's fine."

Mom met my gaze, and she smirked. I could read everything she was saying in that look. Derek looked like a tasty treat to her. And probably something about how *her* looks had won me a boy this attractive. Because how else could I get him for myself? Same old, same old. Unfortunately, it didn't make me feel any less disgusting.

She swung back to Gran. "I want the money. A thousand."

Gran pursed her lips, but she fished out her checkbook despite our protests. She wrote out the check and threw it at her daughter. "Get some help with the money."

My mom rolled her eyes and then slammed back through the door. She was gone as fast as she had come.

"On that note," Gran said with a sigh as she wiped a tear from her eye, "who wants cake?"

25

SAVANNAH

MARCH 15, 2013

It rained the day before Gramps' funeral. The ground was sodden and squelched under our feet. Lila's heels kept sinking down in the earth. She shifted from foot to foot as she held my hand. I was glad that I'd gone for flats. As if I could think about fashion at all. Not today.

The ceremony was short in the church. His body was carried to a plot in a local cemetery. Gran had the spot next to his already picked out for hopefully *much* farther in the future. He was put into the ground. Flowers placed on top of the casket. Dirt shoveled inside. I didn't hear the words spoken. I just stared numbly, and felt like I'd been scooped from the inside out.

Lila kept an arm around me as we walked away from the whole thing. Gran was still speaking to those who had come. Maddox and Teena disappeared as soon as they could get out of there. I was glad that I had Lila here. I could have invited Derek, but it felt too soon. I didn't even know what we were yet. We hadn't defined anything, and he hadn't known Gramps at all.

He'd gone home to his parent's house Monday night after Mom fucked everything up and told me to text or call if I needed anything. I hadn't yet. He seemed to understand I needed the time to grieve and was radio silent as well.

"I missed you, Mars," Lila said.

We stepped up onto the sidewalk and out of the grass, heading toward Lila's awaiting car.

"I missed you too. You could come visit, you know? Maddox and Josie did."

Lila nudged me. "Maddox and Josie aren't in school. They're off being important."

"True."

Lila cast a secretive look in my direction, "Gran mentioned a boy."

"Oh God." I ducked my chin in embarrassment.

"Spill!"

"What did she say?"

"Just that he flew you out here, so you could make the funeral. That's so sweet."

It was sweet. And I wanted to tell her. I just... couldn't. Everything felt too up in the air. I didn't know what Derek and I were, where it was going, or whether I was ready for it.

"It's too new," I said with a peek at her. "I'm not ready to talk about it."

"Oh, come on. I told you about me and Ash."

"And it was an overshare," I said with a laugh.

She squeezed my shoulder. "At least you're laughing."

"Yeah. What's your plan for the rest of the day?"

She winced. "I have to get back to school. I'm free this weekend. Are you still going to be here?"

"I'm leaving tomorrow. I need to get back to school too."

"Damn. I hate being this far away from my bestie."

"Same."

"Where should I drop you off?" she asked when we got to her car.

"Nah, don't worry about it. I'll wait for Gran."

"You sure?"

I nodded at her and then gave my best friend a long hug. She pressed a kiss to my temple, squeezed me tighter, and then headed out. I watched her go with a sigh. I should have told her about Derek. I should have told her all the many times shit had happened with us. But there was just *so* much history that it felt weird to tell her now.

Gran looked like she would be occupied for a while. She caught me waiting for her and strode over. "You can take the car. Someone else will take me home."

"No, I can wait."

"Marley, I love you, but go home. I'll be okay."

She hugged me, passing me the keys.

I handed them back. "I'll call Derek."

She grinned. "Good."

When I dialed his number, he answered immediately and told me he'd be there in ten minutes. It was more like fifteen, but a shiny black Escalade pulled into the cemetery. He jumped out, jogged around the car, and held open the passenger door for me.

"Thanks," I said softly.

He got back into the driver's side and pulled away. "Where to?"

"I don't know," I admitted. "I don't want to go home. I don't want to walk around. I don't want to do anything."

His hand slipped over mine, and he held it easily, as if he'd always been allowed to do that. "I have an idea. You trust me?"

I arched an eyebrow. "No."

He shot me a look that melted me. "Trust me."

"Okay."

* * *

Twenty minutes later, we pulled up into the marina that I'd once driven out to so I could ruin Derek's date.

"I'm not exactly dressed for it."

He shrugged. "It'll be fine. I'm sure I have a jacket and blankets if you get cold on the water."

I responded by hopping out of the car. He immediately took my hand again and led me out onto the dock. A lock had been added since we'd last been here, and he punched in a code that let us into the marina. His same sailboat sat where it had been all those years before. It had been spruced up in the intervening years, and he jumped onto it like he'd been born on the water.

He offered me his hand, and I stepped precariously onto the thing. It rocked under my feet. I stumbled forward, catching the wheel to keep from falling.

I winced. "Sorry."

He chuckled, already moving about the boat with ease. "You've never been out. I've seen worse on a first run."

"Great," I grumbled. I watched him work for a few minutes. "Is there anything I can do?"

"Do you know *anything* about sailing?"

"Uh, that's starboard," I said, pointing off to the right.

"Correct." His smile was megawatt when he glanced back at me. "I can show you some things to do, but maybe you should just sit."

"Sitting isn't so great right now."

He nodded, a flash of sympathy in his expression. "Okay. Untie that line but hold it steady."

The next half hour was spent not thinking about anything at all. Not a thing, except how to make this sailboat functional. It took a lot to make it do its thing. Derek claimed it was all really easy and would become instinctual with a little practice, but I doubted it. He'd been doing it since he was a kid, so of course, he thought that. I thought aerials and a la second turns were also instinctual, but I wasn't about to ask him to do any.

"All right, hold the wheel," he said as he jerked on a rope. "This is tacking."

The boom thumped to the other side of the boat, tilting us slightly to the left. He tied off the rope, the sail caught in the wind, and then we were heading gently in the other direction.

"That's about it. You tack when you want to change direction into the wind. Luckily, we have the wind today."

My mind was whirring. "That was a lot of information."

"You're smart. You can handle it."

"I work in a lab all day, and somehow, this was more taxing."

"Physical labor stretches you."

I shrugged as he came around behind the wheel. I stepped aside, but he kept me in place, wrapping his arms around mine and clutching the wheel. His body encased mine. I leaned against his chest, dropping my head back onto him. He ducked his head down and kissed my neck.

"I'm glad you called me."

"Me too," I said.

This was apparently what I needed. The physical side of getting a sailboat moving. The salty, humid wind in my face. Water surrounding me on all sides as we headed toward the bay.

We stood like that on the water until he had to tack

again. I got the hang of it after we did it a few more times. It certainly wasn't second nature. He had instincts on the water that had come from years of doing this. But I also understood why he loved it as much as he did. He was entirely himself out here. No one else. He didn't have to act. He didn't have to be his father's son. He could just be a man on his boat. A man in control of his destiny.

Eventually, he let the sail back down and sat us in the middle of the bay, overlooking seven different islands. We bobbed in the water as he helped me walk out onto the bow of the boat. He dropped down cushions from the interior of the boat, and we cuddled up together with nature all around us.

"Derek," I said.

He was running a hand down my arm. "Yeah?"

"What are we doing?"

"Sailing."

I laughed softly. "I mean, what are *we* doing?"

He propped himself up onto an elbow and looked down at me. "What do you want us to be doing?"

"I don't know."

"Then, we can keep doing this if you want."

I cupped his jaw in my hand and then drew him down for a kiss. He responded instantly, opening my mouth with his tongue and sliding his inside. We kissed for a few minutes, unhurried.

"You don't kiss friends like that."

He chuckled. "No. Not any friends I've ever had." He brushed back my wild curls. "But you've had a rough week, and we don't have to define anything right now. We can take our time. We can just enjoy what we have."

"Do you want to define it?" I asked softly, meeting those hazel eyes. "Do you want me?"

"More than anything."

I blinked at his blatant statement. There had been no hesitation. No question in his voice. No wondering if he wanted this or not. He'd already made up his mind, and he'd been waiting all this time for me to get there too.

"I want this too."

His smile could have blinded someone. "Then, that settles it. You're mine."

"I'm yours?"

He dropped another kiss onto my lips. "Mine."

26

SAVANNAH

PRESENT

I hopped out of my car at the marina. It was a cloudless day with the most perfect October either of us could have asked for. The sun was shining, the water was calm, and Derek was shirtless. I had no idea what Derek was doing on the dock, but if he was doing it shirtless, it was a goddamn blessing.

"Whoa," I whispered as I approached the docks.

He glanced up as if he could hear my muttered gasp. His smile brightened, and he waved. I punched in the code he'd texted me and headed out on the dock.

"Upgraded, I see," I said, trying not to stare at him and instead focusing on the sailboat. It was twice the size of the little thing he'd had the first time he took me sailing. Bigger than the sailboat he'd had in Boston too. This was all sleek and gorgeous.

"Yeah," he said with a self-deprecating laugh. "Decided I wanted something a little bigger."

A little bigger was an understatement.

"This is practically a party boat."

He shook his head. "No way. Ash has a yacht. That's a

party boat."

"Fair."

He finished whatever he had been doing and straightened up. My eyes fell over to the hard lines of his abdominals. The six-pack that was still on full display and the V that dipped down into the low-slung blue shorts.

He coughed softly, and my eyes jumped back up to him. A flush coated my cheeks.

"You ready?"

I nodded and stepped onto the sailboat. Derek pulled his white button-up back on over his exposed body. It was both disappointing and a relief. I couldn't concentrate with him like that, but also... damn, he still looked the same.

I needed no instruction this time. Even though we hadn't been sailing together in years, I remembered how to handle myself on the boat. We got her out in the water and down the river as seamlessly as possible.

"Damn, I forgot how much faster it is when I have help," he said with a laugh. "It's been years since I took anyone out but my cousins."

"Your wife didn't come out here with you?"

His face darkened. "Wasn't her scene."

I swallowed. "Oh, sorry. I didn't mean..."

"It's fine," he said, tying off a line. "She was more a yacht kind of girl."

"I see."

"What about you? Any terrible relationships?" he asked with a grin in my direction.

"How do you know I only had terrible relationships?"

"Because you're still somehow single," he said cheekily. "And you kissed me."

I blushed again. "That I did, I suppose."

"Well?"

"Two," I admitted. "Thomas Northcott was in my program."

"Why does that name sound familiar?"

"You probably met him at Harvard."

Derek thought about it and shrugged. "Must not have been memorable."

"He wasn't. We dated for a year and a half. He got a job in Idaho and wanted me to move with him. I declined. It ended."

"And the other one?"

I shrugged. "I started online dating."

He laughed and turned to face me. "That doesn't seem like you."

"It wasn't, I assure you. I gave up very quickly and had only messaged a few guys. One of them messaged me, and we hit it off and started dating. For a while, he liked that I was smart and had a great job, and then it began to devolve into the usual *you're not* that *smart* and the worse *when we have kids, you'll stay home to take care of them*."

Derek practically cackled. "So, he was intimidated by you and didn't understand you at all."

"Yeah. Pretty much. What happened with your ex?"

He turned away again, as if just talking about it upset him. "She changed."

I waited for more, but it turned out that was all the explanation he was going to give. If what Amelia had said was any indication, Derek had started the divorce proceedings, and she'd been totally bonkers. I couldn't blame him for still being upset.

"You know, thanks for not tipping off my mom that we knew each other," I said to change the subject.

"Yeah. I didn't think that would be smart."

"For a second, I was worried that she'd remember that she met you at Gran's after Gramps died."

He winced. "I thought about that, but it was so long ago and she only saw me for a second."

"Yeah."

After a moment, he added, "She's... not the easiest client."

"I bet. She's not the easiest mom."

He frowned. "I remember."

I wanted to ask how he could fucking represent her if he remembered all the shit she'd put me through, but what was it going to change? He'd taken the job for his dad. He wanted to move up in the company, and this was a way to do it. He'd made that clear. My mom was a means to an end. Which wasn't any different than she was normally treated.

"We don't have to talk about it," I said with a wave of my hand as Derek went to tack.

"Yeah. Probably should keep business and personal separate."

"Probably."

Derek asked about my research instead, and I filled him in on the years he'd missed, the award I'd won, the paths I was working on. It wasn't fast enough. It hadn't done anything to save Gramps. But it was hopefully going to help some other people down the road. That was the goal at least.

We stopped in the middle of the bay again. It was a calm day with very few other boats out. We'd only passed a few fishing boats on the way into the bay, and now, it was like we had the entire water to ourselves.

Derek came to sit next to me and dropped an arm across the back of my seat. Easy and comfortable. As if his arm belonged there. As if nothing in the world had changed.

I didn't move. I should have, but I didn't. I was mad at him for all the things that had happened. For going off and marrying someone else. For hurting me. For helping my mom. I just wanted him to be exactly what I needed and wanted in every way, and instead, he was Derek Ballentine. Wonderful and insufferable and a mix of contradictions.

"Derek," I whispered, "what am I doing here?"

"We're sailing."

"Smart-ass."

He laughed. "You're here because I wanted you to be here."

I swallowed roughly and looked up. "And why is that?"

"Because I never got over you, Mars." He put one of my curls behind my ear. "And I don't think you ever got over me either."

Everything in me was on fire at those words. They weren't wrong. As much as I hated him, I'd always felt this link with him too. As if I couldn't quite get him out from underneath my skin. Now, he was here, and he was looking at me like that and saying everything I wanted to hear. I could tell him to stop. I could walk away, figuratively speaking. But it had been years, and somehow, we'd still ended up here.

His eyes searched mine for permission, or maybe he was just looking for the same longing mirrored back at him. Because he *wanted* me. I'd forgotten how empowering that one perfect fact was. How much his desire stirred something deep inside me.

"Or maybe I'm wrong?" he asked with an arched eyebrow.

He didn't think he was wrong. He knew he was right. That was why he was a hairbreadth from my lips, heat radiating from him, desire palpable. I'd kissed him after Ash's birthday party like it was college all over again, and now, we were here with years of history between us. Could it be as easy as putting it behind me and giving in all over again? Could I survive it one more time? Josie had told me to go for it. It didn't have to mean anything. Even though that wasn't possible. Not with Derek.

"You're not wrong," I said softly. His smile was serpentine.

"I know," he said, as cocky as ever. Then, he grasped the back of my head and crushed my lips to him as if it had been killing him to wait.

Maybe it had been killing me too, because suddenly, I was feverish. I couldn't get enough of him. There was too much space between us. I wanted more, more, more. I pushed my hands up into the threads of his hair at the nape of his neck and drew him closer and harder against me. He groaned deep in the back of his throat.

His tongue slid across the seam of my lips, opening me to him, as he'd done so many times before. The same flare of desire shot through me as the first time I'd ever kissed him. When we were young and stupid and so hopelessly attracted to one another. The years had changed many, many things but never that. Never this.

The desire, as molten hot as an erupting volcano, had been there from the beginning. And we let it sweep us away, heedless of the destruction in our path.

His hands roved over my body. Derek had touched every inch of my body before, but it was as if he were discovering it all anew. As if the intervening years had scrubbed the memory clean. They ran down my sides, across the planes of my stomach, to the underside of my breasts. I arched into him, wanting more. His finger brushed gently against my nipple through the material of my tank top and lacy bralette. I jerked into his touch, as if I were naked before him.

"Sensitive," he growled.

He pulled down the front of my top, exposing my breast to the open air. His mouth came over my nipple, sucking it in and swirling his tongue around it. I fisted my hands into his button-up. Coherent thought fled as he moved to the other nipple. He was sure to give each breast equal attention.

"Derek," I said, remembering how much he enjoyed me saying his name.

He nipped at my breast as soon as the name escaped my lips. "Again."

He moved me down across the row of seats and kissed down my stomach to the hem of my shirt. He pushed the material out of his way so that he could run his tongue along the edge of my bottoms. A thin cotton skirt that was now bunched high on my thighs.

"Derek." I pushed my pelvis up to meet him.

He looked up at me with a glint of mischief in his expression. "I remember that you liked this," he said, sliding his hand ever so slowly up my inner thigh. "The teasing part."

I locked my eyes shut and tried to shift his hand to where I really wanted him. But damn him, he was right. As much as the sex was phenomenal, it had always been heightened by the foreplay that drove me out of my mind. Derek knew how to take his time when he set his mind to it. We'd spent long days in bed when we were at Harvard with nothing but time.

He pressed a kiss against my knee, dragging his scruff across my thigh. All while his hand traced the line of my underwear.

Another kiss landed higher up and then another and another. Until I was breathing heavy just from the tease as he worked his way to where his hand was. Then, he trailed a finger down the center of my underwear. I bucked against him in response.

"Fuck," I gasped.

He smirked up at me and didn't even have to say what he was thinking. I was already wet. Soaking through the thin fabric that separated me from him. He pushed my knees further apart, and I spread out wide for him as he leaned over and put his hot mouth to the material. My toes curled as he breathed hot air against my clit.

"Derek."

He hummed in response, sliding his fingers under the top of the underwear and dragging them down my legs along with my skirt. I was bare before him from the waist down, and he'd just begun.

His thumbs swept in and spread my lips open for him. I bit my lip hard enough that I thought I might draw blood. He slicked a thumb through the evidence of my arousal, dragging it up to my clit and swirling it in a circle. A finger slid inside of me, just one, and already, I was squeezing tight, wanting so much more than one finger.

"Greedy," he said with a smirk on those pouty lips.

He thrust in a second finger, stretching me and working me to a frenzy. My hips started to move with the thrusts of his fingers. When he added a third finger, I thought I was going to tip over the edge. My body shuddered in his grasp. My vision went black at the edges. I could feel it teetering so close as he stroked my clit, drawing it out of me in a deliberate motion.

"Please," I gasped.

He stilled at my words, and I whined in protest. I'd been

close. Just from his fingers. Jesus, was I that starved for sex? Or was it just him?

"Uh-uh," he teased. "Not yet."

"But..."

"I missed the taste of you."

That was all the warning I got before his mouth landed on my clit. He sucked it into his mouth, and my body rocked straight off of the seat. His forearm came out sharp across my abdomen, holding me in place. When his tongue swept against my clit, I thought I was going to lose it. I couldn't hold still. My feet scrambled for purchase. My head was all fuzzy. His fingers worked in and out of me again. With all the sensations rushing through me, it was only moments before I lost it.

"Derek," I cried one more time, and then I came in his mouth.

He slid his fingers in and out of me a few more times, milking my orgasm for everything I'd give him. Then, he sat back and watched me come down.

His erection was visible against the crotch of his shorts. I reached for him before I had another thought. He chuckled softly as I undid his pants and dragged the zipper down.

"Mars," he said softly. He pushed my hair back out of my face.

I didn't answer him. I pushed his shorts out of my way and reached for the waistband of his boxers. His cock jutted up through the material, and I salivated at the sight.

"Mars," he repeated.

Still, I said nothing. I dipped into the waistband, and I took him in my hand. He was hard as a rock and so much bigger than my brain had processed. I slid my palm across the tip of him, feeling the wet pre-cum.

"Mars," he grunted this time. He grasped my chin and jerked me up to look at him.

"What?" I finally said. "Can't you see I'm busy?"

He chuckled and then pressed a hard kiss to my lips. "I missed you so much."

I stroked him up and down. "How much?"

"Let me get inside that pussy and show you."

"Uh-uh," I repeated with a teasing smile. "Not yet."

His eyes dilated at my gall. He wanted to fuck me. He was already pumping into my hand, wanting sweet release.

I slicked my tongue along the head. He jerked, pushing himself further inside my mouth without even meaning to. I dropped to my knees before him. His eyes rounded in wonder as I slid his shorts all the way off and then devoured him. I might have liked the teasing, but he certainly didn't need it to get turned on.

His hands fisted into my hair as I bobbed up and down on his cock, taking him deep in my throat. Deep enough that my eyes watered and then back again, stroking him with my hand at the same time. His hips lifted each time to meet me, fucking me the way he clearly wanted to do to my pussy.

He lengthened and lengthened. He shuddered once and then twice and then abruptly jerked out of my mouth.

I sat back on my heels with wide, alarmed eyes. "Derek."

"I want you to finish with me." He stripped out of his shirt, tossing it into the hold below. Then, he was on top of me.

We lined up perfectly. His arm around my back, the other with a grip on my hair. He kissed me with all the pent-up desire that had nearly burst out of him and into my mouth. Then, he slid home, and we both sighed with pleasure.

I hadn't planned any of this when I agreed to come sailing with him. We'd had sex on boats before. Plenty of times in college. But this was different. This was claiming. This was him not wasting any more damn time. We'd certainly wasted enough.

His thrusts turned brutal as he hit deeper and deeper inside of me. I drew him down on top of me until we were pressed tight together. His hips jerking against my clit while he drove into me. Everything built up again and again. Until I looked up into his eyes and knew that I couldn't do it any longer. I had no idea what he was holding on to. We were both hanging on to a razor's edge.

"Oh God," I said as I came all over his cock.

He finished inside of me, squeezing me tight to him. Afterward, we both lay panting on the deck of the sailboat. When I was able to move again, I found the little bathroom. When I returned, Derek was collapsed in a small bed at the back of the boat.

"There was a bed the whole time?" I asked, curling up next to him.

"Overrated," he joked.

"Derek?" I bit my lip as anxiety began to creep in where only sexual desire had been before.

"Don't."

"What? You don't know what I was going to say."

"Yeah, I do. And you're wrong. This was right. It was perfect." He kissed my shoulder and then rolled to look down at me. "This is how it should have always been."

"Okay," I whispered, drunk on his confidence.

"Good."

I hesitated a moment before speaking again. "So... my birthday is coming up. Lila and Josie are coming into town for it."

"Oh?" he asked, tensing at the names of my friends.

"Do you want to come out too?"

He searched my face, as if looking for something that he couldn't find in my expression. "Sure. I'm guessing I shouldn't invite Ash?"

I chuckled darkly. "No. Probably not."

He blew out a breath. "And you want me out with your friends?"

"Yes," I said with absolute certainty.

"All right. I'll be there."

We went for round two, lying in the bed, exhausted and satisfied. Finally, we got dressed, and Derek turned the boat around, heading back for the marina. I checked my phone, which I'd ignored throughout our sexcapades. I frowned. I had a voicemail from my attorney. I listened to the message, and my frown deepened. They'd chosen a court date for our meeting with the judge to determine the will challenge.

Derek noticed and quirked an eyebrow. "What's wrong?"

"Did you know?"

"Know?"

I bit my lip. "About the court date?"

His frown mirrored mine. "Yeah. Did you not know?"

"No. Why didn't you tell me?"

"One, I thought you already knew, and two, it's not my responsibility to tell you, Marley. We were keeping business and personal separate."

We'd agreed to that. And still, the entire thing made me unbelievably irritated.

"You should have said something."

He held his arm out, and I reluctantly stepped into him at the wheel.

He pressed a kiss into my hair. "I didn't know you wanted me to."

"Well, if it's important, I deserve to know."

He held me tighter against him. "Just promise we can get through this case."

I paused, considering the statement. What if he won? What if my mom got the house and it was his fault? I squeezed my eyes shut. I couldn't even consider that. It couldn't happen.

"I can't promise that," I whispered.

He sighed. "I'll do all the promising for the both of us then."

It wasn't enough. We'd always been complicated. But I didn't know how we'd survive this if it went south. Why did I always put my heart on the line with him?

INTERLUDE

When I was a child, I'd loved to play tea party with Gran. Not the British stuff that would have made me posh, but good, cold, sweet tea made with buckets of sugar. I'd pour it into our plastic cups and hold a pinkie out and beam, speaking in some fake British accent that was definitely more Scarlett O'Hara than Queen Elizabeth.

Then one day, I decided I was too old for the plastic tea set. Gran wasn't around, but I wanted to play. And I wanted to use her porcelain set. The one she'd gotten as a wedding gift. Passed down from one generation to the next. It had a blue floral design and was the prettiest thing I'd ever seen. Also one of the few things I'd been explicitly told not to touch. Though I was sure they would one day be mine.

Since I knew how important it was, I took out the tea set with care, cradling it against my chest like it was life or death. At the time, it felt like it. Then, I poured myself the sweet tea, getting back into the fun of the game. I laughed and played as if I were allowed to use something this important every day.

I'd never know exactly what it was that shook me so much. Maddox startled me, but I'd heard his clomping steps. I should have known he was coming. But one minute, I was holding the teacup, and the next, the glass slipped out of my hand. I wasn't fast enough by any stretch of the imagination to keep it from falling. The cup crashed to the floor, spilling tea everywhere and leaving broken china in tiny pieces.

When Gran found me, she was furious. But no one was as hard on me as myself. No one ever would be again. I'd taken something delicate and fragile and important and watched it be destroyed by my own carelessness.

So, when Derek and I began a relationship, I knew it was a china set just like the one Gran had. Precious and irreplaceable. I held it with care. I kept it safe. And I waited for the moment when it would shatter.

PART IV

27

HARVARD

SEPTEMBER 13, 2013

The doorbell rang.

"I got it. I got it. I got it!" I called before Derek could get off of the couch.

He laughed and got to his feet.

I swung the front door open, and Josie stood in the doorway, looking as utterly glamorous as always. We both shrieked, throwing our arms around each other and swaying side to side.

"I missed you so much," I told her.

"Same. So much."

I released her and pulled back. "You look amazing."

She laughed. "Thanks. I love this," she said, touching my green dress. Her eyes swept to Derek. "And this!"

"Hey, Josie," he said.

She wrapped him in a hug, forgoing his offered hand. "This is the best taste you've ever had, Mars."

I shook my head.

But Derek quirked a smile. "I couldn't agree more."

"Now, are there bars around here or what? My flight *sucked*. I had to have three vodka tonics to fight my nerves, and if I don't start drinking again, I'm going to lose my buzz."

I rolled my eyes. "So dramatic."

"We know just the place," Derek said with a laugh.

That was Josie. She entered any room and owned it. I loved her for it and envied her just as much.

She dropped her bags in the living room, and we were out the door ten minutes later, heading out to one of the Cambridge dive bars. It wasn't going to be Josie's scene, but I didn't care. She had come here for me, not glamour.

We stepped inside the already-crowded bar, claiming a booth near the back. Derek disappeared a minute later to procure us drinks.

Josie looked around with a dirty grin on her face. "If I wasn't married, I could have *so* much fun here."

I snorted. "Classic Josie."

"Well, I am who I am." She tapped her electric-turquoise manicure against the hardwood table. "And you? You're happy? He's one hunk of a man."

"I am. We are."

I found Derek at the bar. Some girl had gone up to him and was clearly flirting. He put distance between them, and from my vantage point, he politely turned her down.

"How do you keep him on a string? Martin is..." Josie waved her hand.

I snapped my eyes back to her. She'd only married Martin eight months ago. Was it already going poorly?

"Is he cheating on you?" I asked, my voice lowering.

"No, of course not!" She laughed. "It's just Hollywood, you know?" She looked at my blank face. "Or maybe you don't. He has a lot of fans, and they're pretty aggressive. The spotlight isn't always the best place to be."

"I can imagine. Derek gets a lot of attention just because he's Derek. I don't know if I could handle fans."

Josie patted my hand. "You couldn't."

I swatted at her. "Bitch."

She cackled. "I missed you so much. I need more time with people who will call me out on my bullshit."

"That's very clear."

Derek came back then, balancing three drinks in his large hands. He passed Josie a beer and me a sidecar. He winked. "I told them how you like it."

I flushed and took a sip of the drink. "It's perfect."

"Stop. You're adorable," Josie said.

Derek slipped into the booth next to me. He took a sip of his beer and wrapped an arm around my shoulders. "We try."

"Well, at least someone can make my girl happy. I never thought I'd see the day," Josie said.

"You're ridiculous."

"Dramatic," Josie corrected. "It's part of my job."

"Didn't you just win an Emmy?" Derek asked, changing the subject.

Josie arched an eyebrow. "Did you Google me?"

"Maybe."

I rolled my eyes. "I suppose you're perfectly Google-able."

"That I am," Josie said with a wink. "And yes. Best actress actually."

"Congrats," Derek said. "Quite an accomplishment. And this is the third year of *Academy*?"

"Correct."

"You and your costar finally going to hook up?" He leaned forward for the scoop.

She snorted. "Ship has already sailed."

The biggest part of *Academy*, the supernatural show that Josie had premiered, was the will-they, won't-they between her and her costar. Especially considering she'd married him at Christmas, everyone was wondering when they'd finally get hot and heavy on the show.

"Not on-screen," he pointed out.

"A girl never kisses and tells."

I nudged her. "Liar."

"I mean, obviously," she said with a laugh. "I'll just say, the tension is hot on set."

"On and off set," I said into my drink.

"Touché!" she cheered.

A few girls scurried over then. The boldest of them stepped forward and cleared her throat. "Sorry, I couldn't help but overhear you discussing the show *Academy*?" She said it more like a question. "Are you... are you Cassie Herrington?"

Cassie Herrington was Josie's character's name on *Academy*.

Her friend giggled. "Josephine Reynolds," she corrected.

Josie's eyes revealed to me how much she hadn't wanted this to happen. But it was just a split second of annoyance, stripped away so quickly that no one else would have ever seen it. A smile split her face, and she nodded.

"That's me. Are you fans?"

"Huge fans!" the first girl gushed.

The second nodded. "I can't believe you eloped with Martin Harper!"

"He's the *hottest*," a third piped up. "I love him as Cord!"

Derek and I watched in awe as she handled all three of the girls, taking a few pictures, signing a napkin, and then sending them on their way.

Josie plopped back down in the seat as if nothing had happened. "What were we talking about?"

"Damn, you're famous," Derek said with a chuckle.

"It's a pain sometimes," she admitted. "But gotta love the fans. They got me here." She flipped her dark hair over her shoulder as if that was done with. "So, tell me all about you, Derek. Mars is so tight-lipped."

I didn't want to admit why that was as Derek dived into an explanation about what he did for a living. After graduating in May, Derek had decided to stay on with his advisor to be a legal researcher. We'd spent every day together all summer—lost on his sailboat along the Charles River, sneaking kisses in the Law Library, him bringing me food in the lab. It was easy. Tinged with a worry I couldn't ignore or get rid of.

My anxiety was driving me crazy. Misty had laughed at me. She said it was just the first real relationship I'd ever had. *Real* being the operative word because every other guy I'd dated had gone up in flames. Derek was my constant. Somehow, it should have made it easier. But no matter how effortless it was to be with him, I couldn't brush aside what had happened to us in college. The words he'd said to me, the pain of his loss.

Everything had changed when he took care of me after Gramps died. And nothing had.

I was his.

That should have been enough.

Derek smiled over at me, pausing in his conversation with Josie. "What?"

"Nothing," I said automatically.

"That's not a nothing face," he probed.

"Come on, Mars. We're having a good time," Josie teased. "Sometimes, I think you're the mysterious one."

I laughed. "Yeah, right."

"Yeah... we both know it's Lila."

"That's how she always has those two boys falling all over themselves for her," I said.

"Too true," Josie agreed. "I wish she were here this weekend with us."

I glanced down at my drink again. *Oh boy. Here we go.*

Josie cocked her head at me. "Why isn't she here with us, Mars?"

"Uh..."

Derek shot me a pointed look. "Marley hasn't told her we're dating."

"What?" Josie gasped. "Why not? That's absurd. She's been your bestie since second grade."

"She's... busy," I offered lamely.

Derek threw up his hands. "Maybe you can talk some sense into her. She's been saying that all summer."

"She *is* busy," I said. "PT school is very demanding, and she had that internship all summer. I think she was working even more than during the school year, which I hadn't thought was possible."

Josie gave me a blank look that would mean nothing to anyone else, but I knew all too well that it meant she was trying to keep her cool. She was mad at me for not telling Lila. It was one thing to keep it a secret from Lila before we were officially dating, but it was another thing to purposely not tell her.

I'd had the opportunity at the funeral to divulge it all, but it had been so precarious. So unknown still. I hadn't wanted to ruin it by letting anyone know what was really going on. Only Gran had that information. But it was beyond that now... and we all knew it.

"I'm going to get us more drinks," Derek said.

It wasn't the first time he'd gotten irritated that Lila didn't know. And I was going to tell her… I was.

"Marley," Josie said slowly.

"I know. I know. I'll tell her."

"Will you?"

I bit my lip. "I don't know."

"Tell me what's going on here. You like Derek, right?"

"Yes."

"And he's really into you. I can tell."

"Yeah."

"So, what's the problem?"

I shook my head. I wished that I could explain it. Explain the fear that gripped me. I'd lost him once. I'd lost him before he was ever really mine to begin with. And at some point, I'd have to put my trust in him that he wasn't going to go anywhere. I just hadn't gotten there yet. He'd broken something fragile in me. I didn't know how to put it back together. And telling Lila would change it. That was what my gut told me, and my gut was always right.

"You're scared," Josie said intuitively. She gripped my wrist and leaned in. "Because it's not real until Lila knows, is it?"

A tear welled in my eye, and I brushed it aside. "I guess not."

"You can't do this. It's no way to live, Marley."

"Not everyone can easily throw their feelings around like you and Lila," I said, pulling back. "I don't want to be hurt."

"That's part of life."

"He already hurt me once."

Josie narrowed her eyes. "But you're with him again anyway. It's not fair to hold it over him like that. You either move on from what happened in the past or you leave him. That's it, Mars."

"I know," I whispered, squeezing my eyes shut. I couldn't lose him. I was holding on so tight and too loosely at the same goddamn time. "I know, okay?"

Josie nodded, rubbing my shoulder. "You know why you're freaking out, right?"

"Why?"

"Because you love him."

Derek returned at that very moment with a tray of shots. So, I never got to confirm the words that had left Josie's mouth. But her soft smile said that she knew she'd hit the nail on the head.

I was in love with Derek Ballentine. And I didn't want to be.

28

HARVARD

OCTOBER 26, 2013

I stared out at the mountain of powder coming down out of the sky with a pout on my lips. "It never snows on my birthday."

Derek laughed. "We're in New England. It can snow before Halloween."

Which was true but something that I'd never considered in all of my twenty-five years. It was also the first birthday I'd be spending without my brother. Maddox was out in LA for something to do with animation, and Derek had suggested getting a cabin in New Hampshire for the weekend. Just the two of us. I'd expected some wooden cabin with crappy running water and a fireplace for heat. This was a five-star-hotel vibe with fur rugs, central heating, and a Jacuzzi tub with jets. The bed was a California king, loaded with comforters and a plethora of throw pillows.

"You know this is all too much," I told him.

"It's your birthday." His hands slipped under my jacket, dragging me closer to him, and he dropped a kiss onto my mouth. "Never too much."

"Well, thank you. This is an excellent present."

His brow furrowed. "I still got you a present."

"No!" I groaned. "Derek!"

He laughed and tugged me back toward the bedroom. "What did you expect? I like to give presents."

"You got me a five-hundred-dollar scarf once," I chided him.

"And you wore it into the lab, which was my favorite part."

I sighed. "I can't believe you let me do that."

"It's how I knew that you actually liked it."

I rolled my eyes and let him drag me into the bedroom, where a rectangular box rested on the bed with a silky red bow on it. There was no use in arguing. I pulled the ribbon on the box and opened it. When I pushed aside the red tissue paper, I gasped and covered it up again.

"Derek, you didn't."

He grinned devilishly. "You don't like it?"

I gulped and withdrew the tissue paper once more. Underneath was a few scraps of black lingerie. "Are you sure this is a gift for me?"

He kissed my neck. "I thought we could both enjoy it."

"Devious," I said with a shake of my head. His eyes were hungry as he looked from me to the lingerie. I pushed him away. "Well, get out of here, so I can try it on."

He laughed, his eyes ravenous. "All right."

As soon as he disappeared, I stripped out of my jeans and sweater, folding them up on the bed. Then, I shimmied into the lingerie. A small black G-string thong with a matching lacy bra that my breasts practically spilled out of. Plus, a black garter with dangling clips and even a set of thigh-high tights. I felt ridiculous, pulling the tights on and clipping them into place, but as I stared at myself in the full-length mirror, dragging my wild curls out of the bun on the top of my head, I could admit that the set had the desired effect. I looked like a vixen.

Derek knocked once and then peeked his head inside the bedroom. He stepped fully inside with a greedy purpose. His eyes were glazed with desire, and those pouty lips looked ready to devour me.

I turned fully to face him. "Well, do you like my present?"

"Oh yes," he said, striding toward me. "I intend to fully unwrap you."

I laughed as his lips crashed down on mine. Everything was on fire all at once. No hesitancy. No slowing down. Just Derek doing exactly as he'd intended. He'd wrapped me in the skimpy clothing of his desire, and it had worked out for the both of us.

Within minutes, all my hard work of getting into this contraption was for naught. Derek had it all on the floor with his face buried between my legs and his fingers in my pussy, coaxing me to the fastest orgasm of my life. He kissed his way up my body before bringing our lips together.

He drove home inside of me in one swift motion, and everything went fuzzy at the edges. I wanted this. I wanted all of this. Just him.

It had been weeks since I'd realized that I had fallen hopelessly in love with him. I'd kept that knowledge to myself. Told myself that it would be safer to wait until he said those three perfect words to me. I didn't need to rush anything. But somehow, every day that I kept them in felt like a betrayal. Like he needed to know how I really felt. I hadn't said them with words, but my body sure said everything I couldn't get out.

We came together, hot and sweaty and panting. His lips

trailed along my neck, jaw, and collarbone. Then he took my hand and climbed off the bed.

"Come with me," he breathed.

I padded into the bathroom to find he'd started the water and jets. I climbed in, and he pulled me into his lap. His lips continued their mapping of my skin.

"God, you taste so good." He pressed another kiss to my shoulder. "I can't get enough of you."

His hands slid down my body. First touching the planes of my stomach and then up to the crest of my breasts. He palmed one breast and then the other, taking his time in reacquainting himself with the feel of them. Pinching each nipple and making me squirm against his lap.

"You're going to get me all turned on again," I said in what was hardly a complaint.

"Oh?" he teased, running his tongue along the shell of my ear.

One hand moved across my stomach before reaching the apex of my legs. He maneuvered my legs on top of his and then spread me wider open. I tipped my head back onto his shoulder as his fingers found my clit once more. A groan escaped me as he worked my body into a frenzy.

"I'm going to make you come over and over tonight," he commanded.

I shuddered at his words, and he dipped his fingers inside of me. "Oh," I gasped.

I squirmed, nearly dislodging myself from his lap. He banded an arm around my stomach, so I couldn't escape him. I bit my lip as he held me in place, circling his thumb around my clit as he fucked my pussy with his fingers. He nipped at my neck and drove his pelvis against mine. I could already feel the length of him hardening against my ass.

Then all the sensations hit me at once, and I came to his careful ministrations.

He released me, and I slipped off of his lap. I panted in the water, looking up at him with worship in my gaze. He grinned, standing out of the water and showing off his erection, long with need.

"Bend over the tub," he instructed.

I arched an eyebrow at him. "Ready again?"

"Always for you."

Then, he guided me to the side of the Jacuzzi tub. His hands grasped my hips, and suddenly, he was at my entrance. His fingers probed my opening, and I squirmed, wanting more of him already.

"So wet."

The tip of him met my opening from behind. I wriggled backward until I got the entire head inside of me. He chuckled softly and then slapped my ass. I cried out in surprise and jerked around to look at him.

He winked at me. "Like that?"

I opened my mouth to deny it, but then he spanked me again, his dick pushing all the way into me. I moaned instead, my eyes rolling into the back of my head. His growl of approval was all I needed to hear before he drove into me again and again. His hand came down on my ass, and he took me until I thought I was going to explode.

"Derek," I cried out. "Oh God."

"Yes, baby," he said, running a hand down my back. "I'm close too. Come with me."

A few minutes later, he cried out as he emptied himself deep within me. His orgasm triggered mine. I could barely stand as we both finished. When he finally withdrew from within me, I collapsed into the water.

His hands came to help me up, cradling me against his

chest. Sleep felt so close. I was in a euphoric state that I'd never even known existed. New heights that I'd never reached.

He kissed my hair. "That was perfect, Mars."

"Perfect," I agreed, lost to this man.

"Happy birthday."

I snuggled in closer. "I love you."

Derek froze with his arms around me for a whole second. The longest second of my entire life. Then, he relaxed, drawing me in closer. But he didn't say anything. Not a word. Just kissed me.

I swallowed. The fear that had evaporated with our sex marathon came back full force. "You... you don't have to say it back. I just, I don't know. I wanted you to know."

"It's okay."

And somehow, that made it so much worse.

29

HARVARD

NOVEMBER 17, 2013

Derek still hadn't said he loved me.

And I hadn't been stupid enough to say it again.

I'd thought that things would change afterward, but it was all remarkably the same. The same lab dates. The same Law Library study sessions. The same sailing expeditions. We were busy, but we were together. So, maybe it didn't matter that I loved him... and he didn't love me.

Maybe.

"You can't stay in here all night," Misty complained. She'd already changed into something straight out of Martha's Vineyard. "There's a *huge* party tonight. It's Harvard/Yale."

I wrinkled my nose and turned back to my work. "You know I don't care about football."

"I know, but again, it's Harvard/Yale."

"You keep repeating that like I care."

"It's your third year. I'd think you'd get into it by now."

"I care about Duke. The rest is meh."

"Come on. I bet Derek wants to celebrate."

"I'm sure he does, and he is. He went to the game with his boss or something. He said he was meeting friends."

Misty huffed. "Suit yourself. Don't say I didn't ever do anything for you."

I laughed and pulled away from my work. "Is it that important to you?"

"Kyle's bringing a date," she said with a pouty face.

"Ah."

Misty and Kyle had dated fall and spring semester. They'd had a falling-out this summer, and she wanted him back. I hadn't realized he was dating someone new.

"All right. I'll go with you."

"Yes!"

Misty had come prepared. She'd brought me an outfit to wear to the party. A red minidress that was impractical in this weather and that I never wore anymore anyway, but it was what I had. I slipped out of my lab coat and into the dress. Misty passed me red lipstick, and then we were out the door.

The party was not far from the labs. The house party was packed and warm inside with all the body heat. I texted Derek when I got there to let him know I was out with Misty. The text never registered as Read though. I didn't know what he was up to. Normally, he at least texted me throughout the day. His boss must have gotten him drunk at the game.

I shook my head and pushed through to the kitchen. I took a beer and followed Misty into another room. She found Kyle almost right away. He was with a blonde that I'd never seen before. Instead of just going to talk to him, she found Matt and danced seductively with him. I leaned against the wall to watch the showdown, nursing my beer and wishing I were still in the lab.

I checked my phone again. Still nothing from Derek. He'd now read the text at least.

With a yawn into my beer, I stepped into the next room over, and my feet stilled. Derek was at the head of the table, sitting with a half-dozen people that I knew *all* too well. A bunch of his douche friends from high school who had traumatized both me and Lila for years. I disliked every single one of them on sight.

Chuck Henderson was hot but a total bastard. I'd seen Derek throw him out of a party for touching Amelia. And now, he was *here*. With his two cronies, Michael and Joseph. Neither of them had ever had an original thought in their heads. Trask and Hooper sat nearest to where I'd walked in. They'd both played basketball with Derek in high school. He hadn't mentioned that he was having friends in town just that he was going out with friends. Why hadn't he specified?

Derek didn't look up at my entrance, but Chuck did.

His smile widened to pure Cheshire, but he was drunk as hell. "Minivan!" he crowed.

My body seized at that word out of Chuck Henderson's mouth. Derek sometimes still used it affectionately, like it was our little secret. But this was how he'd *first* used that word. To try to tear me down for my circumstances when they were all pretty little rich boys at the private Catholic school. They were above me. That was how that had been used. And how Chuck was using it right now.

Derek's head jerked up. I could tell that he was *beyond* drunk. I'd seen him intoxicated but never like this. He could barely hold his head up. And when that word was uttered, all the other guys started laughing.

And to my horror, Derek followed along. He *laughed*. He actually fucking laughed at that word. Like it was funny and not humiliating.

It didn't matter that I was a PhD student at Harvard. That I'd finally escaped the horror of being the poor girl at school who drove a fucking minivan. It didn't matter that I was on my way to a breakthrough in my research. That I was dating Derek Ballentine of all people. That I was *someone* here.

Suddenly, I was back in high school. Just the nerdy girl to make fun of. Not anyone at all. Not good enough.

"Minivan!" Michael said, cracking up.

"Fuck, I'd forgotten that nickname," Joseph said.

"How could you forget?" Chuck asked with another drunk laugh. "She drove a fucking minivan."

I wanted to open my mouth. To tell them to all go fuck themselves. And yet I stood paralyzed. Stuck in a time loop of terror. Repeating old hurts that I'd thought I'd finally healed over. Instead, the wounds were being ripped open and revealed for everyone to see. Just another poor girl trying to be something she wasn't.

"Derek?" I managed to croak.

"Come on over here, Minivan," he said with another chuckle.

The word felt sour in my stomach. It had lost the edge of an inside joke when it was stolen and appropriated by the enemy.

I took a step back and shook my head. "What the fuck is wrong with you?"

"You're going to let her talk to you like that, D-Man?" Chuck egged him on.

Derek stumbled to his feet. "Nothing's wrong with me."

"D-Man?" I said in exasperation. "Seriously?"

Derek laughed again at something one of the other guys had said, and I just shook my head. I was done. This was fucking ridiculous. I didn't have to stay here and be ridiculed.

"Whatever." I stormed away from the lot of them.

I heard laughter in my wake, and then suddenly, Derek was there. He grasped my elbow.

"Mars, hold up."

"Oh, it's Mars now?" I demanded, snatching my arm away.

He teetered forward drunkenly, reaching for the doorframe for support. "It was just a joke."

"So, I'm a joke to you now?"

"Just lighten up," he said with that smarmy smirk on his lips. "You're overreacting."

My spine straightened at that word. "Excuse me?"

"It's nothing."

"It's not *nothing* to me, Derek. Or should I say, D-Man?" I snarled. "You didn't even tell me your friends were in town."

"Why should I?"

"I don't know. I thought we were dating."

"You hate my friends," he said with a shrug. "I knew you wouldn't want to hang out with them."

"You mean, you knew that you didn't want to introduce me as your girlfriend," I snapped right back.

He glared down at me as he met my rising anger. "Like you with Lila. Tell me, *Minivan*, does your best friend know you're dating me?"

"That's different."

"How? From my vantage point, it's the same goddamn thing," he said. "This isn't real to you, Marley. You say you love me, but you won't even tell Lila. And then you have the audacity to be mad at me. Rich. Real rich."

I balked at the way he had thrown aside the fact that I

loved him. As if it had never mattered. My spine was ramrod straight, and my hands balled into fists. "I should have told Lila. Fine. You're right. Is that what you wanted to hear? You're still a drunk asshole who let your friends make fun of me."

"They weren't making fun of you. They were calling you a nickname. It's not a big deal."

"No big deal to you," I yelled back at him. "Because you have no idea what it's like to be the person who drives the minivan. Who is made fun of for it."

"No, I don't," he said with a shrug. "I'll never know what that's like. I shouldn't have to feel bad that I didn't grow up poor."

My stomach dropped at the words. "The great Derek Ballentine. Forgive me for forgetting your eminence above the rest of us peons."

I shook my head at his stupidity and pushed my way through the party. I couldn't believe that the guy I'd spent the last year with could be this callous and uncaring. He might be drunk, but he was being a mean drunk. And the truth was finally coming out.

Derek and I were from different worlds. Just when I'd let myself think that we were on the same playing field, I was reminded how wrong I was. He would always be the rich legacy kid, and I'd always be the poor scholarship kid.

Still, he followed me out of the house. Oh, how history repeated itself. A year ago, he'd begged me to try this again. And now, he was ruining it all just as easily.

"Marley," he said, stumbling drunkenly out into the freezing weather. "I don't know why you're so mad."

"Then, you're a fucking idiot. I've been *waiting* for this." Tears welled in my eyes, and I swiped at them. "Waiting for you to hurt me like you did before. When people show you who they are, believe them the first time. This is my third time, and it's the same old shit, Derek."

"Then that's your own fault," he said so casually that my heart broke.

Tears fell down my cheeks at the words. The easy way he'd said that, as if it were so obvious. Because the problem was… I'd hoped that he was different this time. I'd waited *months* before giving in to him because I didn't trust that he wouldn't break my heart. Now, he was here, shattering it into a million pieces, just like Gran's tea set.

"You're right," I said with a nod. "I see you for exactly who you are now. I won't forget it."

30

SAVANNAH

PRESENT

"No *fucking* way they're here."

I stalled in the doorway of Dub's as I zeroed in on the group of guys at the center of the bar. Of all the fucking bars in all of Savannah, it had to be the place that Chuck Henderson was holding court.

"Who?" Lila asked. Then, she saw who was sitting there and said, "Oh."

Josie peeked around me. "Do we know them?"

"Minivan!" Chuck Henderson cried as he caught sight of me standing there.

Michael and Joseph cackled at Chuck's lame joke. Luckily, Trask and Hooper weren't in attendance, but his cronies were enough for Chuck's amusement.

My cheeks flushed crimson, and my back straightened. These douche bags were not going to ruin my birthday.

"Fuck," Derek said. He strode around me. "I'll handle it."

"Wait," I said quickly as my blood pressure spiked.

The last time I'd seen Chuck around Derek, it had been a disaster. It had ruined everything we'd built. I didn't want it to all fall apart again because of one douche.

Derek turned back to face me. It was my birthday. I'd invited him out with my friends. An unprecedented thing from our past. Everything had been going great, and yet here was what had ruined us, rearing its ugly head. He'd stop for me. I could see it on his face. That Derek would walk out of this bar and forget it if I told him to.

"What are you going to do?" I asked in a panic.

His face went perfectly still as he realized how upset I still was. His pinkie finger wrapped around mine. "Marley, let me handle it."

History told me not to trust him in these situations. I should get the hell out of there. I shouldn't trust Derek to defend me because he'd only ever defended himself. And yet... and yet...

Derek looked different. He'd *been* different the last couple months. Despite the case between us, somehow, miraculously, he'd grown up.

Finally, I nodded. "Okay."

Derek smiled, pressed a kiss to my lips right in front of them, and then turned to address the douche bags.

"What is going on?" Josie asked.

"Remember the night that Derek and I broke up in grad school?"

Josie's head whipped to the guys seated before her, and her eyes widened. "Ohhh."

Lila shot me a look. "You sure you don't want to leave? I've had my fair share of run-ins with Chuck Henderson."

I shrugged. Yes, I wanted to leave. But I wanted to see what Derek would do.

"D-Man," Chuck said with a laugh. "You and Minivan, huh?"

"Don't call her that," he snapped.

Chuck's eyes narrowed, and he tipped his chair back

onto two legs. He was clearly drunk. I wondered if he was ever in any other state. "Bit of a downgrade from Kasey, isn't it? Prom queen to a minivan."

I winced at the mention of his ex-wife. Derek, however, didn't. He strode around Chuck, grabbed the back of his chair, and jerked it backward.

Chuck shouted, scrambling to keep from falling. But it was no use. Chuck fell backward on the hardwood floor. His feet dangling comically in the air before he rolled over with a groan. "What the fuck?"

"I said, don't call her that," Derek said calmly.

"Jesus Christ, it was just a fucking joke."

"You weren't joking, Chuck. You're just a prick who never left high school behind. Marley has done more in her life than you'll ever do, and I'm done letting your petty insults continue."

Chuck clambered to his feet. Michael and Joseph similarly got up with wide eyes, staring at Derek as if they'd never seen him.

"Fuck you, Ballentine," Chuck said eloquently.

Derek nodded and took a step forward. All three of them jerked backward in alarm. He laughed. "That's what I thought. Now, get the fuck out of here."

And to my shock, they tucked tail and all but ran from the bar. Sure, Chuck threw obscenities at Derek, as if it would make a difference. But they were gone.

Josie leaned in close to me. "Remember how I said that you didn't have to marry him?"

I laughed. "Yeah?"

"I take it back."

Lila's head whipped to us. "What? Marry him?"

"You should definitely marry him," Josie said.

Lila looked between me and Derek and then shrugged.

"It'll be an awkward wedding, but I have to say that I'm with Josie on this one."

I shook my head. "Y'all are ridiculous."

Derek held his hand out to the abandoned table. "Drinks, ladies?"

"We'll get them!" Josie said. She grasped Lila's hand and dragged her away, leaving me and Derek alone.

I stepped forward, brushing back a loose curl. "Um... thanks. That was unexpected."

He pulled up Chuck's overturned chair and offered it to me. I sank into it, and he took the seat next to me.

"Well, that's how it should have gone the first time."

"Yeah," I whispered.

Derek reached out and threaded our fingers together. He dropped a kiss onto my hand. "That was always my biggest regret."

"What was?"

He nodded down. "That I let you go over that."

"Oh," I said softly. "Well, you didn't let me go exactly. You did show up at my house a bunch once you sobered up with no memory of what had happened and begged me to come back."

"Yeah," he said sheepishly. "I did that. But I'd already ruined it."

"We both did." My eyes trailed to my friends at the bar. "I should have told Lila long before I did."

Silence stretched between us, but it wasn't uncomfortable. For the first time in a long time, there were no more regrets between us. We were here again. I still wasn't entirely sure what this was. The case was between us. It was hard to completely separate business from personal when it came to my life on the line. But I'd vowed to do it for the night.

Lila and Josie brought a tray of shots back with them at

the same time that Maddox entered Dub's. He shook out an umbrella in frustration and then found Josie and froze momentarily. She looked up at him and then quickly away.

"Goddamn rain couldn't wait a few minutes for me to get here," he complained.

"That's Savannah for you," I said.

"Hey, man." Derek held his hand out for Maddox.

My brother looked down at it and then sighed, shaking.

"This is a bad idea," he told me.

Derek and I both laughed.

He wasn't wrong. I'd been shown time and time again that Derek could hurt me. I had no reason to believe he wouldn't do it again. And yet here I was, falling head over heels for him. I hated him for our past, but somehow, I still felt exactly the same for him as I always had.

After that, we all settled in for my birthday. Lila discussing the current Falcons schedule and her role as a physical therapist in their training room. The final season of *Academy* was running this fall. Josie chatted about future plans. An indie film, some superhero movie she was in talks about doing, and a makeup line. But I couldn't have been the only one who heard that she was afraid where her career would go without her hit show. Maddox didn't say much about his animating, but he never did. That was who he was.

Derek pointedly didn't mention work. And my research was on a temporary hiatus while I was on sabbatical. I should have been with Gran, but I wasn't. She was missing from the conversation too.

We ended at Lulu's again, just like we had for Ash's birthday. Derek and I looked at each other, as if remembering but refusing to bring it up. Ash would not be a welcome conversation topic. I was still worried about him, but I'd been glad when I found out he was heading to LA to see his buddy Tanner during my birthday. The chance of us running into him was always likely with Lila in tow.

I finished off my chocolate chip cheesecake and leaned backward in my seat, full and just a little drunk. Unlike Josie and Lila, who were as smashed as I'd been the night of Ash's birthday.

"You are good people, Derek," Josie said, slapping his hand twice.

"Thanks, Josie," he said with a laugh.

"I thought I'd hate you," Lila said with a shrug.

"Don't take it personally, but I've hated you for a long time."

She snorted. "I bet you have."

"And yet we're all here together for *moi*," I said with a laugh, dramatically placing a hand on my chest.

"It's my birthday too," Maddox grumbled.

"Oh yeah, and for my little baby brother."

Maddox cast his eyes to the ceiling. "It's only thirty-seven minutes."

"Long enough," I teased.

We all joked around over our dwindling chocolate martinis before heading out. Maddox took Josie and Lila in his Jeep, and I headed out with Derek. Lila winked at me as we left. Josie whistled at us. I ducked my chin in embarrassment.

"Some friends," he said with a laugh.

"They're the best."

"I can see that."

He held my hand again as we walked to his car through the Halloween crowds that had already descended on Savannah.

"Thanks again for what you did with Chuck."

Derek laughed. "He kind of had it coming."

"I can't believe what he said."

"What part? Everything out of his mouth is as outrageous and predictable as always."

I bit my lip. "Um... that you'd downgraded."

He huffed. "Ah. That." He was silent for a moment before saying, "I did downgrade." I tried to yank my hand away in outrage, but he was smiling and held me tight. "I downgraded from you to her."

I opened my mouth as if to protest, but the words died on my lips. "What?"

"You're always the upgrade, Mars," he said and then fitted his mouth to mine, soft and tender.

"Oh, Derek," I breathed. "You're so much trouble."

He chuckled, and we stopped in front of his BMW. "Sounds right. I also... got you a birthday present."

"What? No. You can't give me anything."

He opened the door and pulled out a long, skinny box with a black ribbon on it. "But I did."

"You literally cannot spend money on me," I said in a panic. "It would look bad for..." *The case.* I didn't say it, but it was implied. It could look bad, like he was buying me off or something else ridiculous.

"I thought of that. So, I didn't spend any money."

I narrowed my eyes at him in confusion. "*You* didn't spend money on a present? Who are you, and what have you done with the real Derek Ballentine?"

He laughed and passed me the box. "Just open it, Mars."

I took it with a sigh, tugging off the ribbon and lifting the box open. My heart melted at what sat inside. I withdrew the black, white, and red Hermès scarf that he had given me as a Christmas present all those years ago. When we'd broken up, I'd stuffed everything that reminded me of him in a box and left it at his place.

"You kept it all these years?" I asked, my heart constricting.

"Always." He took the scarf and wound it around my neck. "To Mars and back."

Then, he kissed me.

And I knew I was in deep, deep trouble.

31

SAVANNAH

OCTOBER 28, 2016

"I'm glad that you could make it for this, Mars," Maddox said.

"How could I miss it?"

Maddox pulled a face. "It's not a big deal."

"Well, are you happy, or is it not a big deal?"

My brother grinned, tightening his charcoal suit around his shoulders. "Both."

"Shithead."

He cracked up. "That's why I want you here. If I have too many people telling me that I'm awesome, it might go to my head."

I rolled my eyes. "As if it hasn't already."

"Nah. Us animators aren't usually recognized. Hard to get a big head when no one knows your name."

"Speaking of someone whose name everyone knows, have you seen Josie?"

He flinched at the name and then acted like he hadn't. "I have not."

"Are you two still at each other's throats?"

"I have no idea what you're talking about."

"Okay," I said, drawing out the word. "Sure thing. Play dumb. That's always worked out so well for you."

"You're such a bad sister."

I laughed. "I'm the best sister, and you know it."

"Remind yourself of that when this thing goes all night," he said with a wink and then headed backstage.

I didn't mind that it took all night. The SCAD Film Festival was an annual event that brought hundreds of celebrities to our doorstep. I'd gone to my fair share of films because of it, but I'd never been to their infamous cocktail party. Both Maddox and Josie were being recognized for their achievements after graduation. I spent the remainder of the night bouncing between the two since, apparently, neither was speaking with the other. That part was exhausting. And by midnight, I was ready to bounce.

I was still in my black cocktail dress and heels and had driven to the event with Maddox, which I was now realizing was a mistake. I'd have to get an Uber or something home.

But as soon as my feet were out on the old familiar roads with the old familiar Halloween crowds through Savannah, my exhaustion fell off. I stepped into one of the squares under the Spanish moss and breathed in my home. It had been awhile since I'd been back to visit. Gran had chided me for being too busy, but work had kept me occupied.

I stepped out of the square and out onto Bay Street. It was crowded despite the hour, and I pressed myself back into the overhang to avoid a raucous crowd of ghost-tour revelers. Suddenly, the door behind me pulled open, and I teetered on my heels before falling backward into the stranger.

"Oof," I gasped.

Hands came down around my waist. "Oh God, I'm sorry."

I stopped struggling and came slowly back to my feet. "My bad."

"I didn't expect anyone to be there."

I turned around to thank my rescuer, but when I saw who it was, I ceased breathing entirely. Derek and I gaped at one another. I hadn't seen him in three years. Not since we'd broken up at Harvard. I'd had no idea he was even in Savannah. My brain couldn't process any of it.

"Hey," he said finally.

"Derek," I said, stepping backward.

"Mars."

His eyes swept my fancy cocktail dress, down my pale legs, to the stilettos on my feet. I'd even gone to get my hair and makeup professionally done for the event. I had never really figured out how to make my curls behave. He looked at me as if he'd never seen me before.

"You look… stunning."

I blushed and took another tentative step backward. "Thank you."

He looked just as gorgeous as he always had. Though… rumpled. I'd seen Derek in every state of dress or undress, but I'd never thought of him as rumpled before. He had on a black suit with a white shirt and blue tie. The top button had been undone and his tie pulled loose from around his neck. The suit fit him perfectly, but it was as if he'd been sleeping in the thing. His eyes seemed distant or just exhausted. Even worse than those years of law school, which had wrung him dry.

"I…" He ran a hand back through his hair. It was longer than he'd worn it in college. The slight curl giving way to a full wave. Somehow, I liked it even more. "What are you doing in Savannah?"

"Maddox and Josie had a thing at the SCAD Film Festival." I glanced up at the building we were hovering in and saw the words *Ballentine Law*. "You're working for your dad?" It came out as more of an accusation than I'd intended.

He nodded. His jaw set. "Yeah. You?"

"Emory," I told him. "Neuroscience faculty."

"Of course. Congratulations."

"Thanks," I said softly.

It had been three years. Three long years without his face in my life. I'd dated since Derek. I'd even thought that I was in love. And somehow, one look at him made all the years just disappear.

Even if I couldn't forget the hurt. And I needed to get away before I started to forget that too.

"Well... good night," I said, taking another step past him.

For a few moments, as I walked away from him, I thought he'd let me go. He'd been hurt by what had happened too. A lot of what he'd said was true on my part. It had been both of our fault. Even if he'd driven the nail into the coffin.

But then he was there. "Wait..."

Wait. There was that word. That impossible word.

I stalled, took a deep breath, and then released it. Was I going to do this to myself? I bit my lip. Sometimes, love was messy and painful and made absolutely no sense, but it was still there regardless.

I turned back to face him. "What?"

"Don't go."

"Why?"

"Because... I don't know." He ran his hand back through his hair again. He looked lost, as if he truly had no idea why he had asked me to stop. "I can't let you leave."

I gulped. "I know that feeling."

"Get a drink with me."

I shouldn't.

"One drink."

Then, his smile hit me full-on. I felt like he crushed all the air from my lungs when he looked at me like that. Flashes of memories cascaded through my mind. Nights spent wrapped in his arms. The feel of his arms around me from the prow of his sailboat. A stolen glance over a stack of law books in the library.

I looked down. He was intoxicating, and I was drunk off of him in one glance. Fuck.

We walked side by side down Bay Street, veering toward City Market. We stopped at the bar of an upscale dining room. We were both dressed too nice for the dives, but this also felt safe. It wasn't a place I'd ever go with anyone else. I had no memories at these sorts of places.

I drank a sidecar as I listened to him discuss how he'd come home and taken over right where he'd left off. He was working himself to death, trying to reach partner. I could see the strain all over him. I told him all about my work at Emory. How I'd had a breakthrough with my dementia work. A few years too late for Gramps. But if it helped one person, it was worth it.

And slowly, we both relaxed. His exhaustion evaporated. My unease around him vanished. It was just like old times. As comforting and terrifying as that notion was. We hadn't seen each other in three years. I'd been *so* mad at him then, and somehow, we could still act just like we always had.

We left the bar after three drinks instead of one, of course, and headed to the water. I took the cobblestone steps in my heels like a newborn colt. These steps had been built in the 1800s. They were steep and uneven and terrible. A hundred percent not made for modern high heels. Derek offered his hand to help me down. I hesitated only a moment before placing my hand in his. Sparks ignited between us, and my stomach dipped at the contact. How? How could it still be this potent all these years later?

I made it down to the riverfront. We grabbed frozen drinks from Wet Willie's and then crossed River Street. I sipped at my alcoholic concoction, already buzzed from earlier, and felt all the alcohol go straight to my head. Derek finished his in record time, tossing it into a nearby trash can. Then, he leaned out against the rail overlooking the Savannah River. In the darkness, the water was a black abyss, mysterious and beautiful.

"Do you like being back?" I asked after I threw away my own drink and came to stand next to him.

"Nowhere else ever felt like home."

It mirrored my thoughts so perfectly that I nearly stumbled backward. No matter how much I'd tried to escape the South, it always called me home. I had gotten rid of my accent and worn plain clothes and gotten used to the food elsewhere. And still, Savannah with its Spanish moss and old Colonial squares and cobblestones just *was* home.

"Same. I miss it," I said.

Derek turned to face me. His features perfectly illuminated from the lights of the giant paddleboat. Time slowed to a crawl. My heart thudded in my chest. Derek Ballentine was a problem. He was all of the best and worst of me rolled into one ball of conflicted emotions. And still, I wanted him.

"I missed you," I admitted softly.

"I missed you too."

I stepped forward, leaning into him. His arm came around my back. And for a moment, we were transported to a different time. When I could have had this whenever I wanted it. When we had been meant to be together.

A butterfly whacked against my stomach as I worked up

the courage to look up into his handsome face. He met my gaze. A wanton, pained look in those hazel eyes. He wanted this as much as I did. So, I reached up on my tiptoes to claim the kiss that was within reach.

For a second, I could almost taste the brush of his lips.

Then, he sighed and dropped his forehead onto mine. “I can’t.”

My body shut down. I blushed furiously and pulled back, out of the warmth of his arms, away from the years of want. Because of course, this wasn’t what I’d thought it was. This was… insane.

“Marley,” he said, reaching for me.

“It’s fine.”

“Fuck,” he spat. He turned back out to the water. He was silent a handful of breaths. “I’m getting married.”

It felt like a punch to my gut. I actually gasped, stepping away from him, as if he’d been the one to hit me. I couldn’t even form words.

“Next weekend.”

I jerked another step away from him at the words. “Holy shit, Derek! What the fuck are you doing here with me? What the fuck is this?”

“I don’t know.” He squeezed his eyes shut. “I didn’t intend for it to happen.”‘

“You told me to wait! You could have let me walk away.”

“I planned to. I wasn’t going to go after you.”

“But you did!”

“I know. I… I couldn’t just let you walk away.”

“Why?”

“I don’t know,” he ground out and sounded like he meant it. I baffled him. I was beyond comprehension.

“Jesus, I am such an idiot,” I spat. “Here I thought… well,

it doesn't matter, does it? I almost trusted you. Even though I told myself that I never would again. God, I'm so stupid."

"No, Mars, this is my fault," he said, reaching for me again.

"You're fucking right it is." I stepped away from him. "I hope you're both *very happy*."

"Mars."

I waved him off and stormed away. And for once, he actually let me go.

32

SAVANNAH

JULY 22, 2017

"I'm fine, girls," Gran said. "You don't need to worry."

Lila and I shared a glance. We'd known each other long enough that we almost had the same twin ESP I had with Maddox. Gran was *not* okay. That was abundantly clear.

She was in the hospital. The doctor had said early stages of lymphoma. But they were still doing tests to determine what it was and how virulent. Regardless, she was weak. She was hooked up to oxygen and coughing around most of her words. She'd always looked so strong and resilient in my eyes. And right now, she looked so frail. It was the first time I'd ever wished that I'd gone into medicine and not neuroscience. Then, I could have helped her myself. Instead, I was the wrong kind of doctor.

"Stop worrying. Both of you," she insisted. "You have that reunion of yours tonight. I won't have you staying home because of me."

"But Gran," I said.

"No, *but Gran*," she said. She pointed at Lila. "You make sure that she goes."

"Okay, Gran," she whispered with a nod.

I leaned forward and pressed a kiss to her cheek. "I'll come back tomorrow."

"I love you, chickadee."

"I love you too."

"Love you, Gran," Lila said.

We stepped out of the hospital room without words. Lila put her arm around my shoulders and held me that way as we left the hospital.

It wasn't until we were in the car that she finally spoke, "I'm so sorry, Mars."

"Me too. She looked so rough."

"She's in good hands. They'll take care of her."

"I know. I feel helpless, like there's something else I should be doing."

"You don't like to be out of control. I get it. But I'll be here for you through the whole thing."

I nodded at her and then tried to shake the malaise off. "We should go to your reunion."

Mine had been the night before. It had been pretty fun. Not that I kept up with anyone from my high school, except my brother, who had reluctantly gone with us. But I was going to Lila's more for moral support. Ash would be there, and I knew that she didn't want to see him. Or at least, she acted like she didn't want to see him. Not after the church steps at Christmas. What a nightmare.

"You sure you still want to go?" Lila asked. "We could skip."

"I'm committed."

Lila shrugged. "Okay. Let's go show those bitches how awesome we are."

I laughed as she drove downtown. We parked in a garage near the riverfront property that had been donated by the

Talmadge family for the event. Lila had apparently forgotten to actually *read* the invitation and hadn't even realized that Ash had gotten them the venue from his family's real estate fortune. Typical.

"This sounds like a supremely bad idea," Lila said as we walked up to the reunion.

"You've had a shitty few months. What's the worst that could happen?"

Lila clapped her hand over my mouth. "Don't jinx us. The worst is always waiting around the corner."

I couldn't keep from laughing. "Okay, fine. Chill. It's just an excuse to be in Savannah while Gran is sick. I don't know how much longer she has. I wanted you to be here, and I used this as an excuse."

"Mars," she said, pulling me into a hug, "I'm so sorry about Gran."

"Me too," I whispered. The thought ran unchecked through my mind. All the worst-case scenarios. She was *Gran*. She was my best friend. My rock. What would I do without her? "I don't know what I'm going to do. I have teaching obligations, but..."

"But if something happens to Gran, then take the time off that you need."

I nodded and looked away. "Yeah. I'll figure it out."

I could take a sabbatical to be here with her for a semester. That was about the best that I could do. I'd have to plan it out for my schedule when I got home. So, when we knew what the prognosis was, I'd be ready.

After taking the elevator up to the top floor, we grabbed name tags and entered the cheesy Catholic high school reunion. At least they were serving alcohol. I wasn't sure how we'd have survived otherwise. We grabbed drinks and then proceeded to wallflower the entire event.

"I don't like any of these people," Lila whispered to me.

I snorted. I couldn't agree more, but still, I needed to get her through this. "You were here for three years. You had to have liked someone."

"Yeah, Ash."

"Right." I picked at my nails. "Well, there's Shelly Thomas. Looks like she's coming over here."

Lila took a deep breath and let it out. "Let's just go."

"What? Really?" I asked.

Lila had partially come to this whole thing to show the girl who had tormented her through her senior year that she was successful. But in the end, it didn't matter.

"Yeah. Come on."

I shrugged and turned to follow Lila out. This wasn't my event anyway. I didn't need to be here.

Then, I heard a voice behind us. "Marley Nelson."

The sound of Derek's voice slid down my back. I froze in place and suddenly forgot how to breathe. What was he *doing* here? Derek had been a Holy Cross boy, but he'd been two years older than us. Of course, he knew Ash Talmadge. I just hadn't thought for a moment that he would come to this reunion.

And oh fuck, was his *wife* here? Did I have to suffer through seeing Kasey in all of her tall, blonde model glory?

Not to mention, I'd still never told Lila what had happened between us. I'd compartmentalized it and shoved it so far away from me that I never, ever had to look at it again. What the fuck was I going to do?

I slowly turned, my eyes narrowing to pinpricks. "Derek."

"How are you doing? I haven't seen you since—"

"I remember," I snapped.

Lila glanced over at me with round eyes. She'd felt the

full force of my anger in those couple of words to Derek. She didn't know what it meant, but she knew it meant something. It was the first time Lila had ever seen Derek and me together. Of course, she'd know as soon as she saw him. Fuck.

"Hey, Derek," Lila said quickly as if she could defuse the tension.

But Derek was still looking at me. He was fucking smiling. He'd married someone else, and he was smiling at *me.* In that moment, I hated him. I hated how goddamn handsome he was in his sharp suit. That he'd somehow filled out even more with broad shoulders and a tapered waist. His hair was shorter than ever. I could barely find the hint of curl that had been there for so many years.

Then, he glanced away from me to my friend. The one person he'd never officially met in my life. He grinned as if it were an inside joke.

"Delilah, right?" he asked.

"That's right," Lila said.

"You dated Ash Talmadge."

As if the bastard hadn't already known all of that.

Lila flushed. "I did."

"He's a cool guy."

Lila nodded uncomfortably. "Sure."

And something in me erupted. I couldn't stand here and pretend that everything was okay. Sure, he'd never met Lila before and jumped at the chance. But he was the one who had married someone else. This was *his* fault this time. Not mine.

"Leave her alone, Derek. Can't you see you're making her uncomfortable?"

"Oh, calm down, Minivan," he said with a soft laugh. The laugh that said the nickname with a caress and not the bite that other people had said it with. My toes curled in my shoes, and I hated that he could elicit that reaction from me. "We're just reminiscing."

"Minivan?" Lila asked in confusion.

"We should go," I said. "Good-bye, Derek."

I grabbed Lila's arm and yanked her away from him.

"What was that?" Lila asked as soon as we were away.

"What was what?"

Lila gave me a pointed look. "You *freaked* out on him."

"He's an asshole."

Lila pulled back on my arm, dragging me to a stop. "Okay. But I've never seen you act like this."

I clenched my jaw. What the fuck could I say? How could I explain what I'd held back from her all those years? I told her the bare minimum. "He went to Harvard Law when I was there for my PhD. He's an ass."

"But he's hot."

My face flushed at those words. I pinched myself and looked away. "So?"

"Oh my God, are you into him?" Lila asked, all excited. It was as if she had just sprung water in the desert.

"No!" I gasped fervently. "How could you even suggest that? I hate him!"

"Fine line," Lila said with a smirk.

"Maybe for you!"

"All right." She raised her arms in surrender. "If you say so."

Lila turned back to look at Derek but instead found Ash Talmadge waiting there for her. He smiled at Lila, an invitation for more. For everything with him.

I winced at that look. Ash and Lila were combustible and problematic. I hated how much it reminded me of me and Derek.

"Lila," I whispered, "are you going to talk to him?"

Ash raised his glass toward us. Lila wavered. She wanted to go, and yet she wouldn't let herself. Not after what had happened with her, Ash, and Cole.

"No," she finally said.

I reached for her hand and squeezed. "Are you sure?"

"No."

Ash stepped forward, need scrawled all over his face.

Lila shook her head. "We should go."

So, we left.

* * *

I convinced Lila to head to the riverfront for a drink. We both needed one after that. We'd been sideswiped with feelings that neither of us had wanted to encounter. I still couldn't believe that Derek had been there.

We sat down at a table overlooking the water, nursing our drinks in silence.

Then, Lila broke it. "You know Derek."

"Yeah, I do," I said with a sigh.

"How do you know him?"

My head tipped back. "I know him like you know Ash."

Lila's eyes rounded. Those words had said everything I hadn't been able to say all these years. "Why didn't you tell me?"

"I don't know." I laughed softly and set my drink down. "Yes, I do. I mean, it's stupid, but if I told you, it would be real."

Lila shot me a sympathetic look. "Was it that bad?"

"Yes and no. It was... everything. A whole new world that I'd never, ever understood before. It was like I was really breathing for the first time. And then it burned down over and over again."

Lila touched my hand. "That I do understand. I wish you'd told me. Did Josie know?"

I nodded. "Yeah."

"Well, at least you had one of us."

"And Gran."

"Always Gran," Lila said softly. "So, when was this?"

"It was when you were in PT school and you were so swamped. I don't know. I held it secret for so long, expecting it to fall apart and then it did. A self-fulfilling prophecy."

"Do you still care about him?"

A tear slipped down my cheek, and I swiped at it angrily. "I don't know."

"Mars," she whispered, "no more lying or hiding. It's me and you. You know how I feel about Ash and Cole. Walking away today was one of the hardest things I've ever done."

"Well, it doesn't matter anymore. Derek married someone else."

Lila winced. "I'm so sorry."

"And there was a moment when I thought it could work out again. I was in Savannah for Josie and Maddox's SCAD thing last Halloween, remember?"

"Yeah. I was at a Falcons game and couldn't come."

"That weekend, I ran into Derek. We spent the entire night walking around the city. We nearly kissed, and then he told me he was marrying someone else."

"What?" Lila gasped. "That's terrible."

I buried my face in my hands. All of the pain came crashing down on me all over again. "I wanted it to work out so bad. I've never gotten over him. I hate him so much. I hate him with every fiber of my being for the way he hurt and manipulated me, but..."

Lila stroked my back. "But you love him that much too."

I sniffled, wiping at my eyes, and met my best friend's gaze. She understood like maybe no one else ever would. "I love him even more. And seeing him, it all comes back every time. I want to punch him and kiss him. I want it to all work out and for him to come crawling back to say he made a huge mistake. But… he's never going to do that, is he?"

"I don't know, Mars. But I'm glad you told me, and you're not alone with this hurt anymore."

Lila pulled me into a hug. Our broken hearts were still a crushed mess. Even if everything else was demolished and impossible, at least we had each other.

33

SAVANNAH

PRESENT

Finding parking in Savannah was always such a nightmare. Derek's house was in the heart of the city with tourists rampaging through the goddamn streets at any given day of the week. Finally, I found a spot a few blocks from his place. I shouldered the bag I'd put together for our sailing trip. Amelia and Ash were meeting us at Derek's in twenty for us all to go out on the water. Since I hadn't seen them for my birthday, I'd wanted to do another outing with the four of us. Derek had seemed to approve.

I practically skipped up the sidewalk and knocked three times on the front door. Ever since my birthday, I'd been trying to see Derek as much as I could. It was reckless, considering the case. And being reckless with Derek had always blown up in my face. Still, I wanted this to work. It worried me that I wanted it to work, and yet I was still doing it. Maybe it was Gran's passing that was making me give in to this one more time. But I was happy, and that was all that mattered.

The door swung open, and a gorgeous blonde stood

before me. She was tall, maybe five-ten, with legs for days in a baby-blue romper and wedges. Her makeup was immaculate and hair perfectly Southern. Her pretty features sneered as she asked, "What do you want?"

My smile dropped and eyes rounded. Because I knew who this gorgeous blonde was. I'd never met her in person, but I'd looked Derek up on social media just once to see the miraculous woman that had gotten him to settle down. And that woman was standing in front of me.

"Uh..." I said. "Wrong house."

I backed up, fear and disgust boiling through me.

"Kasey!" Derek barked from somewhere in the house. "Why the fuck are you answering my door?"

She whipped around, her hair flying. "Someone *knocked*."

"We're done here." His eyes passed Kasey in the doorway to find me slowly backing away. He looked panicked and then furious. "Marley, wait..."

Ah, *wait*. That wonderful word that had ruined me time and time again.

Kasey turned back to face me. Her eyes were now scrutinizing. "*You're* Marley?" She'd heard my name before. Oh great. "Seriously, Derek?"

"Leave," he shouted at her. "Just leave. Christ."

Kasey crossed her arms. "Fine. Just... think about what we were talking about."

He glared with fiery hatred on his face as she walked away. I'd never seen him look at anyone like that. Not even people he actually disliked. He'd always been so good at hiding his emotions. But he couldn't do that with Kasey.

"Uh... I guess I should go too," I said.

"No, no, no, no, no," he said quickly, stepping in front of

me. "Kasey and I are so far past over. It wasn't what it looked like."

"What did it look like?"

"Like my ex-wife answered the door," he said slowly.

"That is what happened."

"Yes, but it's not..." He sighed. "We're divorced for a reason. A damn good reason at that. Can I at least tell you what happened and let you decide?"

I arched an eyebrow at his offer. He'd been purposely reticent with information about the divorce. Amelia had been more forthcoming than Derek ever had been. I'd wondered, but I wouldn't push. Finally, my curiosity won out.

"Okay."

He breathed out a sigh of relief because I'd agreed. I had no reason to. Not after all the shit we'd gone through. Not after the way he'd first *told* me that he was getting married. It had been years since that day when I'd stood on the riverfront and he'd told me he was marrying someone else. It felt like a lifetime ago... and also just yesterday.

I followed him back inside his house. I'd never been inside the three-story mansion he'd purchased and renovated downtown. It was walking distance to his office and had to have cost a small fortune. It was also one of the most perfectly elegant homes I'd ever seen. It outshone the giant monstrosity that was his father's house by a long shot. This had clearly been done with love, and I could feel it in every stone and painted wall and carefully curated art collection.

"Your house is beautiful," I whispered softly as I followed him into a sitting room. I took a seat across the small room from him.

"Thanks. My, uh, mom helped me with it."

I blinked at him. "Your mom? She's back in Savannah?"

Last I'd heard, Margie Ballentine had been cheated on by his father. Doug had taken his mistress, a young Kathy, as his wife. Margie had taken a sizable chunk of money and moved to Charleston to be around her brother and his kids. Derek had spent a few summers with his cousins Daron, Tye, and Marina. They were still close, but he never had been with his mom.

"We reconnected," he said with a shrug. "She apologized for leaving the way she did after it all went down, but I don't really blame her. I'd want to get the hell out of Dodge too. But she'd been an interior designer before she left, and she began to pursue her real passion—art."

"Well, it sounds like she got the better end of the deal."

"Yes. Though it has little to do with Kasey."

"I figured you were stalling."

He laughed softly. "God, I've missed you."

My heart warmed at those words. It was so easy to forget all the baggage when I was with him like this. Even after just seeing that his ex-wife was somehow still in his life, I wanted his praise.

"So?" I prompted.

"So," he repeated, "I met Kasey at a golfing event for the company. She played in college, and we played a round together. We dated for two years before we got married. She was old country-club money, and her dad works in the shipping industry. She went to St. Catherine's. We ran in the same circles."

My throat closed at those words. All the ways that Kasey was something that I was not or ever would be.

"After we were together for two years, I thought that I knew her. I was wrong."

I held my breath, waiting to hear that she'd cheated on

him. It felt like that had to be the explanation. Him reliving what had happened to his mother when he was a child.

"So, who was he?" I asked.

Derek narrowed his eyes. "What do you mean?"

"Did she cheat on you?"

He laughed sardonically. "I almost wish that she had. But no, she was faithful, as far as I know.

"Kasey was a successful real estate agent when we met on her way to opening her own firm. She had big dreams. And then we got married, and every single one of them disappeared. She quit her job without telling me and began to spend the hours she should have been at work shopping. At first, it was just designer clothes and shoes and bags. Expensive—obnoxiously expensive—but not a drain. Since she hadn't told me that she quit, I assumed she was mostly spending her own money on it." He shrugged and looked distant. "I was working eighty to a hundred hours a week at the firm. I wasn't around enough then to pay enough attention.

"Then, everything seemed to happen all at once. I found out that she'd quit her job while she was away on what I thought was a business trip. Instead, she'd gone to St. Barts with her friends for a week with a cost in the low six figures."

I gasped. "Holy shit!"

"While I waited to confront her about the spending and her job, I went through the bills. She'd told me that she was handling them. That I needed to just relax after work and not worry about money. I'd been played. She was running up all of our credit cards. Three of them were maxed out, and apparently, she'd opened *seven* more that were well on their way."

My eyes rounded in horror. “Derek, that’s terrible. I can’t… I honestly cannot even imagine.”

“She had an insatiable appetite for money. We had a huge fight when she got home. I cut up all the cards. I put limits on my bank accounts. She was furious and hit me, scratching my arms and face and screaming like a banshee. I’d never seen anyone act like that.” His eyes were so far away. “I still tried to salvage the situation. I wanted her to go to therapy.” He shook his head. “Suffice it to say, none of that worked out. I was saddled with all of her debt during the divorce, but I got out without having to pay her alimony. She had been counting on that money to continue living this insane life, but it didn’t happen, and she still has the audacity to ask me for more money.”

My mind was reeling from this news. And by how similar it felt to my childhood. All the times my mom had train-wrecked back into our lives to ask Gran for money. The way she begged until it happened. Then, she was gone again with some new man who was *the one*. When it inevitably didn’t work, she always came crawling back. And Gran had always given in until the very, very end, the last one that had ruined all of this.

“Believe me when I say that I know something of what you went through,” I whispered. “I can’t imagine the depths of her betrayal, but I do remember what it is like to live with someone like that. To always be looking for the next time they tried to ruin everything.”

He frowned as he realized I was talking about my mom. That little piece wedged between us uncomfortably. “I’m sorry, Mars.”

“Me too.”

“This is why I pursued you when I saw you were back in town.”

"This?" I asked in confusion.

"You were the only person who ever cared about me... just me."

Our eyes met in the distance, and my heart melted all over again. I crossed the sitting room and curled up into his lap. I rested my head against his chest, just listening to the soft beat of his heart.

"Why is this always so hard?"

He kissed my hair. "It's not. You and me, Mars, we've always been easy. That's why I want you back. I want you to be mine. I want all those things we talked about when I was still too young and immature to ask for them."

"But..."

He tilted my chin up to look at him. "Don't think about it. Just be here with me. Just be mine."

I wanted it to be that easy. To not have one more thing between us.

Then, the doorbell rang, and Ash crashed into his house with a boisterous, "Honey, I'm home!"

Amelia giggled behind him. "Shut up, Ash."

They barreled into the sitting room just as I slid off of Derek's lap.

Ash raised his eyebrows. "Are we interrupting?"

Derek threaded his hand into mine. "Nope."

Amelia grinned from ear to ear. "I love seeing y'all together again."

"It's adorable," Ash said with an eye roll. "Can we go now?"

"Yeah. I just had to deal with Kasey."

"More money?" Amelia snarled.

"You guessed it in one."

"She's the worst," Ash said.

I fell into step with them, as if I'd always belonged there.

It was easier than thinking about all the problems that we still had to face. If I even was able to. The case was only a few weeks away, and after that, I had to return to Atlanta to my job at Emory. What would happen then?

When I looked up into Derek's smiling face, I decided I didn't care. This was everything that I'd ever wanted with Derek. I wanted to live in this moment forever.

34

SAVANNAH

PRESENT

Derek docked the sailboat with Ash's help while us girls huddled together. It was always a few degrees colder on the water, and the breeze had chilled Amelia and me to our bones. Thank God for the extra blankets Derek had on board. Besides the cold, we had a perfect day out on the water. The wind had filled the sails. Ash was drinking less and starting to look like a person again. And Derek and I were just *together*. As we should have always been.

"There we are, ladies," Derek said, tying the boat to the dock. "You're all set to return to the heat."

Derek offered me his hand as I clambered out of the boat. Ash helped Amelia out, and then we all headed to Ash's Audi SUV. I let Amelia take the front seat and sat in the back with Derek. He kept his arm around me, pressing occasional kisses into my hair on the drive back.

Ash dropped us off at Derek's place, and I waved goodbye as they drove away.

Derek pulled my hand to his mouth and pressed kisses into my skin. "Don't go."

I laughed. "I've been with you all day."

"So? Stay longer. Stay forever."

I looked up into his eyes in surprise. I was expecting to see him laughing with that pouty smirk on his lips. But he was serious. He was actually serious.

"I'd like that," I admitted. I pulled my hand out of his. "Can I rain-check for later? Maybe tonight?"

He stepped forward into my personal space, cupping my jaw with his hands. "Whatever you want, Mars. I just missed you and want every bit of time you'll give me."

I smiled and leaned into the kiss he planted on my lips. "I want that too."

"Then, hurry back," he breathed against my mouth. "You should just stay the rest of the weekend."

"So greedy," I teased.

"For you. Yes." He hungrily kissed me again. "Just think of all the things that I'm going to do to you when you get back here. I have a whole list in my head. It's probably going to take a long, *long* time to get through it."

I flushed from head to toe. "Filthy."

But I pressed myself into him regardless, devouring all of his kisses and imagining every single one of those things he'd do to me later. Which was likely his intention. He wanted me to rush back to him—or preferably, not leave at all.

We'd waited so long for this. So long. I should have been able to wait a little bit longer. It was hard enough breaking away from him to get back in my car. I didn't want to do that. I wanted to stay and be with him and make up for all the lost time. It was easy to drown in Derek Ballentine.

"Mars," he said, leaning into my car to meet my gaze. He pressed a kiss onto my mouth one last time. "I couldn't let you go without that."

I giggled and kissed him again. "You're insatiable."

"Yes. Come back soon."

He pulled back and tapped the roof of my car. My heart was full, and my stomach was all fluttery. I hadn't felt like this in so long. So very long. I parked outside of Gran's house, skipping up the front steps and doing a little twirl on the porch. The light blinked on the answering machine. I deleted the spam messages and ignored the one from the executor of the will. I didn't want to think about that today of all days. I just wanted to shower the sea salt off of me, drink some of Gran's sweet tea, and answer my work emails for a few hours before going to see Derek again.

I T-shirt-dried my hair, plopping it on the top of my head, and then headed downstairs. I poured myself some tea and got settled in when the doorbell rang. I audibly groaned. Now was not the time.

I pushed my laptop away from me and trudged to the front door. I swung it open, only to find my mother standing on the doorstep.

"No," I said, trying to close the door before she could get her hooks in.

"Marley Sue," my mom said. She held her hand out to stop me from slamming the door in her face.

"What do you want, *Hannah*?" I emphasized her first name and not the fact that she'd birthed me.

She sighed. "I want to talk."

"I don't want to talk."

"I've been worried about you."

"Since when?" I demanded.

"I'm your mother. Surely, a girl can be worried about her own flesh and blood."

I rolled my eyes. "Again, what do you want? We both know that you're not here because you care about me."

And for the first time in a long time, I saw tears come to my mom's eyes. "Oh baby, I'm sorry."

I retreated uncomfortably from the display. My mom was fierce and a train wreck and resolutely stubborn, but she was never vulnerable or sad. Despite everything, I felt for her. Just for a second, but it must have been long enough for it to show on my face. Even when I hadn't wanted it to. She had to be up to something, but she was still a person.

"Can I come in?" Mom asked.

I tipped my head back and then swung the door open. "This better be good."

My mom strode inside as if she owned the place, which immediately got my hackles up.

"What's this about?"

She turned around and swiped at her eyes. "I think we got off on the wrong foot."

My eyebrows shot up. "Our entire life? You might need to be more specific."

"Since you've been back in town."

"Oh, why would that be? Is it because you're contesting Gran's will?" I asked sarcastically.

"That's not personal, honey. You know it isn't about you. It's not that I want you and your brother to have nothing. I just think that Gran changed her will under duress. It was done a mere two months before her death when she was dying from cancer."

"Because of the fight *you* had with her. It was her money. She could do with it what she wanted."

My mom nodded. "I know. I agree. But it was all split up between us for decades. It seems unlikely she'd change her mind about that on her own after so long. I pushed all of her buttons growing up, and she never cut me off before."

"Well, she finally saw who you were."

She tilted her head. "Do you really think that?"

I crossed my arms. "I was there. I remember how upset she was."

"Enough to cut me off forever?"

She had been, but my mom would never accept that. I thought Gran should have done it a long time ago. Mom had abandoned Gran in the same way that she had abandoned me. That was what she did.

"You really think that," my mom said softly. "I thought we could get along. We could see eye to eye on this."

"Why? Why would you think that?"

"Isn't it obvious?"

"No?"

"Like mother, like daughter."

I blinked at her. "I have no idea what you're talking about."

"You're sleeping with my attorney. He has enough money to comfortably take care of you. We can call it even then, honey."

I balked at her words. The horror and outrage dawning on me. "*That's* why you're here? Because you found out that I'm dating Derek?"

"Of course. I understand your long game."

"How did you even find out?"

"What does it matter? I'm not mad. I'd probably do the same in your situation."

My face went slack. She thought I was sleeping with Derek to get his money. Just like she had always done. It was her only logical explanation to finding out that we were together. And I couldn't fucking believe it.

"Gross, Mom. No! Derek and I are not together for his money."

"That's not what his wife is saying."

I reared back. "Derek is divorced. Are you saying that you heard about us from Kasey?"

She snapped her fingers at me. "Kasey. Yes, that's her name. Derek's wife. I met her at a golf tournament this morning with my latest beau."

"Ex-wife," I corrected. "They're divorced. Not together."

My mom shrugged, and a sly smile touched her lips. "You're sure?"

My stomach knotted at that question. At the way she thought that she had me here. "Yes, I'm fucking sure. And if you're here to extort me because the guy I'm seeing has money, you're in a losing battle. That is never going to happen."

I couldn't believe that Kasey was claiming to still be married to Derek. But on the other hand, I could. Or to think about how my mom had heard about it all and twisted it in her head. That somehow, I was *like* my mother. It infuriated me. I was nothing like her. Nothing.

"It's time for you to go," I said, storming to the door. "I thought you were going to actually be a human being, but apparently, I was wrong."

"Marley," she said with a shake of her head.

But I yanked the door open and pointed for her to leave. "Go."

Then, something flipped in my mom's brain. It was like a lightbulb. I'd seen her do it to Gran so many times that I shouldn't have been surprised that she'd do it to me.

"Fine," she snarled. "You want to think we're so different, but Derek is just manipulating you."

I rolled my eyes. "What are you even going on about?"

"You think that he likes you? He's trying to win a case. For being so smart, you sure are stupid sometimes. Don't shoot the messenger."

There was nothing at all that I could say to that. This was classic narcissist bait. No matter how I felt, I couldn't show it. Was it possible that Derek was using me to try to win this case? Sure, anything was possible. Was it probable? No. Not the way he'd talked to me today. Not after all this time. Derek didn't need to resort to that shit to win me over or to win the case.

"Go," I repeated.

"If I were you, Marley Sue, I would make sure that what you're getting out of this is everything you think it is. Because that boy is going to realize that you're not worth it any day now, and you're going to be left with exactly as much as you had before—nothing."

I narrowed my eyes at my mom. "I know exactly what's happening between me and Derek, and I see straight through you."

"If you want to be manipulated by him—"

"I'm not going to be manipulated by him," I snapped. "I've had *years* of practice dealing with a narcissistic manipulator. All thanks to you. So, I don't need to hear any more of your bullshit. I'm done. I'm as done as Gran was when she cut you out of her will. So, *leave*."

My mom glared at me. "I'll see you in court."

"Looking forward to it."

She grinned devilishly back at me. "Looking forward to Derek standing at my side through the proceedings?"

"To watching you lose and getting exactly as much as you deserve—nothing."

Then, I slammed the door in her face.

My hands were clenched into fists, and I wanted to bang them on the door. Or better yet, into my mother's face. She was so fucking horrid. She'd come over here to hurt me. To try to get under my skin.

I sighed and sank onto the ground with my back to the door. I wanted to say that it hadn't worked. But it had. It wasn't that I thought Derek was manipulating me or still married or that I was *anything* like my mother. Those things were fantasies she'd concocted to get to me. It had made me realize something else. Something I'd been avoiding the last couple months.

Derek and I couldn't survive this court case.

35

SAVANNAH

PRESENT

My heart was heavy as I parked in front of Derek's house. I stared up at the front door of the three-story brownstone. The door was a soft blue. Everything carefully and meticulously cared for. It was so very Derek. And for a few scant hours, I'd pictured myself in that house. Seen all the what *ifs* flit through my vision. All the ways we'd make it work *this time*. As if all the times before hadn't prepared me for what was to come.

With a deep breath, I popped open the door of my car. I shouldered my purse and walked up to the steps as if I had lead in my shoes. Each step was heavier than the one before it until I was practically dragging my body to the front door. I couldn't knock. I didn't want to get to the inevitable any faster. I'd stalled long enough by dropping by Maddox's place on the way here. I couldn't put this off any longer.

I knocked on the front door and fiddled with my fingers. I hated this. I hated everything about it. My stomach was in knots. My body ached. All I wanted to do was run. Run and hide and not deal with any of this. But I wasn't a kid anymore. I couldn't run away from all of my problems. I had to face them head-on. There was nothing to be done about this one. No solution that I could envision for it. And that made it all the worse.

Derek pulled the door open, a huge welcoming smile coming to his face at the sight of me. "Hey! You're back early."

I nodded. "Sort of."

His eyes drifted past me to my car parked in front of his house. His smile faltered at the sight of the packed backseat. "When I said stay for the weekend, I didn't know you'd be moving in." He cracked it as a joke, but I saw the worry on his face. He had to know what my full car meant and wanted to deflect.

I finally met his gaze and shook my head just once. "I'm not."

He sighed. "Don't."

"Don't what?"

"Do whatever you're about to do."

"I'm sorry, Derek."

"Don't be sorry either," he insisted. "Just come inside and spend the weekend with me, Mars."

"I wish I could," I told him honestly. I swallowed around the lump in my throat. "You have no idea how much I want that."

"Then, forget everything else." He reached for my hand, and like a weak fool, I let him take it.

I glanced down at our joined hands. If only what I wanted and what I knew to be right were the same thing. But they weren't. And they couldn't be. No matter how we rolled the dice, our time was up.

"I'm going back home."

He tugged me just a little closer. "*This* is your home."

I gulped. "Back to Atlanta."

"Why?" he demanded.

"I can't lie to you, Derek. I'm way past that. My mom came by to see me."

He narrowed his eyes at that. "So... what? You're leaving because she got in your head? What did she say?"

"It's not so much what she said. Though she tried her best to ruin my life. You should know that Kasey is telling people that you're still married and that, I guess, I'm your mistress."

"What?" he practically roared in horror.

I held my hand up. "Do with that information what you will, but I set the record straight with my mom. She both suggested I should date you for your money"—he winced, the hit striking home, as I'd known it would—"or that we were only together so that you could manipulate me to win the case."

"I would never," he snarled.

"I know. I'm not accusing you of anything, Derek. I'm letting you know that I don't believe a word out of her mouth. I never have. She's rotten and spoiled and festering. I'm smarter than her tricks."

He breathed a sigh of relief but then realized I was still leaving. "Then why?"

"Because her point was wrong, but the conclusion was the same. We can't be together."

"Marley—"

"Please, don't make this harder than it has to be."

"Harder than it has to be?" he demanded. "It was hard enough the first time. I don't want you to go."

I nodded and bit my lip. "I know. I know, it was. I don't want it to be like that again. But this just isn't going to work with the case between us. You know that's true. It's why you've been avoiding bring it up."

"We can survive this, Mars."

I barreled forward, saying all the things I never wanted to say. "We can't. It wouldn't be fair of me to ask you to give up the case. You've worked all this time to make partner.. It's your dream. And it's not fair to me for you to stay on the case. We can't survive both scenarios. There's no *winning* here. There's only getting out before either of us gets hurt."

"Too late for that."

"I know," I whispered, swiping at a tear.

My heart was being shredded from the inside out, even though I was doing the right thing. I was approaching this as an adult. Looking at it from all sides. I wanted Derek, but it wasn't that simple. Maybe it never had been.

"We've spent fifteen years trying to make this work. If it didn't work before, it's definitely not going to work now. Not with this between us. Not like this."

"So, you're just going to run?"

"I'm not running," I told him calmly. I wasn't. Running would have meant handing the keys to the house to Maddox, getting in the car, and never looking back. This was the sane, rational way to do this. It was the only way to do this. "That's why I'm here. I'm telling you the truth. It sucks, but it's still the truth."

He looked distraught by my words. As if he could make me take them back. Go back to the moment this morning when we'd been pretending like the case didn't exist. If only I had been able to keep business and personal separate, but that wasn't realistic. My business *was* personal, and that was the difference.

"Deep down, you know that I'm right," I told him. "We were treading water, and as easy as I find it to drown in you, I want to survive this time."

"What if I don't want you to go?" he asked, just shy of begging.

I stood on my tiptoes and placed a soft kiss on his perfect lips. "It's okay."

"Please," he breathed against my lips. "We can figure this out."

"And what happens when I go back to Atlanta at the end of this semester?" I demanded, asking all the hard questions we'd put aside. "What happens then, Derek? Your job and life are here. Mine is four hours away. We can't do long distance forever. I don't *want* to live my life four hours away. It was always going to end. This was just... a summer fling."

"It's not the summer." He brushed a lock of my hair backward, staring down into my eyes. "And it's not a fling."

"I'm sorry," I told him. "I really am. But this is good-bye."

He reached for me, but I backed up. I had to get out of there, or I was going to start really crying. This was the right thing to do. It was going to save us both a lot of pain. Even if it hurt us more in the short-term.

He took a step after me, but I shook my head. This was it. This was the end. No more back and forth. Fifteen years, and nothing had changed. I could want this so bad, but it didn't mean it was going to work. We'd been living in a fantasy. In real life, it didn't work out.

So, I turned away from him and ran back to my car. I pulled out of the street and checked my rearview mirror. He stood on the sidewalk, watching me go. It wasn't until he disappeared in my mirror that the tears started to fall.

PART V

36

SAVANNAH

JUNE 14, 2019

"I can't believe that I'm going to miss the wedding." Gran all but pouted from her hospital bed.

"Don't worry about the wedding. Let's focus on you getting better."

I sank back down into the chair opposite her. She had been doing so well. The cancer diagnosis had come in two years ago, and we hadn't been sure if she was going to make it. But she had recovered slowly but surely. Then, *bam*! It had hit all over again. Stronger than ever.

I couldn't even believe we were here again. That, on the eve of Lila's wedding, I'd be waiting to find out how long Gran had left to live. I had to be back in a few hours for the dress rehearsal. Lila had told me that I could skip if need be, but I wanted to be there for my best friend. But I also *needed* to be here for Gran.

Maddox was asleep in the other chair in the small room. He'd been in LA for the last couple weeks, working on a new movie. He did most of his animation work from with own company in Savannah, but every now and then, he'd disappear to LA. He'd taken a red-eye in for Lila's wedding, and when he found out about Gran's health, he'd come straight to the hospital.

"It'll be fine, chickadee. We've been here before, and we came out ahead."

We had. I wanted to guarantee that we'd be that lucky again. Gran wasn't a spry, young chick anymore. She had always seemed so strong and healthy. But the last two years after her diagnosis had really taken it out of her.

"We want that again, Gran," I told her. "It'll help that I'll be back here next semester."

"Are you sure that you want to put your research on hold for that long?"

"Yes," I said confidently. "I can still manage my lab from a distance, and I won't have any teaching obligations while I'm on sabbatical. It's more important to me to be with you for six straight months. I'll be able to help around the house. You need someone to take care of you."

Gran waved at me. "Don't mother me, Marley Sue."

I laughed. "Are you saying you don't want me home?"

"Of course not. I'd love your company. I just don't want you to give up your career to be with me. I can take care of myself."

"Good. Then, I'll be there. It's not giving up my career anyway. It's just a semester." I hitched my thumb at Maddox. "He's clearly not around enough to help."

She laughed fondly at Maddox. "I'm so proud of both of you. Following your dreams and changing the world."

Tears stung my eyes at Gran's words. She always knew the right thing to say to make me tear up. It was both wonderful and obnoxious.

"I love you, Gran."

"I love you too."

We sat in silence, listening to the beeping of the machines and waiting.

Finally, the door opened. I jumped to my feet, anxiety cresting through me. I wanted to act like I was ready to deal with this all over again even if I could never, ever be ready for what was about to happen.

Then, my mom stepped into the hospital room. "Hi."

I froze, fear replacing my anxiety. This was never a good sign. I should have been glad that the adult was here to take care of the situation, but I knew better. I knew exactly who my mother was.

"What are you doing here?" I asked.

"Marley Sue," Gran said, "be kind to your mother."

My mom shot Gran a reassuring smile. "It's okay, Mom."

Maddox stirred from his chair. He blinked blearily up at the situation in the room. "Fuck, I need coffee."

"Language, Maddox," Gran said.

"You want some too?" He pointed at me.

I stared back at him helplessly. Despite the years, we still had our twin ESP. He sighed and straightened in his chair, massaging a crick in his neck. I didn't want him to go. I couldn't be alone in this room with our mother, but I couldn't leave Gran to deal with her either.

"I'd like a cup," our mom said.

Maddox snorted. "I guess coffee can wait."

"I got your message that you were in the hospital," Mom said.

Gran smiled tentatively. She'd at least learned enough over the years to be cautious. Even if she couldn't quite move to pessimism. If it were me, I'd never have let my mom know about this shit.

"I'm glad you came."

"Of course. Ruth should be here after work."

Gran smiled at knowing that her daughters were both going to be here. For a second, I saw the light in my Gran's eyes. As if everything would be all right again.

Mom stepped up to Gran's side. She wrinkled her nose slightly at the hospital bed and all the equipment. It wasn't exactly her aesthetic. Her hair had been bleached an unnatural blonde. So bright that it was nearly white. I'd never seen that color on the woman who I sometimes thought looked like me. Everything was blown out and painted on and fake. Her dress was a mint-green number with lots of frills and high, *high* heels. Her skin was bronze. She was stunning regardless of age, and at the same time, she was absolutely hideous.

"How are you feeling?" she asked.

"I've been better, but I'm sure they're going to let me out of here soon."

Mom looked up at me, and I shook my head. I didn't think that was likely.

Her smile just widened. "I bet you are. You've always been a fighter. Just like me."

Gran tipped her head slightly. Mom had never fought for *anything*. "If you say so. I'm just glad you're here."

She put her hand on Mom's hand. One spotted with age and the other beginning to show the first signs of aging. One of the few places my mom showed any aging at all.

Maddox and I shared a glance. This had to be a charade. It had to be. When had Mom ever cared about Gran?

"Marley. Maddox. Could you give us a few minutes alone?" Mom asked.

I bristled, ready to throw it all back in her face, but Gran nodded.

"Just a minute, chickadee."

I ground my teeth together but I could deny Gran nothing. I shoved the chair back and followed my brother out of the hospital room.

He glanced at me as we headed to grab some coffee. "What the hell do you think that's about?"

"I don't know. I don't like it."

"Me neither. Why does Gran still let her in?"

"I don't think she can let her go. She has so much compassion."

"That's how you get hurt."

He wasn't wrong. Though I hated to hear it out of his mouth.

We came back with our gross hospital coffee a few minutes later to the sound of raised voices. I dashed the rest of the way and swung into the hospital room, sloshing steaming coffee on my hand and all over the tiled floor.

"What the hell is going on?"

But no one even acknowledged my entrance. Mom stood with her arms crossed over her chest. Gran was sitting up in her hospital bed and staring *daggers* at her daughter. I'd never seen that look on Gran's face. She was eternally patient, forever compassionate, endlessly kind. Maddox and I had gotten into plenty of trouble growing up, and we'd never even heard her raise her voice. Let alone scream at someone.

"How dare you, Hannah!" Gran shouted. "I can't believe that you would ask this of me."

"How dare *I*?" my mom screamed back. "You're the one who has always judged me for my choices."

"Judged you? I have always been here for you. I raised your own children for you. I helped them the way I apparently never helped you. I've always given you everything you could ever ask for. And still, you do this?"

My mom rolled her eyes. "You've always been high and

mighty. As if you're so much better than me. Well, news flash: you're not."

"I never insinuated a thing. I simply wanted what was best for you."

"What I want is to marry a rich guy who is going to take care of me. Tell me that makes you so proud," my mom spat.

"You have no idea what you want," Gran said. She shook her head. "I wish it were as simple as finding a man who loved you, but love was never enough for you. You always had to have more. You always had to take and take and take from every relationship, Hannah Marie. Never satisfied until you drained the relationship dry."

"Stop," I pleaded. "Just take a walk and cool off."

"No. That's not it. What I wanted was a mother who saw me for who I was and not what you wanted to *mold* me into. I'm not you, Mom!"

"I never wanted you to be me! I just wanted to *love* you. And I wanted you to love me for something other than a bank," Gran spat.

Mom shook her head. "So, are you going to give me the money or not?"

I gasped. "You came here for money?"

Maddox whistled. "That's low, even for you."

"She's sick. She called you because she's in the hospital, and you used it as an opportunity to come in here and extort her for more money?" I couldn't fathom it. My mother was a terrible person. But... how? How could she be like this?

"She's sick, but she's not dead," my mom spat. "Not yet."

I gasped at the words. Maddox winced. But Gra... Gran was devastated. Her face fell. Tears came to her eyes. Her body shook at the words. At the callous way she'd thrown it out there. As if she didn't even care if Gran died. She'd finally get a portion of Gran's money. She'd get the house.

She'd ruin Gran's legacy with her obsession with youth and money and men.

"Leave," Gran said, so soft that I barely heard it.

"What did you say?" Mom asked.

"I said, leave. It's over, Hannah. You'll get no more money from me."

"What? Mom?"

"No. I gave and gave and gave. I respected your choices. I had compassion for your pain. I accepted all of that. But I can't accept that you would rather have me dead than alive. I can't sit here and be disrespected any longer."

"That is not—"

"Go!" she shouted. "I don't ever want to see your face again."

Mom's eyes rounded. "Seriously? Just like that, you're going to turn your back on your daughter?"

A tear slid from Gran's eye. She looked away from her. "You're not my daughter."

My mom's jaw dropped at those words. Not because of the pain that she'd caused her own mother, but because she wasn't going to get her way. Maddox and I stepped in front of her.

"Go," I repeated. "You've done enough damage."

She opened her mouth again, but Maddox muscled her forward out of the room. "It's over," he growled before shutting the door after she left.

I rushed to Gran's side. "Are you okay?"

Gran vacantly looked off. "No, honey, I'm not. I should have done that a long time ago."

I agreed but didn't say so. "What can I do?"

She patted my hand. "Just sit here with me."

Tears slid down her cheeks, even as I saw her face harden. "Both of my daughters... gone to me. Hannah was always troubled, but I thought if I was there for her, then she'd come around. She never did. And Ruth..." She coughed around the pain. "Well, Ruth never wanted anything to do with me. I haven't even seen her in over a decade. I've tried, but she wants nothing to do with me. I doubt she's coming today. No matter what Hannah said." She reached for me and Maddox. "At least I have you two. My two children."

Maddox came to her other side and touched her shoulder. "I'm sorry, Gran. Mom is the worst."

Gran looked between us and said solemnly, "Don't ever mention them in my presence again."

I swallowed hard at those words. I'd long ago written off my mother and aunt. But hearing that it had finally gotten through to Gran... that was a whole new level of pain. I hated it for her. That she finally saw the world for how it really was. That bad people didn't change. They kept taking advantage of hospitality as long as it was offered. Seeing that realization on my Gran's face made everything so much worse. As if it had drained the life from her too.

I held her hand helplessly. It was all I could do.

"We'll have next semester, Gran," I whispered once a nurse came in and gave her something to fall asleep. "I'll be here all the time. You'll feel better, and we'll do all the fun things together. I'll be the daughter you never had."

37

SAVANNAH

PRESENT — DEREK

Ash answered the door already holding a beer. His brow furrowed. "What are you doing here?"

I hefted a bottle of whiskey. "Care for something harder?"

His eyes held mine. Ash and I had been friends for a long time. Our parents had thrown us together as kids. Despite me being two years older, we hung out all the way through college. Only drifting apart when I was gone at Harvard and then hanging out more when I returned without Marley, a brokenhearted idiot. He'd been the best man at my wedding. He knew when something was up.

"Always," Ash said, throwing the door wide.

That was the best part about our friendship. Neither of us ever had to fucking talk about it. He'd eventually heard what had gone down with Marley. I obviously knew all the nuances of his relationship with the infamous Delilah Greer. But we never made the other talk before he was ready.

And tonight, if I was honest, I'd prefer to get drunk and forget that conversation with Mars entirely. She hadn't been wrong. It had been impossible to argue. Though I'd fucking tried. I wanted her. I'd always wanted her. One kiss in my parents' house at a Halloween party had sealed that long ago. But that didn't change how fucked up our relationship was time and time again.

Was I an idiot for pursuing her while working against her? A hundred percent.

Would I do it all over again? Every. Single. Time.

I opened the bottle of Four Roses and poured us each a glass. I downed mine before Ash even picked his up and then poured another. Ash took the drink, swirling it around and sipping on it. It wasn't actually for shooting. I just needed something to burn on the way down.

"What are you watching?" I asked instead of answering the look from my best friend. I could hear a game on in the background.

"The end of the Ole Miss-Auburn game."

I took another sip. "Who's winning?"

"Auburn has been leading the whole game. Ole Miss is trying to make a comeback."

"Good," I said, not really caring either way.

Ash took his drink back to the couch, and we sat in silence for the final five minutes of the game. Auburn clinched their win. Neither of us had been raised on SEC football, but it was hard to grow up in Georgia and not hate both teams. Either of them losing felt like a victory.

Ash polished off his drink and set it down. "I know I'm not exactly one to talk," he began. "You let me drink the last couple months and never complained."

"You had a good reason."

He tipped his head at me. "True. I came out of it on the other side though because you never disappeared or pushed or tried to make me feel bad about slowly turning into an alcoholic."

"Are you on the other side of it?" I asked honestly. Glad to not be talking about my own fucking problem.

Ash's eyes went distant for a moment. A pain crossed his face. "I'm better. I don't know if I'll ever be fully over it, but I don't want to drink myself to death anymore. My work is suffering. My life is..." He trailed off. As if admitting everything that had been his last several months of existence would make it worse. "Look, it fucking sucks. I just want to be on the other side of it."

"I'm glad."

"I don't want you there either."

I breathed out heavily and downed the last of my whiskey. "Yeah."

"So, what happened?"

"You're actually asking?"

"I've known you a long-ass time, man. We've been through the wringer. And as much as I hated to see it, you and Marley were happy. Today on the sailboat, you were a different man. Even Amelia has been saying how happy she is for you. And she hated Kasey."

"She didn't hate her." I didn't know why I was defending Kasey when I currently despised my ex-wife.

Ash laughed. "Yeah, she did. She's just good at hiding it. She has Ballentine-level emotional control."

Huh. I knew that Mia hated Kasey now, but I hadn't realized it was the whole time. Maybe she was a better judge of character than I was.

"Marley went back to Atlanta," I finally confessed.

"Why?"

"Why do you think? I'm representing her mom in a case to take all the money and the only home she's ever known."

"Then drop the case."

I blew out a harsh breath. "It's a test from my father. This is how I get partner. It's what I've been working a hundred hours a week to get. It's all I've ever really wanted. And she said it wasn't fair to ask me to quit and that it also wasn't fair for us to be together with it between us. We've had fifteen years to get this together, and it's not working. I asked her to stay, but she left."

"I don't know how to say this gently," Ash said with narrowed eyes, "but fuck you."

I laughed. "What the fuck?"

"Let me get this straight. She left because you care more about this case than her?"

"No."

He continued as if he hadn't heard me, "And have you considered that working a hundred hours a week is why you lost your last wife?"

I glared at him. "She was crazy."

"She was. But you were never home, and she found other ways to entertain herself. Not the right ways, obviously, but it can't be easy to never see the person you're married to."

I sat stock-still under Ash's imperious gaze. He wasn't *wrong* about Kasey, but it didn't make it any easier to hear.

"Well, I plan to work less once I hit partner. It'll be a moment to breathe."

Ash raised his hand. "Just shut up for a second. Stop trying to rationalize this bullshit." His face went suddenly deathly serious. "I would have given up anything to be with Lila. *Anything*. It didn't work, and it wasn't enough. Are you telling me that you can tell your dad to fuck off and drop this case and you won't do it?"

"It's not that simple."

"Yes or no, motherfucker?" Ash asked, getting heated. "Is your job more important than Marley?"

"No," I ground out.

"Would you be fired for dropping this case?"

"No, but—"

"No," he spat. "No, you fucking wouldn't. And even if you were, you're a goddamn Ballentine. So, who the fuck cares? You'd have another job tomorrow."

"That's not—"

"Do you love her?" Ash asked.

I gritted my teeth and then nodded. "Yeah, I fucking love her."

"That's what I thought. You've been happier in the last couple months than I've seen you in years. Kasey never made you happy like this. Not ever."

I looked back at the last couple years of my life. Had I really not been happy with Kasey? I tried to remember what it had been like when we first met. With all the bullshit clouding our past, it was hard to think about it. But even then, even in the beginning, it had always been that we made sense. Not that I felt young and in love and carefree. I hadn't. I'd just wanted someone to make me forget Marley.

I'd told myself that I was as happy as I had been with Mars, but it wasn't true. It was always hard. It was always a problem. I just ignored the issues. It had been easier that way.

Now, I had exactly what I wanted. Was I just going to let her go? Could I live with myself if I did?

I looked at Ash and saw a shell of the person he'd been when he was with Lila. He was just coming out of it and willing to see that he could be someone else without her. I didn't want to go through that. I didn't want a life without Marley.

"Fuck," I spat.

Ash smiled then. "Glad you finally got there."

"I have to go after her."

"Yeah, you idiot," Ash said with a laugh.

I shook my best friend's hand. He looked happy for me and just a touch sad. Sad that it wouldn't be that easy for him. But still, he wanted this for me, and I appreciated him saying the things I hadn't wanted to hear.

"Thanks for everything," I told him.

His smile widened. "Glad to help."

"You're a dick though."

He laughed. "Yeah. And you're an asshole."

"True. We're quite a pair."

Ash pushed me toward the door. "Go the fuck after her."

"I will," I told him with confidence. "But I have to do one thing first."

38

ATLANTA

PRESENT

Cole Davis pulled me into a hug before Lila could even get inside my apartment. I leaned into my best friend's boyfriend and tried to keep it together. Lila had known Cole nearly as long as Ash. They had a history that rivaled that whole problem with Ash. If anyone knew what I was going through, it was them.

"Sorry to hear about all this," he said. "We brought pizza."

"And ice cream." Lila held it up and pushed her boyfriend out of the way. "I brought the goods." She shoved everything into Cole's hands and then gave me a hug. "We love you, Mars."

"Love you too." I sniffled and headed into the kitchen.

I'd gotten back into Atlanta late the night before after talking on the phone the entire four-hour drive back. Lila for the beginning and switching to Josie for the West Coast time on the drive. Lila had insisted she'd come over the next day since it was the Falcons bye week. Josie was jumping on the first flight into Atlanta, even when I'd insisted she didn't need to fly in from LA when she'd been here last weekend.

But she'd laughed at me and bought tickets while we were on the phone.

Now, Lila and Cole were here with pizza and ice cream. They both rolled their eyes when I told them Josie would be here soon.

"It's just like her to do some grand gesture," Lila said with a laugh.

Cole shook his head. "Josie is one of a kind."

"You just like her because of what she did this summer."

"Hey, I can't deny that," he said with a mischievous smile as he dipped his head in for a kiss.

I rolled my eyes at their display. I wasn't mad that they were happy. They deserved it and all, but sometimes the cute was a lot.

I loaded up a paper plate with pizza and sank onto the couch to watch the Sunday night game. Both Lila and Cole worked for the Falcons and had always loved professional football. Cole's dad had been a coach for the team since they were in college. I didn't care much about any of it, but it was mind-numbing enough and had the benefit that I didn't have to interact.

"Patriots are definitely going to hold on to this one."

Cole laughed. "Nah, Sunflower. I think the Ravens have this one."

"They're undefeated. It seems unlikely," she said, nudging him out of the way. She pointed at me. "Drink?"

"I'm okay. I'll take the ice cream though."

"Your wish is my command."

Cole went on about how the Ravens were the superior team. He had a list of facts that mostly went over my head, but Lila could keep up with him. She loved football more than anyone I'd ever met, and Cole Davis had played college ball at UGA. Match made in heaven.

Lila handed me the pint of strawberry, and I dived in.

I'd cried on the way home, but I'd been bereft since then. It was like I couldn't bring myself to cry over Derek anymore. After all, I'd brought the whole thing on myself. I hated him the moment I saw him step up to Gran's front door. I knew how much of a bad idea it was. Over and over again, we'd hurt each other. If only I'd sworn him off like I'd decided after finding out about Kasey.

But no, I went back for more. I convinced myself that Gran's death was a new moment for me. She'd wanted me to be happy. She had always wanted that for me. Derek was the one I wanted. It had never been easy to stay away from him. Especially when he was the person who had been there for me after Gramps. A part of me wanted him to be the one to put me back together again after Gran too.

Instead, I'd put myself in an impossible situation and given my mother ammunition. She really had a relentless desire to ruin every single person around her. She'd even sent Gran to an early grave. That argument I'd witnessed in the hospital was the final straw in more than one way for Gran. Unbeknownst to me, she changed her will the next day. Cut my mom out of it for the bullshit she'd pulled in the hospital and Aunt Ruth for not ever giving a shit in the first place. One daughter who only wanted her money and another who lived in the same damn town and hadn't seen her in more than a decade. Quite a pair.

By doing so, a part of Gran was cut off too. The doctors had bad news about her cancer. It had progressed much farther and faster than they'd thought. Gran didn't have any more fight left in her. Nothing left after the destruction of her family. She'd given everything to me and Maddox, and then she'd left.

I wished she were still here. It was still impossible to

think that she was actually gone. That I couldn't call and ask her advice. To hear her on the other end, telling me something silly and somehow serious at the same time. The best advice that I never expected.

What would she think of Derek? Would she tell me I was a fool for leaving or that I was her brave little chickadee for having the courage to end it? The worst part was that she was gone, and I'd never have an answer.

I stared down into my ice cream, the game forgotten. My emotions were too close to the surface. Everything too fragile. I needed to get back into the lab and try to lose myself in work. That might help for a little while.

Lila snapped in front of my face. "Earth to Mars."

I laughed hollowly. "Sorry. I guess I zoned out."

"You want to watch something else?"

Cole made a sound of protest, and Lila flicked her gaze to him.

"Anything you want," he said with a perfectly innocent look on his face.

"No, I'm fine. We can keep the game on," I told them.

Lila opened her mouth to argue, but then the door burst open.

"Honey, I'm home!" Josie announced. She was all decked out in a black minidress and high heels. Her oversize sunglasses obscured half of her face, and her black hair hung down in waves nearly to her waist.

"You wore that on the plane?" Lila asked with a laugh.

"Some people travel in style." Josie dropped her Louis Vuitton luggage and kicked the door closed. "Now, what the hell is happening here?"

I dropped the tub of ice cream and gave her a hug. "Pizza, ice cream, and football."

Josie looked between Lila and Cole. She dramatically

yanked her glasses off and pointed it between them. "I approve of what is happening here, but you're entirely too cute for a girls' night."

Cole held up his hands. "Hey, I was told to help Marley. I didn't know it was a girls' night."

"It's fine," I said. "Really. All of this is fine."

"Fine," Josie drawled. Her Southern accent coming back for a split second. "Delilah, darling, get the booze."

Lila laughed. "Sidecars?"

"Just like Gran liked them," Josie insisted.

"I really don't want to drink," I said as my two best friends promptly ignored me and rummaged through my apartment. Of course, I had everything for sidecars. I always did.

"Cole, honey, sugar these rims like you know what you're doing." Josie winked at him.

"I'll pretend that's not a sexual innuendo," he said, shaking his head.

"It is," Lila and I said at the same time.

We all burst into laughter, and for a second, as we worked together to make the drinks, I forgot the horror of the last twenty-four hours. Josie might have been ridiculous flying out here for me, but she wasn't wrong. I needed it. I needed to forget. I didn't want to face it tonight.

When the drinks were poured, Josie held hers aloft. "What should we toast to?"

I gulped and pushed mine up. "Gran."

Lila and Josie both shot me looks of understanding.

"To Gran," Lila said.

Then, Josie and Cole and I echoed it. We all took a sip of Gran's drink, remembering her in the sweet taste of alcohol.

Josie squeezed onto the couch, complaining about the calories in the ice cream for a whole minute before digging into the pint. It was her job to stay the same shape, but it was nice to see her say *fuck it* for a night. We all did. It was better having everyone there together. Josie took up all the space in a room, which was good for me. I barely had to think at all.

"I should move here," Josie said a few hours later as she lay sprawled across the recliner, tipsy from sidecars.

Lila and I laughed.

"Yeah right," Lila said.

"I know. I know. Hollywood beckons," Josie said dramatically. "But I miss y'all."

"You know she's drunk," I said. "She's resorted to *y'all* again."

Cole grinned. "Welcome back, Josie."

She waved her hand at us. "Yeah, yeah. Laugh it up. But I like being here. Everyone in LA is so fake. They all want a piece of me, and I want to keep a few pieces to myself."

"This doesn't have anything to do with your divorce, does it?" Lila asked.

Josie sighed. "Guys suck."

I nodded. "Seconded."

Cole shrugged. "You're not wrong."

We all wanted Josie to move back. As much as I wanted it to happen, it never would. Just like me and Derek.

It had been nearly all evening before I let myself think of him again.

I stepped out of the living room with a murmured, "Bathroom," and stared at myself in the mirror.

I hated this. I'd made my choice, and I fucking hated it. I wanted him back. I wanted this to be the right time and place. I didn't want it to be like every other time. But I didn't know how to change it. Or if it was even possible.

A knock at the door kept me from wallowing.

"Mars, want me to get it?" Lila called.

I stepped out of the bathroom in confusion. "Nah, it's okay."

Who the hell would be here this late at night? Probably some stranger who was on their way to someone else's house. I couldn't imagine any other scenario.

I yanked the door open and gasped. "Derek?"

39

ATLANTA

PRESENT

"Hey, Mars."

Derek Ballentine stood outside of my door in Atlanta. And he looked... good. He looked fucking great. He had on chinos and a white button-up with the top button undone and his sleeves rolled up to his elbows. None of the fatigue I saw on my own face from our breakup was visible on him. His pouty lips were upturned and his hazel eyes so bright and endearing. He looked more like a Greek statue in that moment than a man at all.

"What are you doing here?" I blurted out.

My friends rustled around behind me. I had no clue what they were doing, but clearly, they were trying to be stealthy and failing.

Derek shot them an amused look. "Mind if I come in?"

"I..." I blinked at him in confusion. "Sure."

I pulled the door open wider and let him in. That was when I found Cole helping Josie to her feet—maybe she'd had more than I thought—and Lila trying to herd them away.

"We were just going," Lila said in a perky tone.

"You don't have to go," I said.

She waved me away and helped Cole maneuver Josie. "Call me if you need me."

She winked at me and then hustled out of my apartment with her boyfriend. Why did this feel so familiar? Hadn't Josie and I plotted something similar only a few months ago for her? Had they contacted Derek?

"That was... subtle," I said after she closed the door.

"Indeed. I don't think any of them are much known for their subtlety."

"Did they call you?"

Derek furrowed his brow. "No. Should they have?"

"It's their style."

"No, I'm not here at their behest, but my own."

"And why is it that you're here?"

"For you, of course."

"Right," I said softly. My head was fuzzy, and I didn't think it was the alcohol. Derek was here. He was *here*. And I'd ended it. So, it wasn't adding up. "But..."

"You thought I was going to let you go that easily?"

"Derek, it's not that I wanted this to happen. But with everything between us..."

"I screwed up in the past," he said, taking my hand in his. "I didn't see what was in front of me. But Marley, I've been searching for you my whole life. I'd be an idiot to not fight for you. I choose you. I want you."

My mouth went dry as I heard him utter the words I'd always wanted to hear. "But the case..."

"Funny story: I dropped the case."

My jaw fell open. "You did what?"

"I told my dad that I wouldn't do it."

"But... but partner?"

He shrugged. "My dad was pissed, but once he got over

me dropping the case, he was actually impressed. Nothing he'd said made me bend or break to him, and I think he could respect that."

"I don't know what to say," I whispered. It was all so much. Everything I wanted and couldn't believe he was saying. Was it possible that he'd actually given this up for me? "I don't want you to resent me for this."

"How could I? You never asked me for it. I did it because you were right. It wasn't fair to have that case between us. Not when I was pursuing you. And I didn't want to stop that, Mars. I want to be with you. I want you to be mine. All mine." He brought my hands up to his lips and placed a kiss on them. "I know we have a long way to go, but when I'm with you, everything disappears. I just exist here with you."

Tears came to my eyes. Just when I'd thought I had none left. "I want that too, Derek. But what about Atlanta? I can't leave my job."

"And I'd never ask you to. What you're doing is important, and you're fucking brilliant at it. We might have to be long distance for a while, but we can make it work while I figure out my situation."

"Figure out *what*?"

"Dad has always wanted to expand," he said with a shrug. "I floated the idea for me to open Ballentine Law in Atlanta."

I blinked. I couldn't process those words. "You'd move to Atlanta? But your life is in Savannah..."

"You're here," he said, drawing me closer. "You're my life."

"Oh my God, Derek."

"Would you want that?"

"Yes," I gasped. "Of course I want that!"

He grinned. "Good."

"This is real?"

He laughed softly. "It's real, Mars. A hundred percent real. Any other objections to us being together? Please allow me to disabuse you of any other notions."

I bit my lip, shook my head, and then threw my arms around him. "No objections."

"Then, you're mine?"

"Yes, Derek. God, I've always been yours."

He spun me in a circle before slowly dropping me back to my feet. His hands cupped my jaw, and his mouth dipped down to mine. Our lips slanted together, tasting each other, as if all of this were completely new and wonderful. My heart was full to bursting. I could hardly breathe, knowing what he'd done to be with me. That he'd actually chosen me above all else. I'd thought that this was our last and final good-bye, but in reality, it was our next beginning.

"Minivan?" he teased against my lips.

"Yes?"

"I love you."

I shivered all over. "I love you too."

Our eyes locked as those words sealed our future forever. No more barriers between us. Nothing left to pull us apart. This was real. It was *real*.

"I love you to Mars and back."

I kissed him again, breathlessly. We were still tangled together when the door cracked back open again.

"Did it work out?" Josie asked with a giggle.

I broke away from Derek, laughing as Lila and Cole tumbled into the apartment after her. "Were you all listening?"

Derek just shook his head at my friends as they all spoke at once, trying to explain the situation.

"Can you blame us?" Lila asked. "We want you to be happy."

"I guess not," I said.

"You're maybe ruining the moment," Derek said with a laugh.

"Ruining the moment is kind of their specialty," Cole said. He offered his hand to Derek, who looked at it for a moment and then shook. "Congrats, man."

"Thanks. You too."

Lila and Josie wrapped me in a hug, jumping up and down with excitement. They insisted on going out with us tomorrow, and then Derek was carefully herding them out of the apartment.

"Okay, I admit it."

"What?" I asked, taking his hand and drawing him toward my bedroom.

"Lila isn't *that* bad."

I cackled. "I accept this."

"But we have one problem."

I arched an eyebrow as I toed the door to my room open. "I don't see a problem. I see a king-size bed."

"*That* is definitely not the problem."

"Oh?" My hands were already fiddling with his belt buckle. Eager for us to make up properly.

"We're going to have to elope."

I stalled at those words and looked up at him in confusion. "What?"

"I had one more thing to do before I left Savannah."

Then, he dropped to a knee before me. My mind went completely and totally blank as he produced a small blue box.

"Derek," I whispered in shock.

"I don't want to wait another day for you to be my wife. I

don't want to live in a world where you aren't my everything. I want to be tied to you in every way possible." He cracked the box open to reveal a simple cushion cut ring with a tiny band of diamonds around it. It was elegant and gorgeous. Maybe the most beautiful ring I had ever seen in my entire life. "Marry me."

"Oh my God," I gasped.

"Is that a yes?" he asked with a laugh.

"Yes!" I said, my entire body shaking with disbelief.

He plucked the ring out of the box and slid it onto my finger. It fit like it had always been meant to be there. As if it had been made for my finger, just as Derek Ballentine had been made for me.

I kissed him, and we spilled onto the bed with delirious energy. We made love late into the evening, reuniting over and over again and forgetting everything in the world around us. Then, as the sun rose over our new joining, we made plans that I'd never thought we'd get to make together. And I'd never been happier making them with him.

Just him. Always him.

40

SAVANNAH

SIX WEEKS LATER

A diamond was wrapped around my left ring finger.

A matching wedding ring sat on the inside of the engagement ring.

Derek had slid the wedding ring on my finger on a sail-boat a few weeks earlier. We said *I do* with only family present. Maddox on one side and Amelia on the other. The ceremony was at sunset. Simple, glowing, and perfect. I wore a dress Amelia had designed for me. The only other person present, other than our officiant, was our photographer. We threw parties afterward so that everyone was happy and accounted for. But I hadn't wanted anything big like Lila's wedding, and it was Derek's second marriage. We'd done what we wanted and ignored everyone else's wishes.

Now, we were just waiting for the judge to make a decision.

Derek rubbed the knot at my back. "It's going to work out."

"I hope so." I bit my lip, thankful for non-smudge lipstick. "It felt pretty convincing to me."

He snorted. "Your attorney did what she was supposed to."

"And their lawyer?"

"I would have been better."

I narrowed my eyes at him. "Oh, really?"

"Sure. I don't lose."

"You're insufferable sometimes. You know that, right?"

He laughed softly. "Yeah, well, you married me."

"Remind me why?"

"I'll show you later." His eyes filled with lust, and I remembered all the post-wedding sex we'd been having.

We weren't going on our honeymoon until the case was closed and done with. He'd booked us three weeks in an overwater bungalow in Bali without blinking. How could I even object?

The only people who'd had any objection were Kasey and my mother. We'd had interactions with both of them since the wedding. Kasey had been a shrieking mess when she found out, but hopefully, it was the last we saw of her. Moving to Atlanta would sure help that. And my mom…

Well, that would end today.

I chanced a glance to her on the other side of the room with Aunt Ruth. They both looked smug, as if they knew it was all going to work out in their favor. I tried to find the sliver of fear that I was feeling, but it wasn't there. My mom really believed in her case. She couldn't think of anything else. This was how she lived her entire life.

Finally, the judge returned to his seat to make his pronouncement. Maddox squeezed one hand. Our eyes met, and he nodded once. I nodded back. Then, we waited for the end of this long debacle.

The judge cleared his throat. "After carefully looking at

the provided evidence, I move to dismiss the will contest and grant full grounds to Marley and Maddox Nelson."

"Oh my God," I gasped. All the air rushed out of Maddox's lungs. I turned and flung my arms around him. "We did it."

"We did it."

I turned to Derek, and he was smiling brightly. "Well done."

He pulled me tight to him, and I breathed him in.

"Thank you."

I had no doubt that Derek would have been better at his job than whoever had filled in for him. But either way, justice had been served. My Gran's final wishes had been honored. Maddox and I had the house now, and we wouldn't see it sold off for pieces. Gran could rest well, knowing we would take care of her things.

My mom looked ready to spit something vile at me as we all exited the courtroom. But Derek put himself between me and my mother and looked down his nose at her.

"Hannah," he said coldly.

She stumbled on her words, and then we were through and outside. The December air was cold and breezy, but the sun was shining bright. Tomorrow was Derek's birthday, and we could actually celebrate now that everything was finally, *finally* over. We'd won, and life could go on.

I hugged Maddox one more time before he headed off to his Wrangler. I followed Derek to his BMW, and he popped open the passenger door.

"One more thing."

"What's that?" he asked.

"Let's go see her."

He kissed me softly. "Anytime you want."

We drove out of town, and he pulled into the cemetery.

We parked up front and walked the paved pathways. I stopped when I found Gramps and brushed away some stray leaves.

Then, I looked to Gran, buried next to her husband of fifty years. Her headstone read:

Meredith May Christianson
Daughter. Mother. Wife.

Derek wrapped an arm around my shoulders as I straightened.

I leaned my head against his chest. "I miss her."

"I know you do," he said. "She was an incredible woman. Just like someone else I know."

"I hope that, one day, I can look back and say that I lived a life worthy of Meredith Christianson."

He pressed a kiss into my hair. "You already have, and she'd be the first to say it."

I smiled around my tears, twirling the wedding ring around my finger. He was right. Gran had always been so proud of me. We'd lost her too soon. Much too soon. But she'd known me for who I was. She'd raised me into the person I was.

"Thank you."

We stayed in front of Gran's and Gramps' headstones as I regaled them with the story of what had happened in court. Then, I followed Derek back to the car. He kissed me in the parking lot.

"Well, Mrs. Ballentine, where to?"

I laughed and ducked my chin. "I'm never going to get used to that."

He grinned. "Oh, I think I'm going to say it over and over and over again until you do."

"I love you."

He threaded our fingers together. "I love you too. What's the plan now that you're free?"

"The world, husband," I joked.

"You're thinking too small, wife," he said with a wink. "To Mars."

"And back."

THE END

ACKNOWLEDGMENTS

At First Hate was born out of a lot of love. I deeply love tales about classism and how we deal with the power dynamics when we were raised with them. Additionally, stories about smart girls, really smart girls bring me a lot of joy. Navigating the confines of being smart but not too smart or just embracing it and deciding you don't care what anyone thinks. It's a lot for a person to handle and it creates an identity in and of itself. "Smart girl" Also, as many of you know I worked at UNC in 2012 and then I was the head coach of the Duke Dancing Devils. So, the rivalry between the two teams is ingrained in me! It was fun going back to North Carolina!

Plus, I loved getting to incorporate cameos from so many of my other series into this one. When I realized Marley went to school with Jack, college with Bekah and Ramsey, and grad school with Penn and Camden, I couldn't help myself but write them all into the story. Hope you caught them all, but if not, go back and look for them!

Thank you to everyone who helped me with this one. Especially my editor, Jovana Shirley, who remembered that Hurricane Sandy hit Massachusetts in 2012. Becky Kimmerling, for all the help plotting this bad boy out. Staci Hart, for coming to Lubbock for a week to help me knock out the last 30k words of this after my puppy got cancer. It was some of the hardest weeks of my life, and it was much easier to get through it with you there. Also, for the kick ass cover! Rebecca Gibson and Anjee Sapp, who read early versions of this book. I appreciate that Rebecca never backed down from how mean I had to make Derek. And Anjee for loving Ash so much that every instance of him brought you fresh waves of suffering. I promise to write more of him just for you. (and me...who am I kidding? I love Ash Talmadge.)

As always, my husband Joel for cooking, cleaning, and laundry during this madness. For going to all the vet visits with me. For lots of hugs while I cried about Hippo. And for telling me I could do it, but maybe I needed more time and that was okay. You're the best.

ABOUT THE AUTHOR

K.A. Linde is the *USA Today* bestselling author of more than thirty novels. She has a Masters degree in political science from the University of Georgia, was the head campaign worker for the 2012 presidential campaign at the University of North Carolina at Chapel Hill, and served as the head coach of the Duke University dance team.

She loves reading fantasy novels, binge-watching Supernatural, traveling to far off destinations, baking insane desserts, and dancing in her spare time.

She currently lives in Lubbock, Texas, with her husband and two super-adorable puppies.

Visit her online:
www.kalinde.com

Or Facebook, Instagram & Tiktok:
@authorkalinde

For exclusive content, free books,
and giveaways every month.
www.kalinde.com/subscribe

CPSIA information can be obtained
at www.ICGtesting.com
Printed in the USA
BVHW031335310821
615689BV00004B/236